Bonner's Den Ranch

Garry Smith and Danny Arnold

BOOKSIDE Press

BOOKSIDE Press

BookSide Press
877-741-8091
www.booksidepress.com
orders@booksidepress.com

Contents

Dedication

This book is a work of fiction, and all the main characters are entirely fictional.

We want to thank our brides, Charlotte Smith and Peggy Arnold, who gave us invaluable ideas and constructive feedback.

Previous Books
by
Danny Arnold and Garry Smith

Freedom Town Series

Bad Cat Jones
Freedom Town
Freedom Town Winter
Freedom Town Summer
Freedom Town '68
Cannon Mines
Freedom Town West
Gabe's Quest
The Sheffield Plantation
The Gracie Plantation

The Mountain Series

Murder by the Mountains
The Mountains Are Calling
Home in the Mountains
Mountain Retreat
Mountain Riders
A New Mountain Generation
Full Mountain Circle

The Bonner Series

Bonner's Den

Prologue

Fergus and Morgan Bonner own a sprawling ranch in the Bitterroot Valley of Montana Territory. In 1870, Fergus purchased the ten sections with gold he and his family had mined for almost ten years during and after the gold strike near Pierce in Idaho Territory.

Fergus was making their spring supply run to Butte, the town nearest the Bonner's Den Ranch. Butte was a day's ride from his ranch, even with the wagon being pulled by two huge Sheffield Mules. One of his Appaloosa stallions trailed behind the wagon.

It was a beautiful day, and the grass and trees looked fresh and clean after the recent snow melt. The wagon road was still soft in places but the mud gave the big mules few problems.

Fergus planned to spend at least one night in Butte at his favorite boarding house. When he entered town that afternoon, he saw a large, freshly painted sign on a big barn. Fergus glanced at the sign that read *Josh Doyle Freight*. He looked back at the wagon road for a few seconds before pulling on the reins and exclaiming, "Naw! It can't be!"

He recalled a young man named Josh Doyle, with whom he drove freight wagons back in Arkansas after they crossed the Mississippi River into West Memphis, Arkansas.

Fergus wondered, "*Surely he's not the Josh Doyle I knew.*"

He pulled the wagon to the barn's front, set the brake, and stepped down. Fergus entered the barn, walked over to the first person he saw, and asked, "Is Josh Doyle around?"

"Yep, out back in the corral."

Fergus walked out back and saw a man about his age hitching a team of mules to a loaded freight wagon. He walked over and said, "You must be Josh Doyle."

The man turned around and said, "Yes, sir, that's me."

He squinted at the grinning Fergus for a few seconds and then said, "Gosh, Almighty! I recognized the Tennessee accent before I recognized you!"

Josh stuck out his hand and said, "Fergus Bonner! Never expected to see you again, but I'm darn sure glad to lay eyes on you. It's been thirty years! We've got to catch up."

Fergus responded, "You free tonight?"

"Yes indeed!"

"I'm on our spring supply run. Let me get to the general store and place my order. I'll pick it up in the morning."

"Where are you staying?"

"I always stay at the Butte Boarding House, my favorite."

"So am I. I'll meet you there for supper, and we can sit out back and catch up."

"Deal. I'm looking forward to it."

Fergus departed and drove his team to the general store. He gave the clerk his list and ensured he understood everything. The clerk had a few simple questions, concluding with, "When do you want to pick it up?"

"After breakfast tomorrow. Just ran into an old friend, and we have some catching up to do."

Fergus parked the wagon out back and put the mules into the store's corral. He then rode to the boarding house on his Appaloosa and rented a room.

Fergus asked Mrs. Catchings to wake him when Josh Doyle returned. He then went to his room and lay across the bed to catch a short nap. An hour before supper, Josh's sharp rap on his door awakened him.

He opened the door, and Josh said, "We have an hour before supper is served. Let's grab a bottle of 'shine and sit out back."

Fergus grabbed his hat and followed Josh, who picked up a bottle from Mrs. Catchings. After they sat, Josh said, "Fergus, you look like a prosperous rancher. I want to know how you got from Arkansas to here."

Fergus grinned and said, "And you look like a prosperous freighter, and I want to know the same thing. You first."

"Okay, here goes. I'm sure you remember the freighter we caught on with in West Memphis, right?" Fergus nodded.

"I worked for him for more than ten years. We became close, and I looked at him like a second father. He had no family, and when he got ready to quit, he sold me the freighting business for a good price. I had saved enough money to buy it for a fifty percent down payment and paid the rest of it by the end of the War. Business was surprisingly good during the War because of government contracts. After the War, it got tough without those contracts and the railroad expansions back there."

Josh continued, "I realized I needed to relocate to a place where the railroads needed help getting goods to their final destination. So, I moved the operation to Kansas City in '68 and Cheyenne in '75. Lots of business comes through Cheyenne. I realized I was sending many loads to Montana, Idaho, Oregon, and Washington territories. So, I decided to set up a distribution operation here in Butte. We opened last fall."

Fergus said, "It must have been just after our fall supply run, or I would've seen your sign."

"Yes, the sign is brand new. Hasn't been up more than a month."

"Did you ever marry?"

"Yep. Didn't last long. She couldn't abide by my long absences mule skinning. So, she ran off with a riverboat gambler."

"Sorry to hear that."

"Water under the bridge. What about you?"

Fergus replied, "Yep. Married a fine widow woman in '61, Morgan. She had a young son who has grown into an outstanding young man. He changed his name to Jeb Bonner. Morgan and I have a fourteen-year-old daughter."

"So you're ranching now?"

"Yep. Appaloosa horses and cattle. Morgan is farming and growing lots of potatoes. Might expand her operation in the future."

"Okay, back up for me. What did you do after you left West

Memphis? Did you drive freight wagons on the Santa Fe trail?"

"I did. I headed up to Independence when I left. When I arrived, I traded the pistol we took from the slave hunter. The store owner taught me how to use a revolver properly. I got very proficient with it. By the way, I ran into two of those former slaves in Idaho, Horace and Hank, and hired them. They're still working for me."

"Good for them."

Fergus continued, "I made two roundtrips to Santa Fe but didn't finish the third trip. Three locals tried to steal my horse in Santa Fe, and I killed two of them. I had to slip out of Santa Fe. I worked on ranches in the area until '61. I kept getting run out of town because somebody would challenge me to a gunfight and die. I eventually moved over to Pierce, Idaho, to try my hand at finding gold. I was making a living when I got ambushed in camp. They shot me two times, stole my little poke, and left me for dead. The woman who is now my wife and her son found me. I almost died, but she nursed me back to health."

"The shooters were henchmen for a saloon owner. They had also killed Morgan's former husband and stole his gold. I took back my money, her money, and all the gold they had stolen. They resisted and died. We ran into the wilderness and made a good life there. We found a surprisingly large amount of gold, and I started raising Appaloosa horses. We collected up an interesting group of people at Bonner's Den."

"Our child, Mary, was born on Christmas Day in '66. Four years later, I received a letter from my mother back in Tennessee. My father and two brothers were killed at Shiloh, and my surviving brother lost an arm in Chancellorsville. He and my mother were about to lose the farm because of increased taxes. So, Morgan, Mary, and I headed for Tennessee. I paid the taxes, sold the farm, and brought them back to Bonner's Den. We picked up a woman on the way to Tennessee whose husband and daughter had been murdered. She married my brother and came back to Idaho with us. My mother married a good man, and he also came back with us."

"I wanted to expand my Appaloosa herd, but we were in the

mountains and needed more pasture for a larger herd. I looked around the Bitterroot Valley and found what I wanted. I bought it and moved everybody to the ranch. It's ten sections west of here, about a day's ride."

"We moved before we wanted to because we were attacked by a renegade band of Nez Perce. We beat them off but feared they would return with a bigger war party. We left as soon as we could."

Josh asked, "The ranch doing well?"

"Yes. It has excellent grass. We run about a thousand momma cows and have a big sale every fall. We keep about a hundred and fifty Appaloosa horses and a hundred cowhorses. People are willing to pay three and four times for an Appaloosa than a regular horse. A rancher west of here also raises Appaloosas, and we've worked out a deal for trading stallions regularly."

Josh said, "I saw the stallion you're riding. I see why people are willing to pay a premium for them. It's a beautiful horse."

They heard Mrs. Catchings ring the dinner bell and took a break to eat supper. She had a Mexican cook who served chopped beef with onions, peppers, fried potatoes, and Mexican cornbread.

After finishing supper, Fergus and Josh returned to the back porch for more catching up. Josh asked, "Who all did you move to the ranch from Idaho?"

"Morgan, Mary, and I live in the big ranch house. My mother and her husband, Oby, live with us. Jeb married a Nez Perce girl, Kamiah, and they live in one of the four other nice houses with their family. My brother and Zelma live in one of those houses."

"We found an injured Nez Perce teenager, Wolf, years ago and nursed him back to health. He later married Half Moon and moved to Bonner's Den so their children could learn the white man's ways. He's like another son for Morgan and me. We did not officially adopt him, but he asked if he could use the Bonner name, and we agreed. They live in one of the houses."

"We picked up a brilliant Chinese man, Chinn, who was a warrior in China. He married Kamiah's mother, Little Bird, and they also live in one of the houses."

Josh asked, "What about Horace and his partner?"

"They both married Nez Perce women and have several children each. They came with us to the ranch. Not long after Chief Joseph surrendered, their wives persuaded them to return to Bonner's Den to be near their families. Horace and Hank now live in the cabin Morgan, Jeb, and I built. They work our best gold claims on shares. They visit us once a year and bring our share. Interestingly, those former slaves have become quite wealthy. They could live almost anywhere but prefer the solitary life and seem very content."

"Have you had any more problems with the Nez Perce?"

"Not lately. A skirmish broke out on the neighboring ranch before the Nez Perce War. Angus and I armed our hands with the 1873 Winchester rifles and Colt Peacemaker revolvers soon after they came out. They made a big difference, and Angus's hands won the skirmish handily. Fortunately, nothing spilled over to our ranch."

After a moment, Josh said, "Sounds like y'all have a lot of children on the ranch. Is there a school out there?"

"No, but we don't really need one. I mentioned Chinn earlier. He is well-educated and tutors the children in history, arithmetic, and science. My sister-in-law, Zelma, is also well-educated and tutors them in English and reading."

"Sounds like a big operation. How do you get everything done?"

"I inherited an excellent foreman, Colorado, who still handles the cattle herd. Although Jeb's background is in gold mining, he developed an affinity for cattle. Colorado took Jeb under his wing and has been teaching him about cattle ranching. Jeb is an eager student, and Colorado treats him like a son. They've divided the responsibilities over the years. Colorado focuses mostly on the cow/calf pairs, while Jeb oversees the yearlings to be sold. It's worked out well."

"Of course, being a Nez Perce, Wolf has an affinity for horses. He ramrods the cowhorse remuda and helps me with the Appaloosa herd. Several of the teenagers are also helping. We like to handle the Appaloosas as often as possible from birth, so we need a lot of eyes and hands."

"Tell me about the farming."

"Brody and Morgan are farmers at heart. They started out with a large garden and grew almost all the vegetables for the ranch. Potatoes were always their best crop. Morgan pushed to grow even more potatoes, so we bought some new-fangled sod-busting equipment available back east and had it shipped here."

Josh interjected, "Well, I'll be switched! One of my wagons hauled that stuff out here! I remember seeing the name 'Morgan Bonner' but didn't connect it with you."

"Amazing! She has over fifty acres of potatoes and about twenty-five acres of other stuff. The soil grows large potatoes, especially after we let cattle graze over the field. We've had to hire additional help for the farming. In a normal year, they harvest three big freight wagons of potatoes. We keep one wagon load, sell one to our neighbor, and sell one in Butte. We had to build a large potato house to keep them from spoiling."

Josh said, "Fergus, who would have thought those teenaged mule skinners back in Arkansas would be as successful as we've been?"

Fergus chuckled and replied, "Not me, for sure!"

"As soon as I get this operation running smoothly, I would love to ride out and visit y'all."

"Any time."

Josh and Fergus said their goodbyes after breakfast. Fergus rode to the general store, hitched the mules to the wagon, and loaded the supplies. He was delighted to have run across an old friend.

Fergus mulled over his conversation with Josh and thought about the ranch. "*I brought forty excellent Appaloosa mares and a stallion to the ranch. The herd is now up to a hundred and fifty solid mares and five stallions. Breeding the right stallion to the right mare has been a challenge. Rotating stallions with the Gold Point Ranch has helped.*

I couldn't believe it when I heard Chief Joseph's band left many Appaloosas in the Wallowa Valley. I guess they took only what they needed when they fled toward Canada. They couldn't move an entire herd. Colorado, Jeb, Wolf, and I rushed to the Wallowa Valley before the Army found the horses. We returned with ten of the best mares, two mature stallions, and three one-year-old stallions. That has really helped with the breeding program.

Even though Sunny is not an Appaloosa, he has helped smooth the gait of many young Appaloosa without harming their coloring. Even the good mares in the cowhorse remuda have dropped foals with Appaloosa coloring.

I'm thankful that Mary, Colt (Wolf's son, formerly Fighting Bear), and Rowdy (Jeb's son) are interested in helping with the Appaloosa. They're all fourteen and look like they've been riding horses all their lives, which they have. They began helping with the foals when they were five or six years old and still love the work.

Chapter One

The country was charging into the 1880s, and Fergus Bonner thought everything was going well for Bonner's Den Ranch. He felt the weather was their most severe problem — it was bitterly cold in winter. The big house was comfortable in the summer, but keeping it warm in the winter was a challenge. It had a massive fireplace in the great room, but it burned too much wood and let out almost as much heat as it generated. They had wood heaters in all the bedrooms and a big one in the parlor. Once he got the big fireplace and heater going and the two cooks fired up the kitchen stove, the house was much more comfortable.

Mary was usually the first to come bounding downstairs in her gown. At fourteen, she was getting a little old to do it, but Fergus loved it. At almost six feet tall, Mary was nearly as tall as Morgan, her mother. Her shoulders were broad after a recent growth spurt, and she was already stronger than most women. Mary had dark blond hair, somehow derived from Morgan's dark hair and Fergus's dark red hair.

Fergus usually covered himself with a bearskin robe until the parlor warmed up. Mary always crawled in next to him. Morgan soon followed, sometimes in her robe on frigid mornings. She also tried to get under the warm bearskin. It takes a massive bear skin to cover three people as large as they were. At six feet and five inches and around two hundred and thirty pounds, Fergus always lost some of his share to the two females. He kept another robe handy to pull over himself.

Juanita or Lotte brought each of them coffee as soon as it was ready. Mary still wanted sweetened condensed milk in hers.

Maude and Oby walked downstairs together when they smelled breakfast. Fergus looked out the windows and saw smoke rising from the other houses and the bunkhouse. Nobody was outside yet in the icy snow and sleet. Even Brody's boys, Elbert, Bates, and Briggs, had yet to venture out. They would likely be the first to test the day. Jeb's kids, Rowdy, Liz, and Joe, were also inside, as were Wolf's boys, Colt and Little Elk. Chinn and Little Bird were also sitting near their heater.

The cowboys had yet to go out to feed the animals. They would start at around ten o'clock after the temperature warmed up. Fergus was sure the cowboys who stayed in the line shacks near the ranch's corners would remain close to a fire until mid-morning. They rode the property lines to keep cows from roaming too far outside the ranch's borders. Fergus also knew the cows would huddle under the trees scattered around the ranch. It would be a short workday for everyone, including Fergus. He had no plans to roam around the ranch.

Breakfast was excellent, as all meals were at Bonner's Den Ranch. Juanita was a superb cook and Lotte, her younger sister, now helped her. Most of the time, the other members of the Bonner's extended family ate at the mansion house or the bunkhouse, which also had two excellent cooks. Juanita and Lotte lived in a room off the kitchen and were usually the first up and the last to bed.

After lunch, Fergus met with Colorado, Jeb, Wolf, Brody, Chinn, and Morgan. They would review the ranch's numbers for the previous year and start planning for the following year. None of the men were excited about either effort. Even though she let Fergus think he was in charge of the discussions, Morgan was actually in charge.

Morgan had helped Fergus prepare notes for the meeting. He began, "We had a good year last year. We didn't make a real profit but didn't lose much, and the cash flow was acceptable. We'll have a good cattle herd to sell in the fall — almost a thousand one-year-old steers and heifers. They're nice and fat even after half the winter. The railroad is headed to Butte but won't be there until next year. It'll be south of Butte this fall, which is where we'll take the herd. Angus and I have been promised that cattle cars and buyers will be at the end of the track. I understand the railroad is building a town called Dillon, where they had to stop laying track for the winter. Angus and a few smaller outfits will join us on the roundup and cattle drive. We'll have over three thousand head to move."

"The horse herd is in good shape. As sad as it was, the Army killing most of the Nez Perce Appaloosa horses helped us. I'm considering taking some horses to Butte to auction this summer. We have to get our name out there and let people know we are raising superb horses. We'll have to figure out how to get the word out about the sale."

"Morgan and Brody have had a highly productive garden each year, and we have enjoyed the bounty of their efforts. Their potato crops have been superb. Morgan wants to add even more potato acreage this year. We're making good money on the potatoes. I've ordered a new breaking plow to help them break more land and dig up the crop."

"I want us to handle a few more things this year. We need at least one more horse pasture, maybe two. Another barn and shed are also needed. Morgan tells me I must stop spending money on the horses until we sell more. She's right, of course, but I'm not listening again. Do y'all have any ideas we need to discuss?"

Nobody was quick to respond. Colorado, the cattle foreman, was mainly of Mexican heritage, with a bit of Indian and white blood thrown in. He finally said, "Since the railroad is coming, do you think we should drive a small herd to meet them? They've always killed buffalo for food and there ain't many left. They might pay top dollar for beef."

"Good idea. It wouldn't take many cowboys to drive a couple hundred head to the end of the line. The grass should be good all the way. If we take them slowly, they will still be in prime condition. We can take a herd of the largest yearlings from last year, and the cows we know have not produced a calf in the last two years. We'll separate them out in the spring roundup. We can hold them over in the garden area if the timing is right. They'll fertilize it well in a few weeks."

Brody, Fergus's brother, lost his left arm below the elbow in the Civil War. He had light brown hair and was over six feet tall and over two hundred pounds. Brody said, "We should consider adding to the garden beyond the potatoes. Butte will likely grow rapidly when the train tracks get there. I understand the main reason for laying the tracks to Butte is they're taking a lot of copper and other minerals out of the big pit. It'll likely be a boom town soon and a good vegetable and potato market. Of course, the potatoes could be shipped wherever the tracks go. We might want a machine to sack them for easier shipping."

"Great ideas! Why don't you go to Butte to order another set of plows? Check to see if we can order a bagging machine. There has to be one because we used to buy potatoes in big sacks. Any other ideas?"

Morgan said, "If Butte is going to grow and we want to sell vegetables, potatoes, beef, and horses there, we probably should buy property there before it gets too expensive. We don't need much, but enough for corrals, a wagon depot, storage, and so forth will surely be needed."

"Another great idea! You and I need to see what's available when the weather improves. We should chat with my friend Josh Doyle to see what he thinks about shipping potatoes and other vegetables back down the line."

Morgan added, "Another thing, our children are growing up, and most have never been off this ranch. We should take all the children to San Francisco this summer to see a big city. It'll be expensive, and several adults must accompany them, but they need to know something about the world outside these little ten sections of land."

"Okay. Talk with the other mothers to make sure they're on board. I think it's a great idea, and we have the money. What better way to spend it than on our children? Is there anything else we need to talk about?" No one spoke up.

"Let's have coffee and a cigar to celebrate, on the warmest part of the porch. We may have to smoke the cigars quickly."

Surprisingly, it warmed up many degrees while they talked. A chinook wind was blowing off the mountains, and the temperature rose well above freezing. The sun also came out, and the day became bluebell beautiful. The group talked more generally and enjoyed each other's company.

Spring was fast approaching, and work was reaching a peak on the ranch. Brody and the other garden workers had plowed nearly one hundred acres of rich land. The new plow was a great addition to the older ones. Most of the field would be planted in potatoes. They required less hand work than the vegetables, which had to be worked every day from planting to final picking. The potatoes were planted first, which involved hand labor, but the main tasks were grass control and digging when the tubers were ready. The garden would be planted by variety as soon as Morgan and Brody thought it was warm enough to reduce the danger from frost.

A new horse pasture was fenced. It was about three hundred fifty acres. Foals were dropping daily, and the majority had Appaloosa coloring. Fergus was happy with what he saw. Almost all were dark on the front with a spotted blanket. The cowhorses produced loud-colored colts the cowboys loved. The one-year-old herd was still looking good. Most of the males would be gelded, but Fergus saved a few he thought would make good studs for his mares. Occasionally, a colt was born with the golden color of Sunny, the Tennessee stallion. These foals were particularly desired by buyers.

Fergus was not sure he wanted to grow his Appaloosa herd much larger. He now had about one hundred and fifty Appaloosa brood mares and thought two hundred might be a good number. Of course, if the auction he planned in Butte went well, he might change his mind. At least half the two-year-olds showed cattle sense, making them even more valuable.

Right after lunch one day, a line rider rode into the headquarters on a lathered, sagging horse. He said, "About two hundred head of cattle crossed our border. I thought they had just wandered off and went to look for them. When I caught up to them, I saw about ten cowboys pushing them. If we hurry, we can catch them by daylight."

Colorado said, "Go to the bunkhouse and get some rest. Tell anyone in there to get ready for a chase."

Fergus, Wolf, Jeb, and Chinn joined the ranch hands in the chase. Everyone was armed with a Winchester lever action, and most carried a Colt revolver. They occasionally had a few head rustled, but seldom two hundred and not this early in the year. It was apparent the rustlers did not expect a quick response from the ranch, but they should have known better. Two hundred cows were easy to follow even with a quarter moon.

The chasers heard the cattle lowing before they saw the herd and rustlers. The ranch group decided to go around the herd while it was still difficult to see. They also kept just under the horizon. The rustlers were not very industrious and slept until after sunup. When they woke, they were surrounded. Fergus told them to drop their guns, but no one obeyed, which was too bad for them. The bloody dance began, but it did not last long. Fergus and others like Colorado, Jeb, and Wolf were far too fast and accurate. The rustlers got off only a few shots. Only one of the ranch hands needed a little first aid. The rustlers would never see another sundown.

The hands rounded up the herd and ate the meager breakfast the rustlers had planned to eat. Fergus said, "We're not far from Butte. This might be a good time to take some or all of the cows to the rail head and sell them. Jeb, you and Colorado pick the hands you need, drive them to Butte, and see how many you can sell. Drive what's left to the trailhead. Ask top dollar — the track layers may be interested in good beef."

Colorado said, "Why don't we take half this time since we don't know the ropes yet. Won't take long to come get another herd if the price is right."

"Good idea! Sell all you can in Butte. Check with Josh Doyle. He might have some ideas and will surely know where the end of the line is. We'll start driving half of them back toward the ranch, but we'll mosey along slow just in case."

They divided the herd in short order. Colorado's group took half the herd, about a hundred and twenty head.

––––––––––––––––––

When the cattle arrived in Butte, Josh Doyle bought five head and put them in one of his corrals. The boarding house matron also took five and asked the cowboys to put them in her corral. Both buyers would butcher a beef when they needed meat. Four individuals bought one cow each. Everyone paid top dollar — fifty percent more than the ranch could get from the eastern cattle buyers.

Josh described the planned route the railroad tracks. It would take a week to reach the end of the line, so they started moving the herd that afternoon. They made good time and found plenty of grass along the way. But they made a sad discovery that evening— they did not have an experienced cook on the drive. It was an oversight everyone paid for, especially Colorado and Jeb, who had to listen to much complaining. Jeb learned to be a passable cook by the third or fourth day. Even with a cook, the menu was pretty much the same — meat and beans.

The cattle got used to the drive and became more pliable with fewer breakouts. The grass held up well, and they found water at least twice a day because of the spring melt. Some creeks were higher than they wanted to cross, but it was relatively easy to find better fords.

Jeb heard a distinct train whistle in the distance on the seventh day out of Butte. He and Colorado rode ahead while the cowboys held the cattle on good grass. They found a foreman, who directed them to the superintendent about a mile back down the track.

The superintendent was busy cursing a group of workers who were not working as hard as he wanted. One of the workers shot back, "If you'd feed us better, we could work harder! Nothing but beans ain't no way to feed hard working track layers."

He agreed but said there was not enough game to even flavor the beans. Jeb walked up and said, "I might can help with your meat problem."

"If you can deliver meat, I'll pay whatever the price."

"Now you are talking my language! I'm holding a small cattle herd about a mile past the end of tracks, over a hundred head. They're prime beef and not stolen."

"I'll take 'em all. What's your price?"

Jeb gave him a number twice the normal price, and the superintendent did not hesitate to say, "I'll take 'em all and more if you have 'em." The workers cheered.

"I can have another herd here in two weeks. They will be the same quality."

"Go get 'em. A hundred head won't last long with this bunch."

"I'll send a couple of riders to get the herd started this way."

"Could you bring two hundred head next time?"

"Sure. They may come in two groups a few days apart if we can catch the first hundred before they get back to the ranch. They were rustled, but we caught the thieves and recovered the herd. We brought half of them here and sent the rest to our ranch."

"Go get 'em!"

Colorado picked two of the best riders and four of the best and fastest horses. He said, "Don't spare the horses, but try not to kill them."

He told the men what to tell Fergus and sent them on their way. Riding hard, they could get to the ranch in four days but hoped to catch Fergus and the other herd before then. They rode as hard as a man could and changed horses every four hours. Four hours of sleep each twenty-four was all they would get.

When the two riders found Fergus, they gave him the information and the price Jeb had received for the cattle. They were dead on their feet. Fergus told them to rest while the others turned the herd around. Fergus would go to the ranch to pick up another herd and start them toward the railroad.

Fergus thought, *We can turn a nice profit with the railroad. Unfortunately, it won't last but a few years.*

The ranch sold 300 head of prime cattle to the railroads for a premium price, which was an excellent start to the year.

———————————

Spring roundup was launched when all the cowboys returned to the ranch. Roundup was a big operation in the Bitterroot Valley. Bonner's Den Ranch joined the Angus ranch and a few smaller operations efforts. Fergus's horse pastures were fenced, but Angus Ranch and the other ranches had no perimeter fencing. The cattle from each ranch were mingled with the others. Bonner's Den Ranch had the most extensive land holding and the most cattle. Virtually all the ranches were treated like open range.

Every ranch contributed cowboys to the roundup. The cowboys collected large herds of cattle near corrals scattered around all the landholdings and divided them based on the brand. When a branded momma cow had a calf by side, the calf received the same brand.

All the ranches had a branding fire at the collection stations. The system worked fine except for unbranded yearlings missed the previous year. The ranchers had a gentleman's agreement that they would brand the mavericks in proportion to the cattle a ranch owned. Bonner owned about forty percent of the mother cows and branded forty percent of the mavericks. It was a workable system so long as everybody followed it and the number of mavericks was not excessive.

The roundup took over a month of bone-jarring work. Each cowboy needed at least four cow horses. The hundred or so men ate a passel of food. They used two chuckwagons and a supply wagon. Two cooks and four helpers did the cooking. One cook was up well before dawn, getting everything ready for breakfast. A hundred cowboys can eat a lot of biscuits. Breakfast was not over until the cowboys on night duty had been fed.

The other chuckwagon crew then started working on the evening meal, which was some form of meat, beans, or potatoes, with dessert, usually a cobbler made with dried fruit. The cobbler could only be touched at supper. A man could lose a finger or hand trying to snitch the cobblers or the sugar. Lunch was usually beef, often rolled in a tortilla.

The system of feeding the cowboys worked well most of the time. Rain could create soggy food and watered-down coffee. The coffee received the most complaints when it was watered down. They erected large canvases to protect the men as much as possible. Overall, the two roundups each year were the most challenging work for the cowboys.

Fergus, Angus, and the other owners were involved in the operation. Fergus was still one of the best heelers in the group. Angus was past his prime as a cowboy and often did supply runs.

Fergus and the other ranchers knew about barbed wire, and Fergus was sure one or more of the current owners, or, more likely, a new owner, would string wire and open range would be a thing of the past. He did not plan to be the first to string the stuff up. He had heard it could really cut animals up, especially valuable horses.

The roundup was about half complete when Morgan came riding in hard. She went straight to Fergus.

Morgan said breathlessly, "Horse rustlers hit us last night. It looks like they took about twenty-five mares and two stallions. They headed north, but I don't know which way after that. Chinn and Oby tracking them. It's not a hard job from what I saw."

Fergus took Jeb, Colorado, Wolf, and three other top hands to chase the rustlers. They each saddled a fresh horse and rode out. The trail was easy to follow because thirty or more horses tore up the ground, and the rustlers traveled fast. But they could not travel as fast as the chasers. Fergus saw Oby riding low to stay behind the sparse cover.

Oby said, "We have them spotted two ridges over. Chinn is watching them. He thinks we can get the horses back without losing any."

Fergus and the others followed Oby to the trees where Chinn waited. He had been observing the rustlers, trying to determine their vulnerabilities. Their main weaknesses involved no discipline and they did not watch their back trail, which could get them killed.

Chinn said, "If we slip in just before daylight while they are asleep, we can use knives and not fire a shot. We have one more man than they have. Their horses are tethered, and they did not post a guard."

"I like your plan. Everyone try to sleep as soon as it gets dark. We'll have a cold camp. Make sure your knife is razor sharp. We want to avoid a shooting scrape if possible. I'll wake everyone up about an hour before daybreak, so we'll be next to our targets by the time the eastern sky provides a bit of light."

The plan was good and would have worked if one cowboy had not heard the call of nature a little early. He stumbled over one of the attackers, yelled, and rolled around on the ground. All the rustlers awakened and grabbed their pistols. The bloody dance started.

Fergus's men still had the advantage, but only by a little. Fergus stayed a little back initially because his forces had a one-person advantage. He had retained his speed and accuracy with a revolver. He took out three rustlers, and their advantage grew. Everyone concentrated on the person they were assigned to knife, and the dance was over quickly. Most of the rustlers were shot, but Chinn used his big sword to cut his man almost in half.

They herded the horses back to the ranch without further incident. Everyone but Chinn and Oby returned to the roundup, which concluded a week later.

When the roundup ended, Fergus had an accurate head count, including the age composition of his herd. He was happy with both sets of numbers.

Chapter Two

Colorado let a few cowboys go when the roundup ended, but not many. They could help with the potatoes and garden if they could humble themselves enough to work in the dirt. Most would work only from the back of a horse, but a few stayed on for the farm work.

Morgan and the other mothers talked seriously about taking the children to San Francisco in the late summer. Morgan worked on convincing Fergus to go with them in case any problems arose. San Francisco was a city known for its high crime rate. Fergus agreed accompany the group and decided to chat with Oby and Chinn about going along. Oby agreed to go, but the conversation with Chinn was interesting.

When Fergus asked him, Chinn responded, "Fergus, if you were going anywhere but the west coast, I would be happy to go along. But I fear I could bring even more danger to your group."

"Why?"

"I'm sure my father-in-law has agents in San Francisco, and they likely have contracted with the Chinese Tong to keep an eye out for his daughter and me. If they find me, you and your group would also be in grave danger. If you decide to take the children on another trip later, such as to Denver, I would go with you."

Fergus replied, "I understand. I certainly don't want to endanger Little Bird's husband."

The trip took place in August and would last about three weeks. Morgan was not sure she wanted to miss any of the potato harvest, but she knew Brody could handle it. Fergus had organized the ranch operations so no aspect was totally dependent on any one person.

Fergus was a little worried about the children's safety. He and Oby would always be armed with a .44-40 Colt Peacemaker and at least one derringer, and each mother would carry a derringer. He also liked the idea of taking a couple of shotguns. He would also miss having Kota on the trip. Kota died the previous winter at fifteen years old. Everyone at the ranch was upset at his passing, and Mary cried for a week.

The adults traveling were:

> Fergus
> Morgan
> Oby
> Zelma
> Kamiah
> Half Moon

The youngsters traveling were:

> Mary
> Elbert
> Bates
> Briggs
> Rowdy
> Joe
> Liz
> Colt
> Little Elk

They took a wagon to the end of the line. The wagon carried their supplies, the younger children, Zelma, and Oby. Everyone else rode horses. The end of the line was almost to the Dillon settlement. The railroad was busy building structures in Dillon to serve as the tracklayers' winter quarters.

A joyous group of people rode toward the train. They camped for four nights on the trip.

The train mainly hauled copper ore from the Butte mines. It traveled on narrow gauge tracks to get through the narrow areas along the mountainous route. It was a genuinely scenic ride with breathtaking mountains and beautiful valleys. Mary was the only youngster who had ever been on a train. The train was not crowded, but a few other passengers did not like the children.

One man became irritated and drew back his hand to smack Rowdy. Fergus grabbed his hand at its full backward movement. His hand did not come forward a fraction of an inch, which hurt the man's shoulder. His friends wanted to help, but they quickly realized Fergus already had his revolver out. Oby's shotgun was ready, and they saw several women holding derringers.

Fergus said, "If you gentlemen plan to stay on this train, you will not threaten the children. Should any of you strike one of them, you will die. Got it!"

The men moved to the end of the passenger car and started talking, "Who is that man? He has to be a gunfighter. I've seen some fast men but never anyone who looked faster."

They asked another passenger, but he did not know. The second one they asked knew the man.

"He's Fergus Bonner. He's a rancher but I understand he has taken on multiple shootists simultaneously and prevailed. I would give him a wide berth." The men thought that was a good advice.

The train took a day and a half to reach Cheyenne. They rented rooms for the night and bought train tickets to San Francisco. The train would depart at noon, so they had time to explore. Cheyenne was by far the biggest 'city' any of the children had seen.

When the train finally rolled out, Fergus talked to all the children and mothers. He gave each child fifty dollars and each parent a hundred dollars. He explained that they should be careful with their money and spend it wisely in San Francisco. They would find something good before the trip ended, but they should wait until they were absolutely sure before buying anything. Everyone could return and pick up their desired items on the last day of the visit.

He expected the mothers to understand but knew the children would be impatient. He actually planned to give them another fifty dollars toward the end of the trip. This might be the only trip to a big city they ever took. He played a little game with himself, trying to guess what each child would buy. He was sure Rowdy, Colt, and Mary would buy horse-related and shooting-related items. He would ensure the group visited a leather goods store and a gun shop early in the trip. Fergus was clueless about what the others would want. It would be interesting and reveal a lot about each child.

Fergus paid for three train compartments from Cheyenne to San Francisco. The trip was uneventful, and the mountain vistas were beautiful. The train traveled faster than the narrow gauge work train to Cheyenne. It passed near some of the tallest mountains in the country.

After crossing the mountains, they entered a long series of valleys. They saw many food crops, which caught Morgan's attention. They also saw many groves of different kinds of trees. The fields and groves stretched for miles. No one but Fergus had seen grape vineyards before, but they soon figured out they were for making wine. The grapes were not ready for picking, but the bunches of grapes hung heavy on the vines.

The train made a short layover in Sacramento before rolling to San Francisco. The children could see the Pacific Ocean in a few places. Only Morgan and Fergus had seen it, and that was many years ago. Fergus was surprised to see extensive ranching — cattle, horses, and sheep. Fergus pondered, *"Bringing cattle to market in California would not likely be profitable, but the Appaloosa horses might be a hit."*

They finally arrived at the San Francisco depot. It took three rental buggies to transport the people and luggage to the hotel Fergus picked out. It was a grand hotel with a Mexican motif, not far from the bay and downtown. Fergus was told the waterfront was unsafe, especially at night, so he planned to avoid it with the children.

Everyone was excited, but they were also tired. The parents decided to take naps before making an excursion. The older children grabbed literature in the lobby that described what to do and see in the city.

Everyone eventually fell asleep and had a good nap. The children and most parents woke up raring to explore. They had never seen a trolley car and wanted to ride in one. The cars were pulled by horses and rolled along a track like a train car. The trolleys passed by places they wanted to see while in the city. The tall three and four-story buildings amazed everyone.

Several children were hungry, so they got off the trolley and found a restaurant. It was the fanciest restaurant most of them had ever seen. At first, they were told children were not allowed, but the manager relented since it was before the dinner crowd.

Many items on the menu were mysterious to the group, especially the seafood listings. Fergus talked to a waiter and told him about their dilemma. The waiter agreed to help and was very patient with the ordering. Eventually, everyone made their selection. The youngsters tended to pick meat and potato dishes. Some of the adults chose seafood.

Almost everyone was pleased with their order. Zelma, however, chose a dish she thought was seafood but turned out to be mountain oysters, which are the testicles of young bull calves. They ate them on the ranch during the spring roundup, but she could not eat them. Fergus graciously exchanged plates with her. He loved the meal and now had a new name for them.

The waiter asked Fergus to make dessert selections he thought the children and adults would all enjoy. Fergus jumped at the chance. He ordered several different desserts, and everyone passed them around. They were delicious and not baked with the typical dried fruits available on the ranch.

Fergus gave the waiter a ten-dollar gold piece for a tip before they departed. It was much more than the typical customer gave, and the waiter asked them to return any time. He gave Fergus his work schedule and told him to ask for Pierre.

They rode the trolley back to the hotel and walked around to see what was nearby. Fergus always walked out front, and Oby brought up the rear. Fergus scrutinized each person they met. Even in dress clothes, Fergus was an intimidating figure, especially to some of the city's dandies. They could tell he was a man not to be trifled with. The women also looked like they could hold their own, particularly when they noticed the knives at Kamiah and Half Moon's sides.

They visited the bay and enjoyed watching the seals and sea lions. They also spotted a sea otter occasionally. No one had ever seen such animals, and everyone was fascinated. Oby was unfortunate enough to have a seagull defecate on his hat and best shirt. He was not amused, but everyone else was.

Just before returning to the hotel, they passed a shop that advertised 'ice cream.' No one in the group knew what it was, but it sounded good. Everyone got a small bowl and thought it was terrific. It was similar to something they made in the mountains with snow and sweetened condensed milk but much smoother. Oby loved it, and it almost took his mind off the gull incident.

Fergus thought they would sample ice cream again. He also wanted to find out how they made it and buy the equipment. The cowboys back home would pay dearly for something that good, but he planned to provide it to them free of charge.

Even after the afternoon naps, most of the group were ready for bed when they returned to the hotel. Their rooms had a good view of the bay and the ocean. Everyone locked their doors, which they did not normally do at home, and went to bed before the sun was completely down. The salty sea air coming through the windows made it seem cool. Everyone slept well, even if a little damper than on the ranch.

Oby tried to clean his hat and shirt before going to bed and again the next morning. He was mumbling something that Fergus was sure the women would disapprove of if they heard it. He asked the doorman if he had a remedy for the stains before breakfast. The hat was soon returned in pristine condition, and the shirt would be returned later.

Morgan gasped when she saw Mary's hair the next morning. The salty dampness had not been kind to it. It was very curly and sticking out in all directions. Morgan looked in a mirror and realized her hair was just as bad. It would take an hour to get it presentable. She started with Mary so she could go downstairs with Fergus for breakfast. She began on hers and worked herself into a state of righteous indignation. The dry mountain air did not treat her hair this way.

All the women except the Nez Perce came to breakfast with the same complaint. They would figure out a way to sleep without all the windows open. It might get a little warm, but they could not take an hour just to comb the girls' hair. Fergus's hair was also much curlier, and the red shined brighter than usual. He was not concerned about his hair and just pulled his Stetson a little lower.

The day was spent visiting the city's museums. The children got all the history they wanted long before the adults. After several dustups, Fergus and Oby took them out of the second museum and let them run themselves silly on a little grassy area. When they got tired, Fergus found another ice cream shop, which was a hit with everyone. The women came out of the museum about the time most of the ice cream cones were gone, with much being on their clothes. The mothers were unhappy about Fergus buying the kids ice cream close to lunch. Morgan read him the riot act, and he promised not to do it again.

After a short discussion, they took everyone back to the hotel for naps. Most went to sleep shortly after lying down. Fergus saw a leather store near the hotel and decided they would visit it after lunch. They ate a light lunch and headed to the store.

As Fergus expected, the older children were drawn to the fancy Mexican saddles and related tack. He reminded them to be patient before buying, but it was hard to drag them away from the store.

Fergus then led them to a nearby gun store. Fergus became interested in a Winchester 73 rifle in a caliber he did not have, .32-20. It was underpowered but much more capable than a .22. The store owner said the rifle kicked very little and was accurate out to nearly one hundred yards. Fergus ordered a case of twelve. All the children would get one for Christmas.

The group went to a Chinese restaurant for dinner. Chinn occasionally cooked Chinese meals on the ranch, so they knew what to expect. The food was delicious, and the service was superb. The staff was surprised that several group members knew a few Chinese words. Everyone was brought a fortune cookie after the meal. They had a grand time reading each other's messages, which led to many laughs and guffaws.

Fergus and Morgan talked after supper about how to better arrange their days. One museum a day was about all the children could handle. They picked out the ones they would visit each morning for the next five days. The plan worked much better once the children understood they had to 'enjoy' only one museum daily. They actually enjoyed some of their visits.

They spent one day across the bay in a giant redwood forest. The children were awed by the enormous trees and enjoyed the visit. Fergus told them about working up and down the coast harvesting redwood trees to build many buildings in the area. The logging allowed him to make enough money to move to Idaho and meet Morgan. The girls liked the story's romantic element. Little did they know that the couple had been more concerned about survival than romance. They walked around the grove and discussed the lack of insects and birds. It was a strange phenomenon to them. None of the children had ever been in a completely silent forest. They spent three hours wandering around in the redwood grove.

They spent an entire day browsing Chinatown's myriad stores and small shops. The children found many things to spend their money on. The girls bought small dolls and trinkets, and the boys picked up a few items like kites. They had several boxes and bags to carry back to the hotel. Fergus bought food from a street cart for their noon meal. Everyone thought the meal was fantastic.

They returned to the leather store the following day. Almost everyone bought a pair of boots, including the adults. Several saddles with fancy silver conchos were purchased. Fergus knew the saddles were pretty but was not sure about their comfort. He ensured the saddles trees were substantial and made from good hardwood. The leather was less critical than the wooden tree forming the saddle's base. Fergus ensured everyone had enough money to pay for what they picked out. They did with a bit of help from him.

Mary discovered a flyer announcing a performance at The California Theater. It was a play written by a man named Shakespeare.

Mary said, "It's probably boring, but I want to see it. Can we go tomorrow night?"

Morgan responded, "Sure. See if you can talk the others into going. If not, you and I will attend."

On the last day, the women and girls visited most of the dress shops lining the main street. Everyone bought two or three everyday outfits, and most of the women also bought at least one fancy outfit. Everyone bought a couple of nice shirts for their husbands, and several purchased a dress Stetson. Mary bought Oby a bowler hat that fit his personality better than a wide-brimmed Stetson.

Mary worked hard during the day to convince the other children to go to the play. She finally got the majority interested, which meant everyone attended. They did not know what to expect but were enthralled with the drama and the costumes. The children were impressed with the way he put words together, and soon were repeating numerous lines from the play.

The homeward bound train would depart at eight a.m. the following morning, so they rose early to board at seven. The night before, they decided to eat breakfast in the depot. They had been eating so well that the women swore they would all diet the way home.

They needed an extra compartment to hold all their purchases. Four saddles and a case of rifles take up a lot of room, and the extra compartment was crammed full.

The trip home was smooth until they reached the steep Sierra Madre grade. Ten robbers hit the train just after daylight near the top of the grade when the train was struggling and moving very slowly. The robbers foolishly expected little or no resistance. But the train was hauling an Army payroll and had a squad of troops in the baggage car, which had shooting ports. The troops were well-armed with Spencer's or Winchesters. The Bonner group was also well-armed, as were many other passengers. The robbers did not stand a chance, and all of them but one perished. Unfortunately, the one survivor had taken control of the engine.

Morgan and Fergus realized the problem and took steps to resolve it. While in the gun store, Fergus bought two new Greener shotguns that used centerfire shells like their Winchester rifles. They were devastating weapons when loaded with buckshot.

Morgan slipped up one side of the train and Fergus the other. The robber in the engine did not know what to do. The gang had expected little resistance, and he was the only one alive. He kept looking back down the track, trying to figure out what to do. He saw Morgan first, squeezed off a wild shot, and jumped off the engine on the opposite side. Seldom has a man gone from the frying pan into the fire in a more grave way.

He saw Fergus far too late. Both barrels of buckshot caught him square in the chest. He barely knew what hit him.

The engineer was a little woozy, but the fireman had more severe injuries. Fergus decided he could stoke the furnace until they reached a station and found a replacement — at least, he hoped they could find one. Fortunately, the engineer found a spare railroad man at the next station.

A worn-out Fergus returned to join his group. Shoveling coal into a steam locomotive's furnace used muscles he had not used in a long time.

When they arrived in Cheyenne, the depot manager found Fergus and tried to pay him for his efforts, but he refused to take the money. Fergus said, "I knew if we were going to get home, somebody had to stoke the furnace. It's hard work, but I don't want to be paid. Wait! I heard many trains serve rum made by a man in the Purgatoire Valley. Does this train stock it?"

"Yes, we do! Freedom Town Rum, and it's excellent."

"If you could slip me a case, we'll call it even."

"Done! You bailed us out by killing the gang's leader and then feeding the furnace to get the train here. You deserve it."

When the group departed Cheyenne, two cases of Freedom Town rum and one of 'shine were in the wagon. He was a happy man the rest of the way to Dillon. The train stopped only a few miles from Dillon.

Fergus had sent a telegram ahead to Josh, and two wagons and their horses were waiting for them at the end of the line. They were the wagons and teams Fergus left with Josh on the way to San Francisco. They drove to Butte to let Josh's mule skinners off at Josh's barn.

The group spent the night in Butte so they would not have to camp on the way to the ranch. Fergus was glad to be back on his horse and free of the wagon, where chatter about the trip never ceased. He had no idea how much the women and children would love the journey. They would have to do something like it again.

Their arrival at the ranch house was a sight to behold. Husbands and wives hugged with their children between them. Every child took their daddy something, and every wife did the same. New hats and shirts abounded. Fergus was able to slip the crate of .32-20 rifles into his room. They would make great Christmas gifts.

Colorado and a crew helped unload. Fergus brought out enough Stetsons for each cowboy to have one. All the hats were the same color and style so everyone would know they rode for Bonner's Den Ranch until the hats wore out.

Colorado called Fergus aside to catch him up on the news. First, a big shindig would be held at a new shed near the line between the Angus and Bonner's Den Ranches. Everyone was invited, and two beeves would be roasted. Maude and Angus were planning the event. Dance hall girls from Butte would attend to dance with the cowboys, paid for by Angus and Fergus.

The next piece of information was not as positive, "We're losing cattle almost every week, and so is Angus. We think they're only taking five or ten head at a time. It looks like a few head wander off onto land we don't own. I took Wolf and Jeb out there, and Wolf found a faint shod track. It looked like two riders with sacks tied around their horse's hooves. I don't think we could have found the tracks without Wolf. When do you want to go after them?"

"When is the shindig?"

"Three days."

"Okay, I'll talk to Angus, and we'll make a plan. Let's not mention this around the other ranchers. One of them could be the culprit. We'll push hard when we go for them. Make plans to double the guards in the line shacks after the party."

Fergus spoke in his booming voice, "Mom, I hear you've been cooking up some dancing while we were gone. Want to fill everybody in while we're all here?"

"Y'all just leave us alone. We're planning a humdinger shindig."

She told them the party would start in three days and might last a few days. They needed to be ready to camp there one night, maybe two. Everyone was enthusiastic, especially the children. They hoped to meet new people to play and fight with.

Mary wondered if Mr. Angus's grandsons would be at the shindig, *"What was that boy's name? Milam? Yes, it was Milam. He should be almost grown like me. Hmm. Maybe something interesting could develop."*

Morgan had the same thoughts, but she was not happy with hers. This party might launch something she was not ready to deal with.

Chapter Three

The following two days were spent getting ready for the shindig. Fergus sent a hand to help the cook set everything up. The cook would be missed at the bunkhouse, but his assistant could handle a day or two with minimal trouble. Another cowboy drove two fat yearlings to the cook's shed and helped the cook butcher one of them. The cooks decided to wait until the next day to butcher the other beef because meat on the hoof did not need to be iced down.

Fergus rode to the shindig site a day early, hoping Angus would also show up to discuss the rustling situation. Angus rode in shortly after Fergus arrived. Both men were pleased to find their thoughts were similar. Angus also agreed that one of the smaller ranchers might be the thief. They talked all afternoon about different approaches to catch the rustlers, finally settled on a plan, and worked out most of the details. They did not plan to mention the missing cattle to anyone at the shindig.

Angus said his sons and grandchildren were visiting and would attend the party. Fergus thought silently, "*That will make Mary happy and Morgan nervous.*" He did not plan to tell Morgan and to be somewhere else when she heard.

The butchered yearling was put on a spit, and a helper assigned to baste it and keep it rotating. Three big pots of water were set on fire to boil potatoes. The cooks would transform them into potato salad. The cooks deboned the beef and reserved the best cuts for steaks the following day. Everything else went into a huge pot of Mexican stew. Angus still had ice he stored in an icehouse at his ranch. The steaks and other perishables were put on the ice.

Guests began arriving later in the afternoon. A few helped with the cooking, but most visited with friends from other ranches. They typically saw each other twice a year during the roundups, but those times were not conducive to visiting or getting to know each other better. A few cowboys were married, but not many. The typical cowboy wage was a dollar a day and meals, so it was challenging to support a family. Most cowboys lived in a bunkhouse, and few ranches had private cabins for cowboys. The wives all knew each other because there were so few of them.

All the Bonner hands except a skeleton crew to feed and check on the horses attended, but they would be rotated to the shindig the second day. Little stock feeding occurred during the summer because the grass was so good. The stallions needed care since they were put in the barn at night. As soon as Mary arrived, she began looking around for Angus's grandsons, especially Milam. She spotted him standing close to Angus.

He saw her and broke away. They walked off and began chatting. Morgan was more than a little concerned but said nothing. She knew Mary was as headstrong as her mother, but people were everywhere. Morgan began assisting the cooks and their helpers, but they already had enough help.

Morgan asked Fergus, "Did you see her go straight to Milam?"

"Yes, Morgan, but they're just talking."

"That's how a romance starts, and she's too young."

"Yes, ma'am. I'll watch and make sure they stay close to the activities. I could send her to get something, but I'm sure he would want to ride with her."

"I know! I don't like it, but I can't stop them from talking. I'm afraid they will soon be holding hands. I don't know if I can handle that."

"When did you get married?"

That was definitely the wrong question, and she let him know. He would need to step lightly and keep his distance for a while.

Angus walked over and asked Fergus if he wanted to check their borders for cattle crossings while the meal was cooking. The aroma of the Mexican stew already wafted throughout the area.

Angus called Milam over and asked if he wanted to begin his ranching education. He wanted to ride along with Angus and Fergus, as did Mary. Fergus found Morgan to tell her what was happening. The look she gave him would have braised all the meat on the table, but she did not say 'no.'

The foursome rode toward the rougher section of Bonner's Den Ranch. Mary had not been there and asked many questions. Fergus told her it was about a thousand acres of steep, rugged forest land. They wanted to see if any cattle were there. They cantered to the edge of the rough terrain and turned north toward Angus's land. The group rode the edge of the wooded area and found where about fifty cattle had been held in a forest glade. The cattle had apparently been driven higher in the mountains.

Angus showed Milam how to read the tracks. Learning to read tracks well enough to determine the approximate count would take a while. Mary listened and paid attention to every word. She instinctively knew seeing bunched tracks leaving the ranch was not good. Milam had to be told.

Angus said, "Fergus, we should start here after the shindig. These tracks are fresh."

Mary asked, "How do you know they're fresh?"

Fergus stepped down to show her, "See how the edges of the tracks are sharp and distinct? The wind and rain only take a few days to round the edges off, and rain makes it happen quicker. It hasn't rained lately, but the wind always blows up here. Those tracks are less than two days old. It looks like they were being driven fast because the front of the tracks are dragged more than normal. The droppings are also still moist. They'll start drying on the edges after about a week."

"How long did it take you to learn that?"

"A long time. You should see Wolf tracking. He can read tracks much better than I can. He grew up reading tracks because his entire village depended on the men being good trackers. He can see bent grass blades and figure out what happened days ago. He truly amazes me."

Fergus and Angus decided to head back to the celebration. They did not want to give the rustlers a reason to change their methods. Both men thought they should be able to catch the rustlers within a few days. They were also sure the rustlers would fight. Each was thinking about how many cowboys they wanted to take on the chase. Those remaining would start the fall roundup.

The fall roundup was critical. It was when they selected the cattle to sell before winter arrived. Most yearlings are sold in the fall and would be in good condition and weight. In most cases, they would also sell cows that did not have a calf at their side. They would bring the herds together as they did in the spring. But branding and castration would be needed only for the few yearlings missed in the spring. Each ranch would decide which animals to sell and which ones to keep in their herds.

Since most cowboys worked roundup, Fergus and Angus thought the rustlers would likely increase their activity. The small group of cowboys on the chase team would be missed, but if they moved quickly, they might catch the rustlers red-handed.

When they returned, the celebration was beginning to crank up. A six-man band with two excellent fiddlers was already playing. A few people were dancing, but most were eating.

Mary and Milam sat together to eat. They were not sitting close, but they were not very far apart. Neither ate much. Suddenly, they were dancing to a lively song—not too close, but close enough to concern Morgan.

Fergus asked Morgan to dance. She almost refused, but she quickly hatched a plan.

When she and Fergus reached the bare ground serving as the dance floor, she guided them close to Mary and Milam. Morgan suggested they change partners. She danced with Milam, and Fergus got Mary.

Morgan immediately asked Milam, "What are your intentions toward Mary?"

27

He stuttered and looked like a scared fawn, "I don't have a plan. We're close to the same age and just like talking. I think she's a very admirable girl, but I have no immediate plans. You will be among the first to know if that changes. Who knows what the future may hold?"

Morgan felt a lot better but was still not wholly mollified. She could not forget her and Shelby's marriage and what she might have missed by marrying so young. But Milam seemed much more mature than Shelby ever was. He was more like Fergus had always been. Her emotions settled down.

The dancing continued for hours despite the men vastly outnumbering the women. The women had to occasionally beg to sit out a dance to catch their breath. The dance hall women would visit the next day. None of the wives opposed them coming out after the fatigue and blisters brought on by too much dancing.

The cooks butchered the other steer the next morning, and began preparing for a steak meal. Every piece possible was cut into a steak. These were added to the cuts saved from the first day's beef. They needed a large number steaks to feed everyone, and cowboys wanted big steaks. Strangely enough, most did not care which cut they received. In fact, many preferred the tougher cuts like sirloin or shoulder cuts. The only meat left on the carcass was trimmings, which were used in a hearty chili and in the leftover Mexican stew.

Breakfast was biscuits, cured ham, and eggs. The lunch selection was stew or chili. Morgan was less keyed up but not completely relaxed. Once again, Milam and Mary hung out together most of the time. One of the other smaller ranchers had a Shoshone wife and two daughters a little younger than Mary. Rowdy and Colt hung close to the girls, but not as close as Milam and Mary.

After breakfast, the ranch owners and their wives talked, and many men enjoyed a cigar. Fergus went to his wagon for a bottle of Freedom Town rum. He returned and poured his group a cup of rum. Everyone was impressed. Fergus allowed them only one cup.

Everyone talked about their future plans. The plans were all similar except for Angus, "I'm getting pretty long in the tooth, quite a bit more than the rest of you. My sons are not interested in ranching, but one of my grandsons is. From now on, Milam will be living with me so I can teach him about ranching. He'll inherit my ranch when I pass. Don't tell any of those dance hall women about him becoming a major landowner. They'll be all over him, literally."

Everyone but Morgan laughed. She thought, *"Mercy! Milam will only be a day's ride away from Mary! At least he won't be a pauper if anything serious develops."*

The dance hall women arrived with a piano shortly after lunch. They were wearing their most conservative work dresses, which were not particularly conservative. The whooping and hollering could be heard for a mile. The women knew the rules — they were to only dance with the cowboys and not leave the area for a walk.

The band and the tinny-sounding piano, started playing before dark and continued until midnight. Fergus surprised everyone by making ice cream with the three crank freezers he brought from San Francisco. They made two batches in each freezer, with ice and salt being the limiting factors. Few people at the party had ever tasted ice cream, and everyone loved it. Angus wanted to know where he could buy the freezers. He vowed to his hands he would soon have the right equipment, even if he had to go get it himself.

After two days and nights of partying, most guests were ready to shut the party down at midnight. The dance hall girls returned to town, and the families and cowboys went to sleep.

Only Angus and Fergus sat up and chatted. They enjoyed a glass of the excellent rum and smoked a cigar. The topic was chasing down the rustlers. They decided it was time to bring in their foremen, so they woke them up. They wanted to take about ten men on the chase, and they wanted them to be good shooters. The foremen wanted to go on the chase but understood they were needed more for the roundup. Fergus wanted Wolf for tracking purposes and three other cowboys. Angus planned to take Milam and Tall One, a Shoshone, and two more cowboys.

Each foreman selected cowboys who were fearless and skilled with rifles and pistols. The only people likely to be missed at roundup were Fergus and Angus. Their story was that they needed to deal with a big cattle buyer.

Everyone returned home the next day after a breakfast of leftovers, which were ample. Colorado called out the three cowboys he wanted to go on the chase. Fergus explained what had been happening to cattle from Bonner's Den and the Angus ranches.

Colorado said, "Mr. Fergus asked me to pick out the three cowboys who I thought would be the best on chase, and I chose you. When we return to the ranch, pick out two top horses, and get a .45-70 rifle and your favorite pistol. Bring a couple hundred rounds of ammunition for each. You may catch them within a day or be on the trail for two or three weeks, so take whatever you need. Shorty, as I recall, you are a pretty good trail cook, so you have that chore. We'll not discuss what you're doing beyond going with Fergus on a job he wants done. Be ready to leave at daylight tomorrow."

Fergus said, "We're being secretive because some of our neighbors could be involved. If true, we don't want to alert them. They have also taken a few horses, and you know the penalty for that. We're going to ride hard and put a stop to the rustling. We will face a dangerous situation, so if you are not up to going, say so now."

No one raised a hand. One of the cowboys eventually commented, "Looks to me like the biggest danger will be eatin' Shorty's cooking."

The comment drew a few guffaws and a rancorous threat from Shorty regarding what he might cook one night. Elk droppings figured heavily in the threat.

The group rode out just as the sky lightened in the east. They rode hard to where Angus and Fergus had found the cattle tracks a few days earlier.

Wolf dismounted to study the tracks. After a few minutes, he said, "Tracks go in and out here. They must drive them into this tangle, hold them for a while, and then take them up into the mountains. We need to search here before we go up the mountains after them."

Milam rode with Angus and Milam was told to hang back while they weaved through the tangled terrain. Milam asked, "Do you think someone should go to the other side of this scope of wood, just in case someone goes out that way?"

"Good thinking. Why don't you and Dub hustle to the other side while we work through this? If they come out, take your time. Make sure it's not us and blast 'em."

Milam and Dub rode around to the other side of the finger of dense trees, and three riders broke cover and galloped away. Dub and Milam were excellent rifle shots, and two rustlers fell before the third one galloped over a rise. Milam put his horse into a dead run and caught up with the rustler. He leaped onto the rustler's horse and took him to the ground. The fall took the air out of both the rustler and Milam. Dub rode up with his pistol drawn.

The rustler sat up and tried to get his breath, and Milam looked a little dazed. He had no idea he would make such a move, it just happened. Milam's pistol was on the ground, so he retrieved it and held it on the man.

Dub used a piggin' string to tie the rustler's hands and helped him get on his horse. They rode back by the two rustlers who were shot. They had breathed their last — a .45-70 slug leaves a big hole, especially where it exits, and the two men were centered.

The others rode out of the woods, and Fergus asked, "What have y'all got?"

Milam answered, "Two dead rustlers, but one is alive and able to talk."

Angus asked, "How did you catch him alive?"

Dub replied, "Well, sir, the boy took off after him and caught him within a half mile. He jumped and pulled the rustler clean off his horse. When I got there, both were a little dazed. I think this tough guy is embarrassed about a youngster taking him down. Milam will do to ride the river with."

Angus started to fuss at Milam, but Fergus interrupted, "Angus, we have somebody to answer our questions, and the boy will bounce back quicker than us older guys. He did a great job and earned his spurs amongst your hands. He's had a good day."

"I reckon you're right, but dang it, I finally have a grandson interested in ranching, and he takes a big risk on his first day. It scares me to death. What if he had broken his neck?"

"He didn't. And don't tell me you never did anything on the rash side."

"That was me, but this is my grandson!"

"Are you ready to talk to the rustler, or do you just want to stammer and sputter around all day?"

"Alright! Alright! Somebody light a fire and make coffee. I need help getting him to open up. I'll get the branding iron out of my saddle bag. Might need it."

Angus put the branding iron into the fire beside the coffee pot. The rustler's eyes widened with apprehension.

Angus sat by the fire and poured a cup of coffee when it was ready. He picked the iron up to see if it was hot enough. He turned it over and laid it back in the coals, wanting it to glow red.

He sat back down and said, "Now, Sir, who's running this rustling operation, and where do they take the cattle?"

"I don't know anything."

"Okay. Fergus, please hand me the branding iron."

The rustler quickly said, "I can't tell you. They'll kill me!"

"If you don't answer my questions, I'll put my brand on you. How many brands can you take before you die or go stark raving mad? It's pretty simple. You have a chance if you talk and live, but you don't have any chance if you don't talk."

The branding iron was glowing red, and Angus held it. Angus said, "Hold him so he can't move. I don't want to burn myself."

Three cowboys grabbed the rustler, and Angus put the iron to him.

The man screamed and said, "Stop! I'll talk!"

Angus took the iron away and directed another cowboy to put it back in the fire. The man said, "The leader is Scar Wooten. The cattle are taken about ten miles into the hills and held on good grass. We intend to sell them in Cheyenne after we get around five hundred head. They plan to make a couple more gathers before moving out. The three of us were left here to collect fifty head and hold them for the next drive into the hills."

"Okay, I believe you. Men, catch their horses. We'll leave him here. He might make it out alive. If he heads toward the ranch, our men will recognize the brand. He might make it to Butte. It'll take him three or four days."

"You said you would give me a chance!"

"I am. You ain't dead yet, so you have a chance. I didn't say I would give you a good chance. Let's take his boots since he didn't like the first offer."

The rustler made no more comments. He knew they might decide to put a bullet in him or maybe even drag him behind a horse.

The chasers returned to where the trail started up the mountain. Everyone changed horses so they could ride hard. Wolf was out front reading the sign at a fast pace. They made it about five miles and thought they should rest while Wolf and Tall One followed the trail. A quarter moon provided enough light for them to follow the big trail. The two trackers returned just as dusk was fading into black darkness.

When Wolf and Tall One returned, they ate a bowl of Shorty's chili and shared what they found. Ten men were in the rustler's camp. They seemed to have no idea they were being followed. Wolf estimated they had at least four hundred head on good grass. But the good grass was almost grazed down, so the cows had started wandering off to find better grazing.

Wolf said, "If we hit them at daylight, we can take them without them getting many shots off. They'll likely have a couple of night herders with the herd, so we'll have to account for them."

Tall One agreed with Wolf and added, "If Wolf and I sleep a couple of hours and slip back to the herd, we should be able to find the night herders and take them out quietly. Most cowboys sing to the cows, and we both have a bow."

"Good idea. Get your blankets ready and try to sleep as soon as you eat."

Wolf and Tall One ate quickly and crawled into their blankets. Fergus thought it was ironic that two men from tribes who had been fighting each other for generations were now fighting as friends for their ranches.

Fergus woke Wolf and Tall One with a cup of coffee two hours later. They intended to take the night herders out and try to slip back to the main group before the dawn attack. Wolf described where the group should wait for the first light of day.

Wolf and Tall One eased forward on their horses. Once they could smell the herd, they dismounted and walked, with one going right and the other going left. As they suspected, the night herders were singing to keep the cattle calm, making them easy to find. The little bit of moon provided enough light to shoot their bows. They were both close enough, so missing was unlikely. The herders did not know what hit them when the arrows sunk deep into their chests. The herders made only a slight sound when they fell. Like most cowhorses, the horses stopped when the rider came off the saddle. They were caught with relative ease and tied to substantial brushes. Each attacker gave a night bird call when the deed was done. They then rendezvoused at the appointed place and dozed until the group came in leading their horses.

They would need to wait an hour before attacking, which they hoped would end the rustling, at least by this group. Everyone was keyed up and ready to go. Only Milam was a rookie at this type of work. His mouth was dry as he contemplated what was about to happen.

Fergus and Angus walked among the men to ensure all were ready. They would move forward as a group, and Angus would fire the first shot. Two rustlers were making coffee and relieving themselves, making them the first targets. The bloody dance began when Angus shot one of the men. The other man received a thunderous volley all his own. The other rustlers flailed out of their blankets, trying to grab their guns. Only a few men were able to get a weapon out before they were hit multiple times.

Unfortunately, none of the attackers noticed a man sleeping away from the fire. He had grown tired of the cacophony of snoring closer to the fire and moved further out to escape the noise. He jumped up and fired three shots before the men knew where he was. Two of his bullets hit Milam. One was a flesh wound in his shoulder, but the other one was more severe, and it was bleeding badly when Angus got to him.

Angus said, "Fergus, they've killed my grandson!"

Fergus shot back, "Not yet. Let's get him to my place. It's closer. We have a woman who has great skill as a healer."

Chapter Four

Fergus cut poles and cross-members to make a travois. He told Angus, "You should send a good rider on a fast horse to bring a Butte doctor to my ranch. We need to get pressure on both wounds and wrap them tightly. We must hurry, so the ride will be bumpy until we get to the pastures."

They attached the travois to a spare horse. Milam was only semiconscious, which was good. Fergus led the horse pulling the travois and pushed the horses as hard as possible. Angus led a string of three spare horses. The trail got better, and Fergus pushed even harder.

The horses were plumb tuckered out when they were about halfway to Fergus's house. They let the tired horses loose — Fergus expected the group driving the cattle back would find them and bring them closer to the house.

The fresh horses were almost worn out when Fergus saw the ranch house. He fired his revolver three times to alert everyone of trouble. Morgan heard the shots and knew something was wrong. She called everyone to the main house to help deal with whatever was happening.

Fergus stopped as close as possible to the front porch. Morgan, Oby, Chinn, Little Bird, Mary, and all the children ran to the travois. Morgan and Little Bird sprang into action. Mary tried to help but could not because of her teary eyes. She feared Milam was dead.

Little Bird told Lotte to get a clean sheet and put it on the large, sturdy dining table. Angus went to Mary and hugged her.

They carried Milam inside and put him on the table. Little Bird and Morgan worked as quickly as they could. They removed the bloody shirt to inspect the wounds.

Juanita put a large bucket of hot water on the table. Lotte brought all the towels she could carry. The shoulder wound was not bleeding, but the chest wound was and there was no exit wound. They cleaned the wounds and covered them with clean bandages. The bleeding was stopped, at least on the outside. Mary had regained control and helped.

Little Bird said, "The bullet is just under the skin on his back. I need a small sharp small knife to remove it." Oby pulled out one of his small carving knives, which was perfect.

She said, "Wash it in alcohol."

Little Bird slit Milam's skin over the bullet. The bullet popped out and blood gushed. Mary almost lost it again. Morgan first poured the hot water into the wound and washed it. She then poured the alcohol into it, followed by iodine. The sheet was getting bloody and Morgan grabbed another one. Little Bird stuck a wad of cloth in the hole and poured more alcohol and iodine. She then began wrapping a long piece of cloth around his body with Mary's help. She tied it tight after wrapping it four times.

Now, they needed to work on the pass-through wound. They cleaned it with hot water and alcohol. Since the bleeding was almost stopped, Little Bird did not plug the wound. She applied iodine and put a cloth bandage on both sides and wrapped it. It was all she could do.

She looked around and said, "We will change the bandages tomorrow morning. I will bring my strongest herbs to help stave off infection. All we can do now is watch and wait. He's fortunate he was unconscious today. Someone will need to sit with him tonight and probably many more nights. If he makes it until morning, he has a chance. I will make broth. He needs as much as he can swallow, but it may not be until tomorrow. He's lost a lot of blood but seems determined to live."

Angus said, "I plan to stay here tonight and for as long as necessary, if you don't mind."

Fergus replied, "You're welcome to stay as long as you wish. I should go to the roundup to make sure everything is proceeding as it should. I'll leave in the morning and stay for the duration. They don't need us, but I think it's better if at least one of us is there."

The others discussed a rotation for staying up with Milam when Mary said, "I'll be staying wherever he is until he recovers."

Morgan opened her mouth to comment, but Mary said emphatically, "Mother, don't argue with me! I will stay with him. You need to understand that I intend him to be your grandchildren's daddy. Not soon, but in a few years."

No one tried to talk Mary out of her plan. It was now a given.

They prepared Milam a bed near the fireplace. Fergus and Angus made a bed much like the ones in the bunkhouse. Mary stepped out of the room while the men finished undressing Milam because his clothes were soaked in blood. They pulled fresh long underwear up to his waist but did not try to put the top on him.

Milam awakened and groaned when they moved him from the table to the bed. Juanita and Lotte cleaned the blood from the table and floor.

Mary made a pallet near Milam's bed and lay down for a nap. It was nearing sundown, and she was exhausted. She knew everyone else was awake to watch him. But it would likely be only her and Angus through the night.

A few tears trickled down Morgan's face. She knew she had lost her baby daughter mentally, if not physically. She accepted it even though she was not overjoyed about it.

Milam did not stir the rest of the afternoon. Mary did not think he had a fever, but he did not move. She kept him covered, which was easy since he did not move a muscle. Supper time arrived, and Juanita brought her a bowl of thick soup. She ate it sitting on her pallet with her back against the wall. It was as though she was a permanent fixture near his bed. Mary finally went to answer the call of nature and wash up a bit. She still had some of his blood on her arm and thought she should change shirts.

Everyone began drifting off to bed after supper. Morgan said, "Mary, wake me if you need me. I'll come if he starts waking up." She hugged Mary not as a child but as an equal.

Milam groaned a couple of times during the night but did not awaken. Just before daylight, he opened his eyes and asked for water. Mary brought the broth, which had been sitting near enough to the fireplace to stay warm. Angus came over to help.

Mary said, "One of us needs to hold his head up, and the other can give him a sip of broth. Why don't you take his head? Be gentle."

Angus eased his gnarled ranchers' hands under Milam's head and lifted it a few inches off the pillow. Mary gave him a tiny amount of broth, and he wanted more. He eventually got a few ounces down and dozed off quickly.

Morgan was watching from the door. She was happy to see Mary act so professionally in caring for Milam.

Fergus was up and almost ready to leave for the roundup. Juanita had breakfast ready and took a taquito to Mary, who ate it slowly. Angus went to the kitchen to eat breakfast with Fergus.

Little Bird walked in and asked, "How'd he do?"

Mary replied, "He groaned a few times during the night and woke up once about an hour ago. We fed him broth, maybe two ounces. He went back to sleep pretty quickly."

"Good. He did not move much, right?"

"Hardly any."

"We need to talk about our next steps. He has an excellent chance to make it. The bleeding during the night was not as bad as I expected. Maybe he doesn't have enough blood left, but no bleeding is good."

Lotte brought coffee and three cups. Morgan noticed Mary putting a little milk in hers, but less than usual. They all needed the coffee.

After a few sips, Mary asked Little Bird, "What do you think we should do?"

"We need to get my herbs on the wounds, but I hate to start the bleeding again. We should not disturb the plugs in the holes. Let's try to get the wraps off the bandages. The three of us can do it. Mary, you get behind him when we lift him. Hug him to keep him steady, and we'll do the unrolling."

Mary did as she was told. The wraps were removed, and the bandages underneath were a little bloody. The stuffing in the hole was bloody and oozing. Little Bird opened her bag of herbs and sprinkled them on the chest wound. Moving him so Little Bird could get to the exit wound was cumbersome. The bandage was bloodier because of drainage as he lay on his back. Milam's back received a sprinkle of herbs and a fresh bandage. The last step was wrapping him back up. He moaned and moved a little. Mary liked feeling him against her.

The other wound was more accessible, but Little Bird wanted Mary to continue to hold him up. She sprinkled herbs on the wound and applied a clean bandage. As they finished the second wound, Milam awakened with a start. Mary had to hold him tight to keep him from breaking something loose. She liked it, and so did he when he figured out what was happening.

He relaxed a little and they laid him back down. He lay there blinking his eyes. Mary gave him a couple of spoonful's of broth. He wanted more, but everyone told him to make sure everything would stay down. It did, so he consumed the whole bowl. He was tired when he finished but tried to stay awake.

He asked, "Mary, what happened to me? Why am I at your ranch?"

"You were shot twice and lost a lot of blood. Little Bird removed a bullet from your back. Our house was closer than Angus's, and Little Bird is a good healer. Besides, you needed me to take care of you."

"Yes, I did." He grinned.

Morgan sighed. She was not happy about their comments, but neither was she irritated. It appeared some things were inevitable. At least she was getting used to it. They propped him up a little, but he fell asleep in minutes.

Morgan said. "Mary, let me show you how to make elk liver broth for when he wakes up. Liver is the best thing to build blood back."

Little Bird said, "Let me add herbs to it. I have willow bark, which we need to boil first. It can help relieve pain, which will worsen as he moves around today."

Mary watched closely as Morgan chopped the liver into small

pieces. She let it cook until it softened and added Little Bird's herbs. The willow bark water was added last to thin the broth so Milam could drink it. Everything was ready for when he awakened again.

Mary had enough room to sit on Milam's mattress and lean against the wall. His head was lying on her lap and the pillow. She was comfortable and went to sleep.

Maude and Oby arrived, and Maude surveyed the scene. She said, "Morgan, you've lost your baby girl to a good man."

Morgan just looked at her and shook her head. She knew Maude was right but did not have to like it. She was coming around, however.

The doctor from Butte, Doc Boyton, showed up late in the afternoon. He asked Mary, "How's your patient? Has he been resting comfortably?"

Mary replied, "Yes. He's hardly been awake since they brought him in yesterday. He woke up once during the night and drank a little broth. Then he woke up for a few minutes this morning and talked briefly. The wounds are no longer bleeding, but he lost so much blood I don't know how he's still alive."

"I need to look at the wounds. He won't like it, but he seems content with you caring for him. Are you his wife?"

"Not yet, but maybe in a couple of years."

Morgan and Little Bird walked into the room. Doc asked what had been done for the patient and liked what he heard. He asked Mary to stay where she was to keep Milam steady. He gently began unwrapping the worst wound with Mary's help. Milam was completely awake after a few minutes and not particularly enamored with their efforts.

Doc was impressed with the women's job dressing the wound and said, "Y'all did a great job cleaning and dressing the wound. I don't see any sign of infection yet. Unfortunately, we have to take the plug out. Son, it's going to hurt like the dickens. Do you drink? If not, I suggest you start today. A couple of swallows of rum or whiskey might help a little."

Morgan brought him a glass of Fergus's Freedom Town rum. He drank it quickly.

After waiting a few minutes for the alcohol to take effect, Doc moistened the plug to soften it. He then used a tool from his black case to pull the plug material firmly. It did not come out easily because it was beginning to scab. Milam's eyes flew wide open as Mary squeezed him as tight as she could. The squeeze helped more than the rum. The plug finally came out, and the wound started bleeding, but not too severely. The doctor did not replace the plug. He washed the wound, applied iodine and herbs, and placed a thick bandage over it.

They turned Milam over so Doc could access the other side. He used the same procedure on that wound. Doc discussed with Little Bird whether to leave the wound open to drain or stitch it up. She thought leaving it open for a few days was best. She told him she had sewn up many wounds and could stitch him up later. He agreed with her. The wound drained a little as they discussed what to do. He wrapped the wound again with Little Bird's herbs and a thick bandage.

The other wound looked good and was washed and cleaned thoroughly. A new bandage was applied and wrapped.

Doc asked, "What herbs are you using on the wounds? They're working wonderfully. I may have to start using them myself. Y'all are doing a great job. Keep up the good work. Young lady, you're going to have to get some sleep."

"I'm good, doc."

"Figured you might say that. Why don't you at least use the pallet by the bed? He's not out of the woods yet, but he's begun the journey. He needs to start sitting on the porch in a week or so to get some sun. When he can walk, help him or let him. Liver broth is what he needs for the next week or so. No solid food for at least a week. We don't know what the bullet did to his insides. It had to have missed the heart and lungs, although I don't know how. Still, some organs may have been damaged. If that happened, his recovery will take longer."

"Sounds reasonable. Milam, did you hear those instructions? You'll be following them to the letter."

Milam rolled his eyes and said, "Yes, ma'am."

The doctor continued, "I'll leave a pain reliever for him. He's going to hurt as he heals and begins moving around more. Give him only what he has to have. It's habit forming if a person takes too much of it and too often. The willow bark pain reliever you have is effective for milder pain and is not habit-forming. Use it as long as it works, but he will occasionally need something stronger before we get him back to normal."

"Young lady, I don't know the family dynamics here, but you're obviously good medicine for him. You're doing an excellent job. Remember, this is a long race. Keep yourself well so you can help him."

"Yes, sir."

The doctor talked to Little Bird about her herbs. She explained that some were Nez Perce remedies and others were Chinese because her husband was from China. They seemed to complement each other. He wrote down the names and inspected the herbs she had drying. She gave him a few and told him about their use. Medical school taught him a few things about herbal medicines, but not nearly as much as Little Bird knew.

Angus had been listening to the discussions about Milam. He decided to go to the roundup to help. It was half over, and Angus was excited to get back with the cattle. Sitting around with little to do was not his style.

Fergus and Angus thought they had lost at least a couple hundred head of prime beef. They would look around to see if they could find where the cattle were sold after the roundup ended.

This would be the largest herd the combined ranches ever sold, even with the missing cattle. The plan was to take most of the herd to the end of the line if enough cattle cars were available. The others would have to be driven to Cheyenne for shipment back East. A small herd would be taken to Butte where Fergus had holding pens. Those would be sold mainly to the mining interests in the area.

Fergus and Angus departed before the roundup ended to check on cattle cars at Dillon. Unfortunately, they found cattle buyers and cars were unavailable, so they would take the herd to Cheyenne.

On the ride back to their ranches, they talked about how to organize the trail drive to Cheyenne. They wanted Colorado to be the trail boss and Angus's foreman to be the ramrod. Wolf would serve as the scout. The herd was moved out as soon as every rancher decided which cattle to sell. It took two days to get the cattle used to the trail drive and moving as they should.

Milam became more and more alert but remained weak. Mary helped him to the porch each morning and afternoon. The wounds had stopped draining after a week, so Little Bird closed them with stitches. The stitching was challenging because too much tissue was lost to close them completely. The herbs apparently helped keep infection at bay. Milam took a good swig from the opium bottle before the stitching began and slept all afternoon.

Before Fergus left with Angus to sell the herd, Milam asked him, "Do you think you can teach me to use a pistol as well as you can."

"I'll try to teach you when we get back. For now, practice pointing your finger at different objects. Just try to point at something without aiming. You'll feel a little foolish, but you'll learn to aim from your side without bringing the gun up to your eye. After a week, try it with an unloaded pistol if you feel up to it."

Fergus left the room and returned with a .44 Colt Peacemaker, "This is the best pistol I know about. Learn with it. We can get you pretty good with only a few weeks of practice. Being good with a pistol is a great responsibility because some people will come for you if they hear you're good. But out here, it's better to be good if you are going to wear one."

Morgan was actually beginning to like Milam. He was such a gentleman. She had come around to thinking he would make a good husband for Mary, although she did not share that thought with anyone, including Mary and Fergus.

They decided Milam was well enough to move upstairs into the extra bedroom. Oby and Chinn had to help him up the stairs. Mary still spent most of the night on a pallet near him, but she did get a little sleep in her bed.

———————

Fergus and Angus rode ahead to Cheyenne. Rowdy rode with them to learn about dealing with cattle buyers. Many cattle buyers were in town and ready to buy. They had dealt with Angus for decades and Fergus almost as long. The buyers knew their herds would be in prime condition and the headcount close. Both of those items were sometimes not the case with other ranchers. They had a deal nearly completed when the cattle arrived. All that remained was a quick inspection and finalizing the number of cattle.

Wolf rode in to find out where to hold the herd. They had about three thousand head of prime beef. Fergus rode back with him to show the men where to hold the herd about ten miles out of town on a good spot of grass. The pens were full because another herd beat them to Cheyenne. They could move the herd into town in four days. The cowboys wanted to go to town to blow off some steam — the trail had been long and without liquor.

Fergus said, "If you men stay here and hold the herd for four days, you'll receive a nice bonus." A few were not happy, but they all agreed.

Some of the smaller ranchers were with the herd. Fergus brought them together and told them the price they would get. They were more than happy with Fergus and Angus and the negotiated price. For most, this would be their best year ever. They could make it through another winter if it were not too bitter, but you never knew about the weather.

Garry Smith and Danny Arnold

Little Bird and Mary became more concerned about Milam's slow recovery and lack of stamina. The walk to and from the porch, even with Mary's help, sapped his strength. Little Bird expressed her concern to Mary after ten days.

Little Bird said, "Mary, I'm concerned. Milam should be regaining his strength more rapidly. He also looks much too pale and is not eating very much."

"What can we do?"

"I think we need to get Doc Boyton back out here to examine Milam."

"I'm worried and agree with you. I'll ride to Butte tomorrow."

"You are the best one to go, but you should not go alone. I'll get Chinn to ride with you."

"Okay. We'll have to spend the night."

Mary and Chinn departed after an early breakfast. They did not ride hard because they knew they would have to spend the night. When they arrived at Doc Boyton's office, he was away on a call. They waited on his small porch until he returned. The fact that Mary rode to fetch him made Doc understand how concerned she and everyone were about Milam. He canceled his appointments the next day, and they rode out after breakfast.

Doc Boyton examined Milam as soon as they arrived. He walked out of Milam's room and said, "As I mentioned earlier, I'm concerned about internal organs being damaged. If not, he would be recovering more quickly. I can't tell which organ is the problem, but I suspect it's his liver. If so, it will repair itself. But it will take a while, several months. Hopefully, y'all will see progress in a few more weeks. He needs as much bone broth as he can take and whatever solid food he can keep down."

Chapter Five

Each rancher carried a large sum of money on their trips back home. Bandits always seem to know when ranchers sold their herds. Cheyenne was a large cattle market, and large sums of money flowed from cattle buyers to ranchers. Angus and Fergus each carried over ten thousand dollars. The smaller ranchers carried lesser amounts. When the cowboys were paid, they did a lot of celebrating.

Angus and Fergus went to find and purchase Freedom Town rum and 'shine. The railroad sold them a case of each, plus a bottle of rum for immediate consumption.

Most of the crews planned to take the narrow rail train to Dillon and then ride back their separate ways. But most of the cowboys would stay in Cheyenne long enough for a bath, a woman, and a drunk, usually in that order. The women demanded a bath come first. They might handle a drunk and take his money, but the cowboys were a dirty, smelly mess at the end of a cattle drive. Most decent houses of ill repute would not let a rank cowboy in the door.

It took two nights to get all the celebrating out of the cowboys' systems. More importantly, most of them were dead broke after two nights. Fergus and Angus asked around about any cattle wearing their brand being sold early, but they found no useful information. The cash taken from the dead rustlers was likely the best they could do.

The train ride to Dillon was pleasant, with about half the cowboys trying to sleep off their hangovers. A large group of robbers hit the train expecting only token resistance, but they received a major surprise. Almost everyone armed themselves to repel an attack when the train slowed down quickly in the middle of nowhere. Nearly fifty rifles opened up at the robbers before the train rolled to a stop. The first volley put down over half of the robbers. Other volleys followed quickly, and almost all the robbers were down. The robbers realized their mistake too late.

A large tree across the tracks was a problem, as was a robber in the engine compartment with the engineer and fireman. The robber realized he was in a serious predicament, jumped off the engine, and raced for his horse. He was cut down by more rifle fire.

When the passengers were sure the remaining robbers had departed, a group checked on the engineer and fireman. The two men were not hurt. The group rolled the tree off the track and began dragging the dead robbers to a flat car for loading. The total delay was less than an hour.

When they reached the end of the line just south of Dillon, the track-building crew gave a resounding cheer. Someone had been stealing their pay from the train, likely the same bunch of train robbers.

The passengers retrieved their horses and saddled up to return to their ranches. They rode in groups in case anyone else was dumb enough to try to rob the owners.

Most of the riders stayed together until they neared their respective ranches. All the ranchers had at least two or three riders with them. Fergus and Angus had almost twenty riders between them. Wolf and Tall One rode in front to scout the route.

Angus and Fergus's group went to Bonner's Den Ranch to check on Milam and rest a little before Angus and his riders continued to his ranch.

Milam and Mary were in the yard, walking close to the house. Milam was still weak and told Angus he might need to stay longer at Bonner's Den Ranch.

Angus looked at him sideways and said, "I bet you want to stay longer because a pretty gal is taking care of you. How long are you gonna' milk this?"

Milam grinned and replied, "At least another month or two. I would hate to start bleeding on you."

Fergus and Morgan also understood his motive. They just rolled their eyes and looked at Mary. They both knew they were looking at a grown woman.

Milam added, "Fergus will try to help me improve with a pistol. Surely you want me to be able to protect myself?"

Angus just grunted, "Yeah, yeah."

Everyone knew Milam would want to stay regardless of his wound, and the odds of him getting snowed in were good. Morgan was resigned that the two would be out of each other's company as little as possible. But she was not unhappy. Morgan realized Milam was more of a man than Shelby had ever been. She thought wryly that the two of them would be amongst Montana's wealthiest ranchers in a few years, likely before they were thirty. Not bad for a girl born in the wilderness only fifteen years ago.

Mary was afraid Milam would break open his wounds — he had not ridden a horse since being shot. But he had been practicing with the pistol Fergus gave him. Fergus reached into his saddle bag, grabbed a holster designed for a fast draw, and threw it to Mary.

Fergus said, "Help him put it on and check the fit. He's gained some weight with the good care he has been getting."

The holster fit perfectly. It was designed to accommodate a Colt Peacemaker revolver, and the shell loops were for .44-40 cartridges.

Milam was so excited he moved a little too fast. It made his wounds hurt, but the sharp pain did not slow him down.

Angus said, "I expect you to be able to beat me and Fergus on the draw when you come home. Remember, fast is good only if you hit exactly what you shoot at. You need to try to get well. The young lady is a real magnet for you staying here, but you must come home to learn how my ranch operates. That's why you moved out here, ya' know."

"I hope to start riding soon, within a week. I plan to get as good as I can with the pistol. I've seen Fergus draw and wonder if I'll ever be as fast. Surely I'll be able to ride home by Christmas."

"Morgan, when you have all you can take of those spooners, tie him on a smooth riding horse and send him my way. I know he's imposing on you."

"He's okay. I've accepted the idea of them being a couple. It took me a while, but I'm now content with it. He's a real gentleman, and I'll welcome him into our family.....one of these days. My main problem was I had a bad marriage when I was too young. But he's nothing like my first husband. I had to get over my fear before I could accept him completely. I kinda' like him now."

"Good. I think he's a fine young man, but I'm a little biased. You know they'll be among the wealthiest landowners in Montana. I think they can handle it. Deciding where to live and run the two big ranches will be challenging."

"I believe they can handle it without too much trouble."

Angus and his cowboys headed home early the next morning. Angus would be happy to get home and put the cattle money in his safe. He hoped Butte would get a bank before long. A new bank had recently opened in Butte, but he wanted to see it operate for a couple more years before he deposited his money in it. The group enjoyed a quiet ride home.

Angus was almost seventy. Chasing the rustlers, the long cattle drive, and ride home had worn him down, and he needed his own bed. When Milam returned home, he would have to quickly get ready to manage the ranch. The time between the sale of the yearly crop and the spring roundup was not particularly busy, so it would be okay if he returned home before the spring roundup.

Fergus and Milam practiced with the revolver every day. He was accurate but slow at first. Once he hit the target every time in the very center, Fergus began working on his speed. He told him to pull the hammer back as he was drawing so he could fire as soon as the pistol reached level. He told him about 'wannabe' gunfighters shooting themselves in the foot by trying to draw and shoot too quickly.

Fergus said, "You must ensure your barrel clears leather before squeezing the trigger. Don't stop to admire your shot. Get it cocked immediately for another shot."

Milam's speed and accuracy improved rapidly. He and Fergus took longer walks and talked about being a shootist. Fergus spent much time telling him how he had to make sure he was willing to take a life before he got into a gunfight.

"You can't hesitate or think about anything else when facing someone ready to draw on you. The decision to take a person's life must be made before you face someone, except you don't always have a choice. I was sick to my stomach the first time I killed a person in a gunfight. Using a gun places a great weight on a person. Never treat it lightly."

They talked about running a ranch on some walks and about married life. Fergus said, "I'm not sure I should have taught you to be the gunhand you are. If you mistreat Mary in any way, I'll have to come for you. You might be good enough to beat me, but don't count on it. But, you'll beat most other people already."

"I've heard you braced three men at one time and got them all. How can you do that?"

"Mainly because they weren't very good. I first went after the one I thought was the most dangerous man. You have to be able to read men and know a split second before they go for their gun. Try not to face multiple men, but when you do, just draw and keep shooting until they're down. Most people are not as deadly accurate as you are. I usually go for a headshot on the first one — I don't want him needing another round. Most of the time, I go for a heart shot, but some men don't die quickly even with their hearts blown up."

On another walk, Milam said, "You and Morgan have had a long satisfying marriage. What's the secret?"

Fergus chuckled, and replied, "Welp, I'd say mostly satisfying. A couple will always have some ups and downs. Two things to think about. First, a man can argue with a woman's logic, but should never argue with how she feels. Second, after you marry, make sure you treat her like you want to get married again next month. It's a challenge sometimes, but you have to try. If you do those two things, everything else will be fine."

"Hmm. Sounds simple."

"Ha! Just wait and see."

Mary helped Milam with horseback riding. The first few times they rode caused a minor blood seepage around his wound. They discovered a little bile in the discharge, strengthening the theory that his liver was hit. They took it easy riding, adding a few miles each week. When the wound showed no discharge, they started going for hour-long rides. Little Bird was ready to declare him fit to ride home when a historic blizzard hit.

Within twenty-four hours, the snow was almost three feet with six-foot drifts. It shut down all unnecessary travel for a few weeks. Before the snow completely melted, another blizzard hit and piled the snow even deeper. It was one of the worst Decembers anyone could remember. The snow did not melt before the next storm hit. To Mary's delight, it was still far too dangerous for Milam to head home.

Christmas was a joyous occasion on Bonner's Den Ranch. All the extended family came together in the main house on Christmas Eve. They ate a sumptuous meal and planned a grand celebratory meal on Christmas Day. Oby had managed to kill a turkey without freezing to death. The turkey and a big smoked ham would be the lunch's centerpieces.

Fergus had erected a tall spruce tree in the house, and Morgan, Mary, and Maude decorated it. Fergus pulled out the Winchester rifles he bought for the youngsters in San Francisco. He put two boxes of shells with each rifle. He had also bought fireworks in San Francisco. Chinn knew how to make fireworks, so he made large firecrackers with paper and black powder. They were not colorful but made a loud boom.

The children were up at daybreak on Christmas Day. Juanita and Lotte cooked a batch of delicious doughnuts, but the kids ran past them to the rifles. Many did not realize the rifles were real at first. The cartridges convinced them otherwise, and they were overjoyed.

Fergus said, "As soon as the weather clears, we'll teach y'all how to shoot them."

Everyone enjoyed the fireworks after supper. All the adults appreciated the vivid colors and flinched at the detonations of Chinn's homemade firecrackers. Cowboys came out of the bunkhouse to watch the show. The stallions did not care for the show at all. The mares were far enough away that the noise did not bother them much.

January's weather was about as bad as December's. The cowboys gave the stock supplemental feedings of hay. Fergus worried they might run out of hay, which could be disastrous, especially for the horses. The cattle could take the snow and cold even better than the Appaloosa horses. Range cattle become almost as wild as buffalo and learned to dig snow with their feet and horns to reach the brown grass below. The horses also dug snow but were less efficient than the cows.

One morning, Jeb said, "This soil should be great for growing oats. Oats would help keep the stock fed in weather like this. I think we should plant forty or fifty acres of oats and maybe a little corn next year. I don't know if corn would have enough time to mature, but I believe we should try. I feel certain the oats would have time to mature."

"Hmm. Interesting proposition. What equipment would we need?"

Milam listened intently to the conversation. He knew something about growing grain crops but was not an expert. He said, "They grow a lot of grain near my dad's place. You'll have to have a harvester, like a thresher. It will harvest much more than fifty acres in a couple of weeks. Perhaps our two ranches could buy one together and use it on both ranches. You'll need a plow unless you can borrow one from Mrs. Morgan."

Both men turned toward Milam. It was one of the few times he had made a suggestion about the ranch, and they thought it made sense. They started asking questions, most of which he could not answer.

Milam mentioned, "Dry storage is critical. If the oats are just piled on the ground, they'll ruin. Most eastern growers use a silo or a round brick structure with a roof for storage. I've also heard men talking about the loss from rodents."

Fergus said, "We can turn some of the boys loose with a rifle to take care of that."

Morgan walked by and said, "You'll get someone shot!"

Milam said dryly, "I don't recommend shooting them. But you might want to find a clowder of cats."

"Huh?"

"Huh, what?"

"What's a clowder?"

Milam chuckled and responded, "A clowder is a herd of cats. Most grain farmers have cats all around their barns and storage facilities."

Milam knew he was strong enough to make it to the Angus Ranch if someone rode with him. When and if the weather broke, he planned to head home.

Milam approached Fergus to talk, "I'm ready to return to Angus Ranch. I have a lot to learn in a short time. But I think someone should ride with me in case I have a problem."

Fergus said, "I'll ride with you. Angus and I need to talk about growing grain."

Mary heard the conversation and said, "I'm going with y'all."

Fergus started to tell her she did not need to go. She looked at him sideways and said, "Dad, I didn't ask for permission. I'm going in case he starts bleeding and needs help." The argument ended abruptly.

They departed the following day after breakfast. Occasionally deep snow drifts were challenging for the people and horses. Those struggles hurt Milam's wound, and he was bleeding a little when they arrived.

Mary told Angus, "Get alcohol, iodine, and bandages. We have to clean the wound and get the bleeding stopped. I don't think it'll take too long, but I still need to hurry."

Mary had brought a bag of Little Bird's herbs. As soon as she cleaned the wound, she sprinkled it generously with the herbs and put pressure on it. The bleeding stopped.

She gave Milam a little peck and said in mock irritation, "Don't do that again! You'll have to stay inside the rest of the week."

Milam sighed and responded, "Yes, ma'am."

"Dad, I may need to stay a few days until he heals up a little more. This wound is frustrating. It hangs around almost healed, but not quite. Doctor Boyton said liver wounds take a long time to completely heal. But I'll bet he'll be ready to go by roundup. I'll be here to make sure."

"Always thinking of his health, aren't you?" Angus snickered at Fergus's comment.

"I've got a lot invested in the boy! Got to protect my investment, don't I? He's going to make a great daddy if y'all don't kill him first."

Angus asked, "Milam, did you learn to shoot fast and accurately? Remember, you must beat me and maybe Fergus for your extended stay to have been worthwhile."

Milam put his gun belt on and walked gingerly to the porch. The wounds were such that they did not hinder his draw. Angus placed pebbles on a hitching rail at the side of the porch.

He said, "Let's see you do your stuff."

Milam pulled his pistol and fired before Angus could get a good look. But he saw the pebbles turn to dust quicker than he could imagine.

He looked at Milam and said, "Dang, son! I got no chance against you. Fergus, what do you think?"

"He's as fast as anyone I've seen, except maybe me. He hasn't missed a target in a long time. The one thing we don't know for sure is how he'll do when his target is shooting back. But he's faced gunfire before and lived. I would not want to go against him in a fair fight. The difference between me and him is not enough for me to count on. He's good, I guarantee."

Mary yelled out the door, "You boys quit playing and come inside so Milam can rest. He was doing good coming over here until one bad drift. His horse made an awkward step and jarred him enough to start the wound seeping again."

"We have to go down to let the boys see my new gunhand. Don't want any of them trying to take him on because hell own the place before long. A little fear and respect can be a good thing. His draw would give me a little fear, for sure."

Mary replied, "Maybe tomorrow after he has rested today."

Angus did not want to go up against Mary and replied, "Tomorrow it is."

Milam slept well that night, and the wound did not bleed. The next morning, he was a little stiff from the long ride because he had not ridden much in months. He would have to get in riding shape before roundup, which would crank up in a few months when most of the snow was gone.

Fergus and Angus talked extensively about partnering to grow oats the following year. Angus did not need as many oats as Fergus because owned many more horses. But they were always a little thin during the spring roundup. A little extra feed would keep them in better condition. They talked about the equipment needed and where to grow the grain.

Fergus said, "If we run a herd of cows on a fifty or sixty-acre tract, the soil would be good and fertile come spring. It would give the oats a good jump. But how do we hold cattle on such a small pasture?"

Milam said, "Maybe we need enough barbed wire to surround the field. It wouldn't take long to drive pointed posts in the ground, even in the icy soil. We'll have a fence if we string a couple strands of wire around it. We'll need to keep the cows inside for a while, but away from the oats later."

Angus said, "I have a couple of rolls of wire, which should be enough for now. Where do you think we should put the field?"

"I'll use most of the oats for my horses, so maybe near my ranch. But I don't really care — a couple of wagon loads won't be hard to move to either ranch. Hmm. On the way over, I noticed a small space, likely forty acres, that had already been blown free of snow. It probably would make a good oat patch."

"Sounds good to me."

"Let's get three glasses of the good rum and go to bed. We need to think this over. I do better sleeping on big decisions. Never wanted to be a sodbuster. Brody is the farmer in the family."

Milam and Mary were pleased the men were listening to Milam.

They also included him in the excellent rum, which was a big deal. Everyone went to bed, with Mary staying near Milam so she could check on him. It just seemed natural for her to be close to his bedroom.

Mary went in to check on Milam early the next morning. She pronounced him ready to come to the table for breakfast. He ate a large breakfast as they continued to talk about the grain. The grain field was insignificant in the scope of the two huge ranches. But it was a noteworthy change for the ranches. It was also something they needed to gain experience in.

Angus and Fergus rode around the ranch to check on the cattle. They were in okay shape, and all seemed to be pregnant. They did not find any lost fetuses. The rough winter may not have ruined them.

While Angus and Fergus were away, Mary taught the cook how to treat Milam's wound if it started seeping. The cook had watched Mary treat it when they arrived and thought she could do it. She understood the steps and why each was necessary. She had treated wounds before, but not one involving the liver. Those people usually died within a day or two.

Fergus and Mary decided to leave the next morning. She was not ready but realized she would never get ready in this lifetime. Mary slept on her pallet near Milam just to be close to him. She was not sure how long she could wait for a wedding. She wondered if being away from him for a couple of months might cool the relationship. But she knew better.

The goodbyes were not easy on the young couple. They did not want to be separated. When Mary left, she had big alligator tears trickling down her cheeks, and Milam was fighting back tears. She and Fergus rode in silence for over an hour.

Fergus asked, "Are you okay?"

"No, but I'll live, I think. Dad, I love him even if we are young. We know what we want and will care for each other. This is not a short-term thing. I may be riding this trail a lot. I don't know how to convince Mom we're ready."

Garry Smith and Danny Arnold

"Just keep doing what you're doing. She's almost there, you know."

Chapter Six

The weather finally cleared, and Fergus gathered all the children over twelve and took them to a small hill in the prairie to provide a backstop for shooting. He spent a long time giving them a thorough safety lesson, and everyone listened closely.

They went by age and shot first from prone at fifty yards. Fergus a board for each shooter. He hammered them into the ground and told Mary to load one round. She was not a rookie because she had shot air rifle previously. In fact, all of the children had shot air rifles and .22s. He explained aiming, although it was not really necessary. Mary's first shot centered a mark on the board. She shot one more time with only one bullet in the gun. The shot almost touched the first. He told her to put five rounds in the rifle and shoot them as quickly as she could shoot accurately. The five were all within an inch or so.

Fergus said, "I think you're done. And, more importantly, you are good."

Colt went next. He had also shot quite a bit. His shooting was good but not quite as good as Mary's. He shot about a two or three inch group. He was crushed that a girl beat a Nez Perce warrior.

Fergus said, "Your shooting is still good. If you aimed at a rabbit, it would be a dead rabbit."

Rowdy went next. The shooting had evolved into a competition. His target was about the same as Colt's. Again, he was crushed to be beaten by Mary. Fergus told him the same thing he told Colt. It did not help much.

Liz was the last shooter. Her target was not as good as Mary's but better than the boys by a little. The boys were totally wiped out.

Mary asked what would happen if they had been shooting a .44-40.

Fergus explained in depth and everyone listened closely. Rowdy asked about a .45-70. Fergus explained the bullet had a lot more velocity and would not drop much at a hundred yards, or at least would hit about where it hit at fifty yards. He took the time to explain.

"All bullets start dropping as soon as they leave the barrel." He drew the parabolic arc of the bullet in the air. They were amazed at his knowledge.

"Shooting at long distances is very difficult because you have to allow for drop. All guns of a certain caliber will drop about the same distance. You also have to worry about windage at long distances. You have to shoot a lot to be able to do that automatically. When you learn these guns, you will likely move to more powerful rifles. Each caliber has its own characteristics."

Rowdy said, "I didn't know a person had to know so much to be a good shot. We need to be practicing a lot, don't we?"

"Son, all of us who shoot well did a lot of missing to get accurate. It may look like we're just shooting without thinking, but we've shot so much that we don't have to think."

"We'll try to practice at least once a week, and a little later, you can practice on your own. You need to clean your guns when we get back. I'll show you today. A dirty gun is a sign of a lazy person. It may not work when you need it, making you dead."

The spring roundup finally ended. The cattle and horses on Bonner's Den Ranch and the Angus Ranch came out of winter in excellent shape. The grass was high, and the cattle were fat. Life was good and relaxed on the Bonner's Den Ranch. The cowboys took it easy and to get over the bumps and bruises from roundup. Few men made it through without at least a minor injury, but no one suffered a severe injury.

The only busy people were Brody, Morgan, and the farm workers. Potatoes were the first crop planted, followed by the new forty acres of oats and corn. The vegetable garden would be planted last, spread out over several weeks.

Brody, Morgan, and the workers began complaining about oats and corn during planting. They said it was too much planting to complete in the proper time frame. Fergus tried to help and tried to get others to help. Most cowboys viewed farm work like the plague. They helped harvest the hay and might help harvest grain. But most cowboys viewed planting crops in the ground as beneath their cowboy dignity.

Mary wanted to see Milam for the first time in weeks. Angus had begun feeling bad during the roundup and had returned home, so she also wanted to check on him. She decided to head to Angus's ranch to spend a few days. She left at sunrise one morning to make sure she could easily get there before dark. She had made the trip several times, and Milam had come her way once.

Milam had been extremely busy during the roundup, especially after Angus had to return home. Although young, he was readily accepted as the ranch's big boss. All the cowboys needed was to see him working beside them from daylight until dark. He performed well, and the snide remarks about the 'kid' quickly became a thing of the past.

Interestingly, Milam decided to visit on the same day Mary rode to visit him. Much to Fergus's surprise, Milam rode into Bonner's Den Ranch mid-afternoon after Mary rode out early in the morning. Milam had not seen her on the trail they used, which alarmed both men. Fergus sent a rider to get Morgan and another rider to find Wolf and Jeb. He saddled the horse Morgan preferred and his favorite, which looked like Sunny, the Tennessee stallion, and could move at a good clip seemingly forever. Milam saddled one of Fergus's Appaloosas to replace his fatigued horse. Fergus left word for Wolf and Jeb that Mary went missing on the way to Angus's ranch. They were to get fresh horses and follow them as soon as possible.

Fergus and Milam were worried, but Morgan was almost hysterical. She was holding it together but barely. While on the trail, they met a rider heading toward them. They did not recognize him as a cowboy for either ranch. When the rider neared them, he stopped abruptly, wheeled his horse around, and galloped away. Fergus and his group thundered after him.

Fergus grabbed his rope and went after the man hard. He rode by far the fastest horse and overtook the runner in about a half mile. His loop settled over the man, and Fergus's horse skidded to a stop as he was trained to do. The man was jerked off his horse and hit the ground hard on his back.

Fergus looked like he was throwing a calf after roping him. He was on the man before he got any air back in his lungs. Fergus disarmed him as he lay on the ground struggling to get air back in his lungs. Milam and Morgan were right behind Fergus.

Fergus pulled up on the guy's belt and helped force some air in. The man had no fight left in him. When he was breathing somewhat normally, Fergus asked about Mary. The man said he did not know what Fergus was talking about.

Fergus searched him and found a ransom note in his pocket. He roared, "You lie to me again, and I'm going to let her mother and fiancé take turns peeling your skin! They're both really good skinners, and I bet they can skin you and keep you alive for a long time. Are you ready to talk?"

"I have nothing to say."

"What's your name? I like to know who I am hurting."

"Adrian Lomax."

"Mr. Lomax, you will talk. Where is Mary being held? How many partners do you have?"

Lomax shook his head. Fergus hit him with his big right fist, hardened like iron from years of work. Adrian did not look so defiant now.

"Mister Lomax, you are looking at Mary's father, mother, and fiancé. I repeat, where is Mary being held? How many partners?"

Adrian again shook his head. Fergus drove his fist into Lomax's gut almost to the backbone and then kneed him in the face when he bent over. Adrian's nose, lips, and teeth would never be the same.

Morgan said, "Fergus, and me your knife and let me get to work. We don't have time to mess around."

"Just give me one more lick at him. I think he wants to talk but can't bring himself to. One more in the solar plexus might do it. Are you ready to answer the simple questions?"

"Yes. Three of us. My daddy and brother, Leon and Alphie Lomax. She's at a line shack not too far from here."

"Which direction?" Lomax pointed northwest.

"My tracker will be here soon, and if you're lying, one of us will drag you until you're dead."

They found a tree, tied him to it, and waited on Wolf. Milam did not like waiting. They could do anything to her while waiting.

Fergus said, "I see them in the distance. They'll be here soon. Wolf will make sure we're on the right trail."

Wolf, Jeb, and two cowboys arrived, and Wolf began backtracking Adrian. The tracks led to a line shack in an almost straight line. They stopped behind a low rise when they saw the shack in the distance. Wolf took Fergus's binoculars and walked about fifty yards until he could see the front of the shack.

When Wolf returned, he said, "Two men are sitting in front of the shack. Let's circle around behind it, and I'll approach it from the rear to see what's going on."

Wolf was like a ghost slipping through the grass and brush. When he got closer, he saw the line rider lying in the corner in a pool of blood. He was sure the line rider was dead.

Wolf crawled close to a small window in the back and saw Mary tied and bleeding in the corner of the shack. He could not tell how badly injured she was, but it was apparent she had been treated unkindly.

When Wolf returned to the others, he said, "Mary's in the left corner. If we attack the cabin head-on, she could be shot through the shack's thin boards. She's been hurt, but I don't know how bad. Her head is bleeding, and she's tied to a chair. The window is not big enough to crawl through. We need to get one or two people inside to protect her from these lowlifes."

Milam asked, "Can we take a board off and get inside?"

"We can try. It might work if we get rifles on each side in case they hear us."

Milam said, "I'm going in for her. Who wants to flank the cabin with rifles, and who wants to help me with the boards?"

Fergus decided to help him remove a couple of boards. Everyone in the group was excellent an excellent shot, so they could handle the sides with a rifle. The dried boards were a little loose, which gave them a finger hold to start prying them off. The first one resulted in bleeding fingers and fingernails. They took one more off to give Milam enough room to slip inside.

As he eased in as quietly as possible, Mary stirred a little. He hurried to get to her before she made a sound. He muffled her scream until she realized who it was. The men had mistreated her badly.

Milam cut her ropes off and passed her to Fergus through the hole in the wall. He hissed to Fergus, "They've hurt her bad. Take her and tell the others to stay out of the fight. I'll take them myself. They'll hurt before they long for death."

Milam gave Fergus time to let the others know Milam's plan, and then he stepped out the front door. He yelled, "You two kidnapped my fiancé!"

The two men whirled around and grabbed for their guns. Neither cleared leather before Milam's shots hit them. They started falling backward, and Milam shot twice more.

Wolf ran in and said, "What happened? Both of your shots are low."

"Yep, exactly where I intended them to be. I want them to live for a while and suffer before they die. A little dragging should speed up the process if it takes too long. We need to build a fire and let Morgan check Mary to see what she needs. "

Mary came around the corner, hurried to Milam, and hugged him hard. Large tears streamed down her face. Morgan also had tears in her eyes. Fergus tried to not let his show, but everyone knew. Morgan and Mary walked into the shack to check on her injuries.

When Morgan asked if they had raped her, she replied, "They tried.

If you check the older one, he likely has injured privates. The other one has serious scratches on his face and elsewhere. They decided to beat me up after I fought them off and wait until I had less fight. I'm sure they would have tried again tonight."

Morgan got water and helped her clean up. Then Morgan walked outside laughing. She told the story of the attempted rape and how Mary had stopped it. Everyone but Milam and Mary thought it was funny.

The group mounted and started toward the Bonner's Den Ranch headquarters. Fergus sent Wolf and Jeb to load Adrian on his horse and take him to Bonner's Den Ranch. He also left a cowboy to make sure Leon and his other son died. The dead Bonner line rider was loaded on his horse to be taken to the ranch to bury.

Fergus asked everyone to ride ahead so he, Morgan, Mary, and Milam could chat. They planned to camp on the prairie and return home tomorrow. Mary needed to rest up a little and take it easy riding home. Fergus found a tiny grove of trees with dry limbs on the ground to make a big fire. They had jerky and coffee for supper.

When everyone finished eating, Milam asked Morgan to walk with him. She had a bad feeling about what was coming. They walked a hundred yards away from the fire, talking about the beautiful stars and full moon. She asked about Angus and tried to make small talk.

Milam finally turned to her and asked, "Mrs. Bonner, I want to ask Mary to marry me. Will you bless our marriage? I know this talk is usually held with the father, but you've always had the strongest reservations."

"I won't stand in the way, but I prefer y'all get married after the next spring roundup. We have a lot of work to do before the wedding, and Mary is my only daughter. I will welcome you into our family."

"We can wait that long. I need to get back and talk to Mary."

"I'll get Fergus to walk with me and give y'all a little privacy."

She and Fergus took a walk. Milam walked to Mary's seat and said, "Will you marry me?"

"Of course! You know that's always been my plan."

"I mean officially. Will you marry me?"

"What will mother say?"

"She has blessed us getting married. She wants us to wait until after the spring roundup next year. I talked with her, and she's telling your dad now."

"Yes, I will certainly marry you! We can wait if that's what it takes to please her. It's not very long — less than a year."

She jumped up and almost knocked him over when she rushed to his arms. Fergus and Morgan walked up to the fire.

Fergus said, "So I'm losing a daughter and gaining another son. If you ever hurt her, we will see who's the fastest draw. If you love and care for her, we'll be partners. When will it happen?"

"After next year's spring roundup."

"Why are you waiting so long?"

"Mrs. Morgan will bless our wedding if we wait until then."

"Hmm, works for me."

Mary jumped back into his arms. They talked long into the night, working out a few details. Morgan insisted the wedding take place at Bonner's Den Ranch.

Morgan said, "You need new clothes and a wedding dress. We can make you a beautiful dress, but it'll take a while to get it done. We need to visit Cheyenne soon to find or order the material and clothes. It'll be a grand wedding, although only the cowboys on each ranch will likely attend. We'll also have a wonderful fandango. It'll be so beautiful. I never had a big wedding, but you'll have one."

Fergus thought, "*This is going to cost me a fortune.*"

He wisely only thought it and did not say a word. Morgan was surprisingly in her element and would not change her mind because of anything he said. Mary was sitting closer to Milam than ever before. She gave him a solid peck every few minutes.

Morgan finally said, "Why don't you get up and give him a proper kiss like a betrothed woman?"

Mary jumped up and gave him a kiss to remember. He was so shocked he fell off the log he was sitting on, and Mary fell on top of him.

Morgan said wryly, "Maybe not that much of one! A certain amount of decorum is still appropriate."

Fergus just laughed. He and Morgan soon snuggled into their blankets. Milam and Mary talked a little more before she put her blankets near his, close enough to make him a little uncomfortable. She was not.

Everyone woke up with Fergus making coffee. Morgan noticed how close their blankets were and wondered if she should let them marry sooner. She thought about it but decided Milam was a gentleman. She was more worried about Mary. It was Mary's blankets that had been moved.

Morgan did almost all of the talking on the way back to Bonner's Den Ranch. Fergus thought it strange that she had opposed the marriage but now was all hyped up about planning it.

Morgan said, "We need to go to Cheyenne, Denver, or Sacramento soon. We have to think about what you have and what you need. I think you will need a lot of stuff. So will I."

Fergus absentmindedly said, "How many clothes can a person need for a wedding attended only by cowboys who work for you?"

As soon as the question was out of his mouth, he knew he had blundered. After Morgan heightened his sensitivity, he vowed to keep his thoughts about the wedding to himself. He would be told everything he needed to know. Milam was reminded that he should also remain quiet. Fergus thought, "*Welp, Morgan has agreed to bless the marriage. Better let her have her fun planning it.*"

Morgan said, "Milam, do you have a ring for Mary?"

"No. I thought I would go to Butte and find one the next chance I have."

"You did not come prepared to ask for her hand, did you? You better go to Butte tomorrow so everyone will know she is engaged."

"I need to check on my grandpa first. He's been having chest pains, and I'm worried about him. You know he's getting older and doesn't want to slow down. I was shocked when he decided to return home early from the roundup."

"You might want to take him to the doctor in Butte."

Milam, Fergus, and Mary agreed with Morgan. When they arrived home, everyone realized Morgan had talked most of the way. It was apparent she had thought about this impending wedding for a while.

Wolf and Jeb had locked Adrian in a barn storeroom. Before they left him, Wolf said, "If you try to get away, I can track you anywhere. I will catch you and turn you over to Mary and her mother. You might not survive again."

Milam spent the night, and all the extended family congratulated him and Mary. They even threw a little impromptu party at the mansion. Juanita and Lotte made their wonderful Mexican stew with many spices for supper. They made three pots of it, each getting a little more spicy. One was hot — too hot for the gringos but just right for the Indians and Mexicans.

The evening was joyous, with many jokes aimed at Milam. A few were a bit crude, and Maude shut down the offender every time. The men retired to the porch for a few fingers of Freedom Town rum and a cigar. Fergus did not share his excellent rum often. He needed to make sure he had enough for the wedding.

Milam returned to Angus Ranch to get his Grandfather. Angus was not thrilled about going to see a doctor. He had never visited one.

Milam convinced him to go by saying, "You know you can't do much without your chest hurting, along with a few other body parts. The doctor may get you back to where you can participate in the fall roundup."

"I'll go, but I intend to die in my own house. I'll be buried next to your Grandmother in the little stand of trees and flowers. I've been visiting there and talking to her more lately."

Milam promised they would return after they visited the doctor, and he handled some business.

"What business do you have?"

"Well, Mary and I are getting married after the spring roundup. I want to buy her a nice ring to show she is engaged."

Angus's eyes lit up, and he walked to his safe. He returned with a stunning diamond ring.

Angus said, "Your Grandmother wore this in her later years. I didn't have the money to buy one until we were older. I thought you might like the ring when you found the right woman. I would be honored, as would she, if you gave this to Mary."

Milam had no idea Angus had such a ring. His Grandmother died when he was very young.

"I would be more than elated to give her Grandma's ring. It's gorgeous. I don't remember her wearing it. It's perfect. I'm sure Mary will love it."

"It cost me a hundred dollars we did not have, but she was so proud of it. It took a long time to save that much money thirty years ago. I think I still have the box it came in."

"Okay, let's plan to leave early tomorrow so she and her family can see it. I'm sure she and her mother will still want to ride with us. One other thing. We can put some of your money in the Butte bank. What do you think?"

"I'm a little leery of banks. Never used one. But it makes sense to keep less money on the ranch. Getting to be too many bad people around, like the ones who kidnapped Mary. But we can deposit half of it in the bank. Fergus may also want to open an account."

They departed the next morning in the seldom used six-person surrey. Milam tied his horse behind the rig. It was mid-afternoon when they arrived at Bonner's Den Ranch. Mary ran out to meet them. Her hug and kiss delighted Milam and Angus. Milam left the team hitched when they walked inside. He would need it later.

They visited a bit with the Bonner bunch. Everyone was excited about Milam becoming one of them in less than a year. They all got to know him well while he recovered at the ranch.

After an hour or so, Milam said, "Mary, let's take a ride in the surrey. I have a couple of things to talk to you about."

She looked at him sideways but would never miss an opportunity to be with Milam. They rode to a beautiful spot overlooking the Appaloosa horse herd.

Milam stopped and began, "I told Angus I needed to go to Butte to find you a ring. He surprised me by giving me the ring my Grandmother wore. He said he was saving it for me when I found a wife. Would you consider wearing this used ring?"

"Oh, my goodness! It's beautiful! Yes, I'm honored to wear it. It's perfect. I love you and Angus so much. He's like the Grandfathers I never knew. You're the best man I know. Let's go show it to Momma."

"Don't I get a big kiss for the ring? I don't think Morgan can see us out here to chastise you."

She grabbed him and gave him a kiss that tingled his toes. It was almost more than a cowboy could handle. They returned to the ranch with her arm intertwined with his. She gave him a more reserved kiss when they stepped down.

When they walked into the house, his mind was still whirling. Only Angus noticed the ring at first, even though Mary was trying her best to get the others to notice it.

Morgan finally said, "What's that on your hand?"

"It's my engagement ring. It belonged to Angus's wife. He wanted me to have it."

"Come here, child. It's exquisite and huge. Angus, are you sure?"

"Well, I'm not looking for another wife. I've been saving it for Milam's bride. It's been sitting in my safe for nearly twenty years. We, my Anna and me, want her to have it. I don't know what one costs today, but they can use the money for something else. You know, one of the wealthiest women in Montana ought to have a diamond ring."

"It's a wonderful thing to give to them. Maybe my husband will get me one someday. 'Course, the way he's working me farming, I could never wear it. The forty acres of grain you two came up with has just about put me over the edge on farm work. I don't know how y'all plan to harvest it. But I'm telling you now that my hands don't fit any scythe

I've ever seen." She gave them a look so they knew she was not joking.

Fergus said, "I'll go to Cheyenne to see if they have a harvester or if I can order one."

"Yeah, and we might just go with you."

She had been complaining about the more challenging farming workload. Fergus would have to do something, but he did not know what.

Chapter Seven

The group departed early the next day and arrived in Butte late afternoon. They dropped Angus and Milam off at Doc Boyton's office and took Adrian to the jail.

After introductions, the Sheriff asked, "Why should I put him in jail?"

Fergus responded, "He, his brother, and his father kidnapped my daughter. The other two are dead."

"Hmm. Why ain't this one dead?"

"He told us where the other two were holding Mary after a little encouragement."

"I can see the results of your encouragement."

The Sheriff turned to the others and said, "So, we have Mary, her mother, father, and fiancé. If you want, I could go to the café for coffee and leave y'all here with him."

Mary replied, "It's tempting. But he knows if any of us see him again, he will be gutshot, skinned alive, and dragged behind a horse until he dies. You can have him for now." The wide-eyed Adrian turned pale and shuddered.

Morgan added, "You forgot to mention castrated." Adrian fainted.

Doc Boyton's office was upstairs over the general store. Angus began clutching his chest before they reached the top of the stairs.

The doctor examined him and asked, "How bad are you hurting?"

"Bad enough to think your office shouldn't be upstairs."

Boyton gave him a pill and told him to put it under his tongue. He was better in a few minutes.

Angus then said, "So, am I well now?"

"I'm afraid not. The problem is your heart, something we call angina. The pill is nitroglycerin. It opens up the arteries and gives you relief. Angina can't be cured and will likely get worse. You're going to have to take it easy and carry these pills at all times. I also want you to visit a heart doctor in Cheyenne to see if he agrees with me."

"Am I gonna' die?"

"Someday. It could be soon, or it could be many years. You should consider getting your affairs in order and learn to take it easy."

"What do you mean 'get my affairs in order'?"

"Your will and other such matters should be set up exactly like you want. Let your relatives and attorney know what you want done with your property."

Angus and Milam rode to the boarding house and rented rooms. Morgan and Mary checked the stores but did not plan to buy anything unless they found something perfect, but they came away empty handed. The general store carried material that could work for regular dresses, but they wanted to look elsewhere.

Fergus talked to Josh Doyle about mules and farm equipment. Josh had four mules he was willing to sell, but no one in town carried the farm equipment Fergus wanted. Butte was primarily a mining town, and most of the equipment available was mining-related.

Angus broke the news at supper about his heart condition and Doc Boyton's desire for him to see a doctor in Cheyenne to confirm the diagnosis. The news meant everyone would be going to Cheyenne. They planned to leave the horses at Josh's so he could feed them.

The railroad's end-of-the-line was just south of Butte, and it had an office at the depot they built in Butte. Fergus bought six tickets for Cheyenne. Josh agreed to take them to the train at noon the next day.

Angus had an episode at the boarding house, but the pill quickly relieved him. He said, "I'm glad the train is not earlier. I need to see my lawyer tomorrow to ensure my desires are followed. I plan to transfer the ranch to Milam now rather than wait. The attorney can draw up the papers while we're in Cheyenne."

Milam asked, "Do you think it's really necessary? It's left to me in the will."

"I don't want to cause a family squabble when I die, which could be soon. I plan to live the rest of my life there and help you and Mary learn more about ranching. But I don't think y'all have much more to learn. I also want to check out the bank to see if I want to make a deposit."

Fergus said, "I just remembered something. Josh told me the bank is having problems getting deposits from cattlemen. They concentrate on the mines, mostly owned by large interests in Cheyenne and Denver. The bank is a temporary holding place for their money. He says the manager is not very good. He also believes a cattleman should buy at least part of the bank. I know nothing about banks, or we might look into it."

Milam added, "My brother is vice president of a bank in St. Louis. Owning a bank is something to consider."

"Listen to the boy! I tell him I'm giving him close to ten thousand acres of land, and he's already considering buying a bank."

"I'm just musing and certainly not thinking about it anytime soon. But Fergus and I may want to be bigshot bankers someday." Everyone laughed as they looked around at the buckskin-clad crew.

Angus, Milam, and Mary visited William Eshee's law office early the next morning. Mary went with them so she could understand the deal they made. Angus explained that he wanted to deed the ranch to Milam. Eshee agreed it was a good idea because other heirs can always challenge a will. He also explained that it would be much cleaner if Milam paid for the land. They settled on a hundred dollars and half of the profits for the next two years.

They walked to the bank after Eshee said he had all he needed for the paperwork. When they entered the bank, Milam and Angus were ignored. Most bank employees appeared to be doing nothing, and they kept doing it.

Milam observed, "I don't believe this bank is run very well. A couple of the largest ranch owners in Montana walk in, and no one even says 'hello.'"

Angus did not take kindly to being ignored. He yelled, "Is anyone in here interested in taking my money? Do I need to pop a round off to get your attention?"

Finally, a wimpy looking man with a rumpled white shirt walked over and said sarcastically, "How can I help you?"

"I'm thinking about putting money in this bank. Can someone tell me about the bank?"

"How much are you thinking about depositing?"

"I don't know, maybe twenty-five or thirty thousand dollars."

"Where does someone like you get that much money?"

"Sonny, I own over ten sections of prime cattle dirt and run several thousand head of cattle on it. I got that much and more. Now, can I talk to someone who is willing to explain this bank to me and take my deposit?"

"Oh, you would be one of our largest depositors. I'll get the President."

He walked into an office and returned with a chubby man who Angus figured had never spent a day doing real work. His handshake was soft and clammy.

"Come in. Let's talk about your deposit."

This guy talked better than the guy in the rumpled shirt. Angus explained that he owned a large cattle ranch. He had never used a bank but thought that, with all the thieves on the range, he might want his money in a safer place than his small safe. He wanted the account set up so he or his grandson, Milam McCullough, could withdraw money.

With much skepticism, Angus put thirty thousand dollars in the Miner's Bank and Trust. He was planning to deposit fifty thousand until he was treated so poorly.

He and Milam later told Fergus about their difficulty at the bank. Fergus said, "Hmm, I might wait 'til we get to Cheyenne to find a bank. They'll have to show a little respect to this old mountain man to get my money."

"It surely is a poorly run business. If they were ranching, the cattle would be strewn all over Montana. Josh might be right about it needing new owners."

Josh had one of his men drive the group to the railhead the next morning. When they arrived, the engine was already belching smoke. Fergus had purchased six seats because the passenger cars did not contain compartments, so they would have to sleep sitting up. The trip took only about fifteen hours, and they would arrive in Cheyenne before daylight or a little after.

The trip was mostly uneventful. But a couple of miners with a bit of change in their pockets made crude comments to Mary. Morgan heard them, and so did Milam.

Milam stood and said, "Sirs, it would be best if you went to another car and left my fiancé alone."

The miners bristled, and one of them walked toward Milam. Morgan woke Fergus with a sharp elbow. He and Angus both stood up and drew their guns.

Milam said, "I'll take you on one at a time. These gentlemen will make sure no one else interferes. Who's up first?"

The conductor walked up and said, "If you damage anything in the car, you'll have to pay for it. If you want to fight, we'll stop for water in a few minutes. Get off and do whatever you want."

When they stepped off the train, Milam removed his shirt and put on work gloves. A big miner said, "This won't take long. Look at the skinny cowboy. He ain't got a chance."

The miners were bulked up by the hard work in the mines, but they sat around town drinking heavily most nights. Angus whispered to Milam, "Stay away from the haymakers. They look soft in the gut. They got no wind. Just don't let them get in close." Milam nodded.

Milam had boxed when he was in school. His muscles were the long, sinewy type. His build was not very impressive, but his punch was surprisingly potent. The first miner charged at Milam, who stepped aside and delivered a kidney punch. It made the miner mad, but it also made him more cautious. He approached again, and Milam landed a hard right on his chin and sunk a left into his belly. The belly punch hurt him badly. The miner returned for another try, intending to grab Milam in a bear hug. A left and right to the gut and ribs took more out of the miner. He was stumbling on his next effort and trying to protect his midsection. Milam delivered a left, right, left combination to his head. The last punch to his temple knocked him out cold.

Milam said, "Okay, are you next?"

"Mister, I'll apologize to the lady and take Jack Hammer to another car. Never see'd anyone who could whup him that easy."

Fergus asked, "Where did you learn to fight like that?"

"Did a little boxing in school. He's probably pretty good in a barroom brawl, but he was easy to read. We better keep an eye on him. Jack Hammer will likely be irritated when he wakes up."

When they arrived in Cheyenne, everyone went their separate ways. The women went shopping, Angus and Milam visited a doctor, and Fergus checked out the two banks in town.

Angus's visit was not pleasant for him and Milam. Unfortunately, he received the same diagnosis.

Angus grimaced and asked, "What do you think I should do?"

"Well, it's going to get worse. Eventually, you will not be able to do much work at all. Even walking will be challenging. Within a few years, you will have to spend most of your time on the porch in a rocking chair. I know it's a hard way to go. Someone will surely find a cure in the future, but the pills are all we have right now."

"How long do you think I have?"

"Hard to say. It will gradually get worse. One day, the pain won't abate, and your heart will stop. I wish I could tell you more, but we don't understand much about the heart."

"Anything I can do to help?"

"Not much that I know of. Some doctors say to eat more vegetables and less meat. It's a good idea, but it helps only sometimes. As a cattle rancher, I'm confident you won't shift to vegetables only. I don't know if I would either. I'm sorry I don't have more to offer."

"My grandson is getting married at the end of spring roundup. Do you think I'll make it?"

"I would bet on it if you take it easy. If he hurries, you'll likely see your great-grandson or great-granddaughter."

"Whoa, her momma would skin us both if she heard that talk!" Milam turned pink.

Fergus had better luck at the banks. Both banks treated him like they wanted his business. He put fifty thousand dollars in the Cattlemen and Farmers Bank of Cheyenne.

The women may have had the best luck. A store manager agreed to order a wedding dress from Sacramento and ship it to Butte. They also found material for all the other dresses and shirts they needed. They could order a nice western suit for each man if they came by to get measured. Morgan made sure they did.

Fergus's trip had been successful, and it was about to get better. He rode to the railroad office and bought two cases of Freedom Town Rum. He might run out before the wedding, but he would enjoy it while it lasted. One case was for Angus.

The trip home was uneventful, with no fights or other mischief. Milam and Angus went to the lawyer's office to sign the papers. Milam instantly became one of Montana's largest landowners and was still a teenager. Mary and Milam talked at length about their future. Morgan just listened. Angus and Fergus enjoyed a couple glasses of the excellent rum while sitting on the porch.

Fergus said, "I need to plan for my demise. I have two people I want to leave with a ranch, but I don't really want to split up the Bonner's Den Ranch. I may have to buy another ranch for Jeb. Think I'll start looking around for ten sections or so for him. I also need to make sure Wolf is taken care of. I like the way you gave Milam your ranch. A person can die out here from many different things. Most of us won't get the heads up like you did."

Angus responded, "It eases my mind to know the ranch is in Milam's name. I don't want the family to get crosswise after I'm gone.

Milam is the only one who really wants to be a rancher. You have to love ranching to be able to do the work. He and Mary seem to love it and are learning so much."

Mary walked out to talk to Fergus, and Morgan came with her. "Dad, I want to learn how to shoot a pistol better. If I had one with me, those three men would not have been able to kidnap me. I don't know a better person to teach me than you."

Morgan started to protest but stopped. It made sense for a person of the West to be good with a gun. A person who carried one needed to be better than anyone they might have to face.

Fergus said, "Yes, I will teach you. Do you have a choice of pistols?"

"What do you recommend?"

"If you can handle the weight and recoil, the .44-40 makes the most sense. Your rifle should be the same caliber. Take mine, and let's see if you can hit with it. Remember, accuracy is more important than speed. How much did you practice finger-pointing with Milam."

"A lot." Morgan gasped a little because she was not aware.

"Just as I figured. You're ahead of the game. We'll go out after breakfast tomorrow and see where you are."

After supper, Morgan said, "You know I'm not in favor of Mary learning to be a shootist, but I know if she carries a revolver, she needs to be very good. I'm torn, but I'm not mad at y'all. She will be a wealthy landowner and a potential target for too many evil people. You make her as good as she can be, but her carrying a gun will always scare me. I know I always carry a pistol, but not in the open."

After breakfast, Milam, Fergus, and Mary rode to a good shooting spot. Mary quickly showed Fergus she was already accurate. She hit five out of six on her first try and six the next time.

"Well, your accuracy is good. Put this holster on and show me your speed."

Her draw was not nearly fast enough. Fergus talked about pulling the hammer back as she took the gun from the holster.

"Keep your finger off the trigger until you clear leather. Many gunfighters have a missing toe. Try it with an unloaded gun first. Practice to get your draw smooth and clean. We will then try to draw and shoot."

Mary looked better with each try. Her draw was smooth and fluid and promised good speed with more practice. Fergus loaded her pistol.

"Try again. Clear your head and draw and shoot all in one motion. Don't think. Just pull the gun and fire."

She drew much faster and drilled the rock she was shooting at.

"That was much faster."

Mary responded, "I have a question. You said, 'Don't think,' yet I know I can't be shooting randomly. How can I not think and still be careful?"

"Good question. Before you get into a potential shooting situation, you must be convinced the person you're facing needs shooting. If you see a rattlesnake, you know it needs destroying. It's really the same with a man. You must be committed before you draw and shoot. Once you decide an hombre needs shooting, quit thinking and start shooting. It's worth a split second in getting a shot off, and a split second can be the difference between living and dying."

"What if I don't know I'm going to fight ahead of time?"

"Honey, sometimes you have to hope and pray you're doing the right thing. You might be surprised how many times a shooter makes a wrong decision, and you would be surprised how much it affects you. Several people quit wearing a pistol because they made a mistake. Doing your best to avoid making one is a heavy burden."

Mary looked at him a long time before saying, "Hmm. I knew wearing a gun was a big responsibility, but I never really thought about shooting the wrong person by mistake. It's something to think about."

"Yep. You need to work through it before you're in a scrap. You can sometimes make the decision early. For example, would you have shot those three men who kidnapped you? You certainly would have. Another thing, don't try to wound the bad guy. Aim to hit him dead center. It might not kill him, but he'll go down. Keep shooting until he is dead. Dead men have killed a lot of men who turned their back at the wrong time."

Mary's head was spinning a little. "Let's try again to see if I can clear my head quickly. It's spinning right now."

She loaded her revolver and stood ready to draw. She was faster by a fraction but not quite as accurate.

Fergus said, "You need to practice as much as you can. The key is getting the gun into action as quickly as possible and still be accurate. Also, practice on horseback. About a third of my shots have been from a horse, even though I don't like to do it. It messes with both speed and accuracy. When you start with live rounds, you want to be far enough away from the house for your mother to not hear it, even though she's taking this better than I expected."

"Maybe I'll go with Milam and Angus to help care for Angus."

"I'm sure Angus is why you are going." Milam and Mary, especially Milam, turned a dark shade of pink.

Fergus added, "Take plenty of ammo, and both of you practice. I'm sure Angus would like to watch you both shoot."

Fergus asked Jeb to come over to chat with the close family after supper. When they were seated, Fergus said, "I've been thinking about the future when Morgan and I are too old to work and pass on. I want to share what we're thinking and find out what you think. I don't want Bonner's Den Ranch divided up, and I want you and Mary to inherit ample land. So, we're thinking about buying another ranch. Most of this ranch would go to Mary, and we want a new ranch for you. What do you think?"

Jeb replied, "Sounds fair to me. I'd be interested in looking for a new ranch. What about Wolf?"

"We're considering deeding him two sections of this ranch, including the rough forested land." Jeb smiled and nodded his head.

Fergus continued, "Jeb, we'll start looking for the right property after roundup."

Morgan was not happy to see Mary going to Angus Ranch. She saw through the 'need to care for Angus' excuse as quickly as Fergus had, but she did not object too much. Mary tied her favorite horse to the surrey the next morning, climbed into it, and scooted close to Milam.

Angus made a comfortable nest in the back seat. He had talked to Little Bird and Chinn about herbs for his angina. They recommended a few and told him they might help but were not a cure.

Angus had accepted his fate but could not take sitting around and having people wait on him. He had always been a hard worker and worked just as hard as his cowboys, or harder. It was the way of the West. Landowners did not just give orders — they worked to get everything done. He did not know if he could sit around and watch others work. Knowing his ranch was in good hands with Milam and Mary was among his many joys.

Milam and his foreman, Dutch, talked at length about Angus's condition and about Milam being the new owner. Dutch had been with Angus through the lean years and the good years. He was almost like a son to Angus. Both knew Angus would not sit around the house and twiddle his thumbs. They work on an old buckboard to convert it into a more comfortable rig Angus could drive all over his ranch.

Most cow ponies were trained to stay put when their reins were dropped to the ground, which was called 'ground tying.' A bridle with a harsh bit was used to train a horse to stay put. The horse was tied to a stake in the ground, and water was not far away but out of reach. The horse was left for an extended time until it quit fighting the bit.

They wanted to find a horse that had never been trained to that level. Angus owned a beautiful black four-year-old with no training to be ground-tied. They picked it to train for his new duties. The horse seemed to understand that he was unique and had special work.

Mary and Milam practiced every day with their revolvers, and Mary quickly improved her speed and accuracy. She was almost as good as Milam, and better on some days.

In the summer, they spent much time riding over the ranch to learn as much as they could about it. Dutch often rode with them to talk about the land and the work needed. Angus even rode occasionally when tired of piddling around the ranch house. But he rode in his buckboard since a horse was too hard and caused him chest pains every time.

Mary had stayed twice as long as Morgan expected her to stay. One afternoon, Fergus and Morgan rode to Angus's house. Milam, Mary, and Angus were out on the eastern side of the ranch. The grass was less lush, but Angus explained that it was rich in nutrients, and cattle loved it. Morgan and Fergus were on the porch when they rode back to the ranch. They were dusty and looked like they had spent all day riding.

Morgan said, "I was hoping you were still here and not off on a honeymoon somewhere. I thought you were staying only a couple of weeks."

"Mom, we've been exploring the ranch to gain the insight we need. It's a big place."

"I wasn't worried much, but don't you think it is time to come home and prepare for the fall roundup. It'll be starting soon. I'm sure you intend to be there this year to help count your cattle."

"I surely am. Are you going?"

"I might for part of it. Being in a saddle every day for weeks is not as easy as it once was."

After supper, Fergus, Angus, and Milam sat on the porch with a cigar and a couple of fingers of the excellent rum and talked about the upcoming roundup. Angus had always planned the order of the pastures they worked. Fergus thought he should continue to do it and check on the progress from his buckboard. Angus looked forward to still being part of the roundup.

Chapter Eight

The Bonner family started home early the following day. Mary and Milam shared a satisfying kiss before they saddled the horses. Mary had not even departed but was already feeling lonesome. The roundup would start in a couple of weeks, and she would only have a little time with Milam for an entire month.

They could get home early afternoon if they hurried. Everything was going well, and they were almost halfway back when a large rattlesnake lay coiled on the trail. Everyone saw and heard it at about the same time. Morgan heard a massive boom coming from each side of her.

She asked, "Did both of y'all shoot?" Both nodded.

Morgan said, "I heard only one roar. Y'all must have shot at the same time!"

Fergus said, "That was fast girl! You've been practicing, and I don't think I've slowed down."

Mary grinned, and Morgan said, "I'm glad she's good, but I'm still concerned about my baby walking around with a gun, inviting other people to try her. I know it's better to be the best, but, my lord, I didn't even see her draw!"

They rode into a bevy of activity at the ranch headquarters. All the horses used on the roundup were getting their shoes checked, and most cowboys would use four horses. Roundups wore out horses fairly quickly, even quicker than the cowboys.

The chuckwagon was also being checked and rechecked. Every cowboy carried at least two ropes, and the chuckwagon had a few extra, along with rolls of pigging rope. Of course, the main thing in the chuckwagon was food. The food stored in the Bonner's Den and Angus Ranch's chuckwagons was based on the meals assigned to each wagon. Bonner's Den Ranch was responsible for breakfast and desserts, and Angus's would handle lunch and supper.

The day to launch the gathering phase finally arrived. The smaller ranches drove their cattle to the holding pens on the eastern edge of Angus Ranch. Bonner's Den and Angus ranches brought many more cattle from their ranches. The roundup had officially begun.

The focus of fall roundup was to select the cattle to sell, and brand and castrate the mavericks missed the previous spring. The ranch owners sat on their horses, or in Angus's case, a buckboard, near the chute each animal passed through after being separated into groups to be sold and kept. Cowboys collected more cattle from the pastures, and others cut out the ones to take to Cheyenne. It was challenging both physically and mentally to get the right ones. They worked through the herd more than once to ensure they had it right.

The momma cows and six-month-old calves were checked and returned to pastures emptied during the collection. The grown yearlings to be sold were kept in large pens at the work sites. Many of these work sites were scattered around the ranches — about one for each two sections.

Mary and Morgan stayed close to Milan and Fergus to help them keep a tally of each rancher's cattle to be sold. It was easy to tell when a rancher was in trouble because he sold momma cows and young calves, which diminished future production. Two ranches on the eastern border of the Angus and Bonner's Den Ranches were obviously having trouble. Selling mother cows was the last stage before throwing in the towel. Fergus made a mental note to talk to the two ranchers when the roundup was over. Their combined ten or twelve sections would make an excellent ranch for Jeb.

Collecting, separating, and dispersing continued for over three weeks. Fifteen catch pens were used, taking roughly two days at each site. The work was hard, and most cowboys used three or four horses a day. Some horses were barely broken to ride, so many rodeos erupted when they mounted each morning. A few riders received bumps and bruises each day, but fewer than in the spring when the men had to handle many more cattle.

The herd was finally ready to drive to market. Fergus and Angus rode ahead to check on railroad cars at Butte. They had stock cars this year, but only enough to handle a quarter of the over four thousand head the ranches had collected. They could drive them to Cheyenne again but preferred to use the railroad. They decided to split the herd into four groups and drive the groups one at a time to Butte. The train made a round trip every other day. They held the herd outside of Butte and drove a thousand at a time to Fergus's half section of fenced pasture near town to wait for the train. The pasture would be crowded but would be okay for a few days.

Morgan and Mary decided to stay in Butte at the boarding house. A nice shower and clean clothes awaited them whenever they wanted. Angus also stayed. Fergus and Milam rode the train to Cheyenne with the first load and a contingent of cowboys to hold the cattle outside of town on open railroad land.

Their plan worked well. By the time the last thousand head arrived in Cheyenne, the herd had been sold with only the count to be completed. They received top dollar — even more than the previous year. It took two days to run the cattle through the chutes at Cheyenne and load them for the trip back East.

All the owners were present when the bank drafts were drawn and received their share based on the counts done as the herd was assembled. They lost only ten head on the drive, likely to struggling settlers. Milam and Fergus received the largest share of the money, and the ranches would be profitable again this year.

Morgan and Mary checked on the dresses they ordered earlier in the summer. The men's western suits and a few of the dresses had arrived. The wedding dress had not arrived, but it would be there before Christmas, along with the other dresses and shirts. Mary was disappointed because she wanted to see the dress, but Morgan was satisfied.

Morgan assured Mary, "I'm sure it'll be here in time. We still have six months before you have to have it."

Milam and Fergus sat on the hotel porch in Cheyenne waiting to put Fergus's draft in the bank when it opened. Milam said, "I saw much predation on the range. Most appeared to be by cougars, but one pasture with many yearlings had wolf damage. A pack went through the herd and killed cows until they got tired. I think we need to do something."

"I agree. What do you propose?"

"I talked to a man yesterday who brought a pack of hounds to some ranches east of here. Ben Lilly, a man in Louisiana, raised and trained the hounds. Ervin, who brought them to the rancher, said they only chase predators. They're best on bears and cougars because there are few wolves to chase in Mississippi and Louisiana."

"How much would a pack of ten hounds cost?"

"About a hundred dollars each, according to Ervin. When they get on the trail, they don't stop until they tree the animal. Gonna' be pretty hard to find a tree on some of our land."

"Find Ervin and tell him we will take a dozen as soon as he can get them here. I'll try to find a trapper to work on the wolf population starting now."

Fergus found a rough-looking man with a wagon and numerous traps hanging from the side. He talked to the trapper, Lucas Batch, and agreed to pay him ten dollars for each wolf pelt he brought in.

They started back to Butte the next day and arrived after dark. The Bonner's and the McCullough's stayed in the boarding house. Milam opened an account and put his money in the bank, and a few others joined him. Fergus rose early to chat with Josh about whatever struck them. The others came downstairs about an hour later. Mary and Morgan took another shower before they came down.

Milam said, "You ladies surely do smell good. I'll look for a way to put a shower in the house."

"Why don't you figure out how to put an outhouse inside like some of the hotels have? Sure would be nice in the winter."

"I'll look into it."

Angus shook his head and said, "What is the world coming to?"

Since they had several stops to make in Butte, the others went to their ranches. Colorado and Dutch stayed to help make sure no one tried to rob them. They made a salty group for someone to take on. No one tried.

Fergus visited a few mines and asked if they were interested in buying prime beef if they were left at the Bonner's Den pasture. They could pay Josh for them, or keep up with the count and pay him when he returned to town. Everyone he talked to said they would take at least two a week.

Fergus said, "I'll have fifty head there within the week." They would pay twice the price he received in Cheyenne.

They left for home in mid-morning and arrived home just before dark. Once again, Milam and Mary would be torn apart, and neither liked it. Milam told her he would be back within a couple of weeks. She was not happy but accepted it. Their wedding would be in six or seven months.

They stayed in their separate rooms in agony not to be closer. Angus slept in the other extra bedroom. Colorado had found a woman in Butte a few months earlier and married her. They lived in a small cabin next to the bunkhouse. Dutch stayed in Colorado's previous room in the bunkhouse. Colorado and Dutch talked about how they could put up all the cowboys on both ranches for the wedding. It would be warm enough to sleep under tarps like they did on the roundup.

Angus did not have a great night and had to take a couple of pills. His color was not good, likely because he had pushed it a little too hard on the roundup and at the cattle sales. He had to get home and rest for a few days, and Milam agreed to drive him home. Angus had a comfortable chair on the porch and planned to use it extensively.

They met Lucas Batch on the way home trying to pattern the wolves so he could set his traps. The traps were mainly snares rather than foot holds. It was hard to trap wolves because they were smart and found most of the traps. They avoided the traps once they knew where they were. Lucas carried some rank-smelling juice to hide the human scent and a wolf scent to help attract them. Lucas also used poison on recent kills to try to wipe them out. He was ruthless about wolves.

When they arrived home, Angus lay down on his bed. He was worn out after working too hard for the last month. Milam decided he had time to ride around the ranch for a few hours.

Milam found a couple of dead wolves he assumed were poisoned. He also found where a cougar killed a large calf. He sat to see if the cat returned to eat before dark, and it did. Milam killed it and brought it back to the barn to skin and prepare it for making a rug.

Angus felt much better the next morning. He spent all day in his rocker watching the activity around the ranch. He did not see much activity because everyone was recovering from the roundup. The cook made his favorite spicy chili. It was a bit too spicy for Milam, but with a little cornbread, he could eat it.

Angus said, "I think we should name the ranch the McCullough Ranch now that you're the owner. What do you think?"

"It makes sense, I guess."

"What do you think of the A and MM ranch? We could keep our brand as it is with an A."

"I like it, but what about A2M. We could change the brand starting now and make sure we get a big start on changing it in the spring."

Angus responded, "Sounds good. Changing the brands this fall will be pretty tough on the hands."

"We can get some Bonner's Den hands to help since it's mainly for Mary. I can go over tomorrow and check on it."

Angus grinned and exclaimed, "Any excuse to ride over there! Can't say I blame you."

Milam left early the following day and arrived at Bonner's Den by early afternoon. His horse was a little tired but not overly so. He talked to Fergus, Morgan, and Mary about the proposed ranch name and brand change. Mary felt honored, and so did Fergus and Morgan. Fergus sent for Colorado to talk about helping rebrand all of the Angus cattle.

Colorado said, "That's a big job. It'll be bigger than either the fall or spring roundup. Plus, we will have to work with large cattle — lots of 'em. Something like three thousand momma cows and calves, and about the same number of yearlings. We're looking at nine thousand head with six thousand being large and sometimes wild. Sure, we can help, but we'll not be able to do much around here. But many cowboys are usually laid off after roundup. We might hire some of them to help."

"Okay. We should help with as many hands as we can. Go to Butte and on to Cheyenne if you have to. See how many you can hire. Keep a skeleton crew here to feed and look after the horses. We can make a dent in the branding before Christmas if the snow doesn't fly too early. I don't want to have to add all of the branding to the spring roundup."

"I'll tell the boys to start getting ready, and leave for Butte tomorrow morning. I'll need to talk to them about bonuses. How much should I offer the new hires?"

"I'll pay double wages to those who stay until the end of branding."

"That'll get you some help. Someone needs to go to Butte to buy supplies. I'd feed them well, not just beans and biscuits.

Colorado talked to the Bonner hands, and after some griping, he told them they would receive double wages for the duration of the extra work. No one opted out.

Colorado headed for Butte the following day to see if he could find cowhands who were out of work and had empty pockets. He found twenty hands he knew were competent and ten he knew nothing about.

They had enough hands to complete the job if everything went reasonably well. Colorado also picked up a couple of boxes of leather gloves for the cowboys. Handling the big cows put heavy wear on gloves. He also bought more lariats because the big cows could break a lariat. The branding would be tough on men, horses, and equipment.

Fergus and Mary took over sixty cowboys to the McCullough Ranch to join their thirty. The process would be much like a roundup. The cowboys started by making drags through the ranch to find cattle with the A brand. They grouped them in a large working area near catch pens.

The cowboys put a group in the catch pen to work them. Five sets of headers and heelers worked through the cattle. A large fire heated the branding irons. The cow was thrown with a rope on the head and the heels and dragged close to the hot irons. The A2M brand was applied. The 2M was burned into the hair beside it for those already with the A. If the cow was unbranded, it was done the same way except with an A2M branding iron.

Once the brand had been changed or applied, the cow was moved into a larger work pen. They stayed for a short time and then were moved out into the pasture. Most of the cowboys were out rounding up more cattle. The most challenging work was the roping and branding. It was also the most dangerous for minor and major injuries. The cowboys traded tasks to even the workload out.

Fergus was still one of the best heelers and took his turn with the other heelers. Dutch and Colorado were also good heelers. About forty cowboys were good ropers. With ten roping at a time, they had time to rest and change horses often.

Everything worked well, and many cattle received the correct brand by the end of the day. The supper consisted of steak, potatoes, and a peach cobbler. It was an excellent meal to cap off a hard day's work, which the cowboys appreciated. The cowboys went to their blankets as soon as they finished eating.

The catch pen was full the next morning, and a small herd was waiting to go inside. In fact, the cowboys had collected enough cattle to work the entire day.

One group of cowboys was sent to the next set of pens to begin collecting cattle. The others would likely finish the cattle already gathered in the late afternoon. They would move on to the next set of pens for supper.

The workdays became routine and were going as smoothly as everyone had hoped. Ervin rode into camp one day and told Milam that Ben Lilly would be along the next day. Milam asked why they were not together.

Ervin replied, "Ben don't ride horses anymore. Just doesn't like them. He's walking from Butte to here and will arrive tomorrow. He can cover more ground than most men can on a horse."

Fergus and Milam just smiled and shook their heads. They had heard Ben Lilly was a strange man.

The next day, a wild-looking man walked into camp surrounded by a pack of hounds. The man looked like he was walking as fast as most men ran, covering the ground rapidly.

When Lilly stopped, he asked, "Who'll work these hounds? I need to show 'em what to do so I can head back to Louisiana."

Angus and Fergus had already picked Wolf and Tall Man as the dog handlers. They told the two men to go with Ben.

Lilly asked, "Do you have a biscuit for a man who's not eaten for a while?"

He had not eaten since he left Butte two days earlier. He ate a biscuit and a slab of ham left over from breakfast.

"Where do you think we can find a track?"

Wolf had seen a cougar kill three miles from where they were working. They rode to the kill site, and the dogs immediately picked up the trail. Ben kept up with them on foot. The cat went straight to a little piece of rougher land with a tree-lined creek and treed. Wolf shot it and put it on his horse, but the horse was unhappy with the new passenger. They rode a short way up the creek, and the dogs hit a bear track. The bruin fled into a jumble of rocks and decided to stand his ground and fight.

The men arrived to find the hounds and bear in a vicious tussle. Tall Man pulled out his rifle to end it, and Ben yelled, "No! Them dogs are valuable. You might hit one."

Lilly drew a large, oddly shaped knife from his belt and waded into the melee. He approached the bear from the rear, plunged the blade in behind the left front leg, twisted it a couple of times, and the bear died. Wolf and Tall Man looked at each other and asked to see the knife.

They had seen many knives, but never one like this one. The blade was at least fourteen inches long and had a double curve, making an 'S' shape. It was razor-sharp on both sides.

Ben explained, "I want the knife to do a lot of damage. The crooked shape cuts a wide path going in. I then twist and let both sides cut as much as they can. Most bears don't last long. If you shoot them while they're fighting on the ground, you can kill or hurt a dog."

Wolf and Tall Man shook their heads. They skinned the bear and headed back for supper.

Ben said, "I'll hunt with you one more day to train you to the dogs. The four older dogs work on their own. Just find a track and put 'em on it. Four other dogs are trained but not as good at cold trailing as the first four. They'll likely get better. Four dogs are young and need more training and experience. They should not be worked by themselves."

Lilly ate supper and walked out away from everyone, along with the dogs. He lay down with the dogs surrounding him and was asleep when his head hit the ground. It was cool to cold at night in Montana, and Lilly had no blanket or other covering. Everyone supposed he used the dogs for warmth.

Wolf said, "We have a lot to tell you. Ben Lilly is a mighty strange man. He's smart but different from anyone I've ever met. He killed the bear with his knife. He's less than six feet and two hundred pounds, but he drew a knife, jumped into the fight, and killed it. I hope he's on my side if I ever get into a bar fight!"

Ervin said, "It won't happen. He doesn't drink, smoke, or chew. He will not work on Sundays at all. He does not go to church but reads his Bible all day Sunday. I've never heard him curse."

All the men were frowning when the stories were over. They had never met anyone like Ben Lilly and probably never would again. The fact he walked rather than ride a horse was different enough. A cowboy would not walk a hundred yards when he had a horse saddled.

Chapter Nine

After a month of hard work, the cowboys were nearly through with the A2M branding. Angus figured they had branded at least eighty percent of the momma cows and yearlings. Everyone expected it to snow any day, so they began to pack up and head home. The larger cattle led to broken arms and dislocated shoulders, but the cowboys had the winter to heal. Milam hired four of the cowboys Colorado hired for the branding, and Fergus hired eight.

Ben Lilly had departed a week earlier. The stories about his time with them took up several nights around the campfire. Ben gave Wolf one of his S-shaped knives. He possessed the skill to make them from scratch because he had been a blacksmith before being given a plantation by a man with no heirs.

Ben had asked Wolf, "Do you think you can jump into a tussle with a bear? I've never been seriously injured doing it. I don't think I'd try a cougar because they're too fast." Wolf could only shrug.

Fergus later asked, "Wolf, you gonna' jump on a bear with the crooked knife?"

"Only in self-defense!"

The group of hands who remained on the ranch during the branding had built a square stone building to store the oats they would soon harvest. It was time to harvest them when everyone returned. The crop was good, but Fergus was unsure it would be enough for both ranches. In previous years, they had bought oats from a homesteader, Mr. Jenkins.

Jenkins drove up one day with a wagon load of oats, and Fergus bought them. Jenkins said, "I'm throwing in the towel. Even with my two teenage sons, I don't have proper equipment and cain't grow enough to make any money."

Fergus said, "Suppose I bought you proper equipment. Could you make it?"

"I have only one old mule, and he ain't much good anymore."

"Let's sit on the porch and talk. Maybe we can work something out."

They enjoyed a couple fingers of rum, and Fergus said, "I need more oats, so I want to make you a proposition. I'll buy your land and lease it back to you on shares. I'll also provide three of the latest two-row breaking plows and a harvester. Plus, I'll provide three teams of strong mules. At the end of the year, my share will be one-third of the crop, and I'll buy your two-thirds. What do you think?"

"What's the catch?"

"No catch. I need grain. We grew oats this year, but to tell the truth, we don't know much about farming grain. And cowboys don't like to farm. My wife and brother grow potatoes but complained about the extra forty acres of oats. I really don't want to hear the gripping another year."

"How much do you plan to give me for my farm?"

"Three dollars an acre."

"Can you get the papers drawn up? I'll do it. My wife will be happy with this deal."

"So will mine. We can go to Butte and get my lawyer to draw up the papers. We'll order the equipment while we're there. I need to wait a week before we go. Will that be okay?"

"Shore it will."

"I'll pick you up a week from today in my buggy. A couple of other people may go in with us."

The next day, Fergus and Jeb rode to see the two ranchers who sold off many momma cows. They rode around one of the ranches and discovered the remaining cattle were in good shape. They rode to the ranch house and talked to the owner, Mr. DeLoach.

Fergus asked, "I noticed you sold some of your momma cows at the fall sale. Are you interested in selling your ranch?"

"I'm barely hanging on, and my wife wants to go back East, so, yeah, I'm interested in selling."

"How much land do you have."

"About five sections."

"How much do you want for it, along with the cattle?"

"Four thousand dollars for the land and another four thousand for the cows. I have about five hundred head of cows remaining. I think it's a fair price."

"I agree, and we will meet your price. Can you be in Butte in a week to sign the papers? I have to go in on some other business."

"What day?"

"Next Tuesday."

"I'll be there. My wife may want to go in with me and not return here."

They rode to the next ranch and repeated the process. Mr. Belcher, the owner, was also interested in selling.

Belcher said, "My health is failing, and I just can't take it any longer. Ranching killed my wife last year. It wore her out, and she gave up."

"How many acres do you have."

"About five sections and three hundred head of cows."

"How much are you asking?"

"Eight thousand for the whole shooting match."

"Sounds fair to me. Can you meet me next Wednesday in Butte to sign the papers?"

"Absolutely! I'm surely glad you came along, Mr. Bonner."

Jeb said, "That's a lot of money to get me a ranch. Sixteen thousand dollars is more than I can wrap my head around."

"We can handle it. We'll get you a better horse remuda later. Both these places can handle more cattle than they're running. The combined ranches will make you a good living if you run it right. I expect Kamiah and your mother will make sure of that. Let's get back to the ranch."

They got back after supper was served, but Juanita had their plates warming in the kitchen. Fergus said, "Why don't you get Kamiah and come over to talk?"

They sat around the table, and Fergus told Morgan, "I spent some of your money today."

"What do you mean?

"I bought another ten sections that will be Jeb's when we get it running right. I bought Mr. Jenkins' farm yesterday, and he'll be growing our oats and corn next year. You can go back to just your garden and potatoes."

Morgan was more excited about the farm than the ranch for Jeb, "Are you telling me we don't have to mess with grain next year?"

"Yep."

Morgan jumped and gave Fergus the biggest hug he had received in a long time. "So, I get a big hug for spending twenty thousand dollars? I thought you might get a little irritated."

"Not if Brody and I don't have to farm forty acres of grain. We're potato farmers, not grain farmers. When does all this land buying take place?"

"Next Tuesday and Wednesday. I'll pick Jenkins up and let him pick out three two-row breaking plows, a seed spreader, a harrow, and a harvester. We'll also give him our small harvester. I can buy four good mules from Josh. He'll need at least six with this equipment. Do we have any extra mules?"

"We can get by with a couple less. What I would like is four of the big gray mules you bought. They each replace two regular mules and give you a little change."

"Don't know how I can get down there to buy them, or even if they have any for sale. They don't sell many of those each year."

"Well, if we ever make it to Denver, we'll try."

Mary, Jeb, and Kamiah listened intently to the conversation. Fergus said, "We'll own the two new ranches now. I'll transfer the title to them when the ranches are operating properly. They need more momma cows, and we'll put a horse herd over there. We'll check out their cowboys and probably have to hire more. You'll also need a good foreman."

Fergus continued, "Jeb, take Colorado to help you determine how many cows the two ranches will support. We'll try to find more momma cows next spring."

"Kamiah, you should check out the houses to see if you want to live in one of them. We did not look at them. They seemed big, but I don't know about the inside. Morgan, you and Mary may want to help her look them over."

Kamiah responded, "Yes, I want them and Little Bird to help me decide."

"Y'all wait until the papers are signed. Don't want to jinx the deal. I didn't expect to find two good ranches side by side and close to Bonner's Den Ranch. The location is near perfect. We'll have about thirty sections bordering each other."

Colorado and Jeb rode over the ranches to evaluate the land and the cattle. About eighty percent of each ranch had good grass, much like the Bonner's Den and the McCullough ranches. The other twenty percent was a more scrubby high desert. It would support cattle, but only a few. The cattle counts DeLoach and Belcher gave appeared about right. They would have to wait until roundup to get a more accurate count.

Colorado figured they could handle about five hundred more cow/calf pairs, which would translate into fifteen hundred total animals on the acreage, or five hundred cow/calf pairs five hundred yearlings held for market.

When they returned to Bonner's Den Ranch, they talked with Fergus. Colorado said, "It's hard to get an accurate count over that much territory in just a few days. We should do separate roundups on the two ranches in the spring to get a good count. I know the herds from each ranch mingle, but we can handle the tally for each brand. By the way, what will you use as your brand."

"I have not thought much about it. They now use the BL- and the rocking DL. I can't think of any way to brand over those like we did for Milam. I might use the JBK. I want to avoid the hassle of changing all the brands already on the cows. We can start using the new brand on the unbranded cattle in the spring."

"Good decision. Rebranding took it out of the hands. I'm afraid the cattle on those ranches don't see riders as often as our cattle and might be wilder. They didn't look very friendly when we rode through them."

Fergus asked, "Do you know where to find a herd of good cows?"

"They're hard to find. Someone selling a herd of momma cows is likely to be selling their ranch. Maybe you can find someone who's overstocked. I don't think Bonner's Den or McCullough Ranches are overstocked, so we're not a good source. The high prairie around Denver can get overstocked, so you might find some there. Those cows would think they had died and gone to heaven when they see this grass."

Tuesday arrived quickly. Fergus picked Jenkins up early, and they were in Butte by late afternoon. They went to Eshee's office and found DeLoach waiting with his wife. The paperwork did not take long to complete because it was a straight transfer of property for cash. Fergus drew a draft on the bank in Cheyenne.

Mrs. Deloach said, "We'll cash the check when we get to Cheyenne. I don't intend to go back to the ranch. Everything in the house is yours. We are moving back East." The papers were drawn up accordingly.

Eshee said he could finish the Deloach deal before closing time and start the Jenkins deal the following day. Jenkins agreed but asked, "Where will we stay tonight?"

"I'll get us rooms in a boarding house. We can shower, have a good night's sleep, and eat a good meal. I'll pay, so don't worry about the cost."

Fergus took Jenkins to the general store to look at a catalog of equipment. They took the catalog to the boarding house to study it. Since only a few companies produced farm equipment, they should be able to make their decisions easily, or so Fergus thought. The decisions would have been easy had Jenkins not become so engrossed in the equipment catalogs. He had never seen them working and had a hard time deciding. His poor reading skills also slowed the process.

Fergus had to help him over supper. They finally made their choices. They ended up picking three two-row breaking plows, a seed spreader, a harrow to cover the seeds, and an oat harvesting machine. A one-row corn planter was bought for corn, but the corn would still have to be pulled by hand.

Jenkins was awestruck. He said, "My sons and I should make a bumper crop with the equipment and the mules."

Josh came over after supper and sold Fergus four good mules. Bonner's Den Ranch had two mules they would also provide to Jenkins. Jenkins had suddenly gone from an equipment-deprived operation to one of the best-equipped farms in Montana. Josh said he would send wagons as soon as the equipment arrived. Jenkins was elated.

Fergus and Jenkins returned to Eshee's office the following day after they placed their equipment order. They arrived before Eshee and sat talking.

Jenkins asked, "Why are you setting me up so well?"

"I hate to see someone working hard but unable to make it because they can't afford the necessary equipment. Like you, my folks tried to make a living back in Tennessee against impossible odds. I got lucky and made money in the gold fields. Besides, my wife hugged me when I told her she did not have to raise grain next year." Jenkins chuckled.

Eshee arrived, and they settled everything quickly. It was the most money Jenkins had ever held in his hands.

Jenkins said, "I need to buy supplies. Living on what we've had to eat has been hard."

"When we return, cut out a yearling from my herd. You can have two a year."

Belcher arrived just before noon, and they immediately consummated the deal. Belcher and Fergus were happy, so it must have been a fair deal. Belcher planned to return to the ranch house, load some furniture, and head for Oregon Territory. He had enough money to set up a smaller ranch there. The memories of his wife dying from a broken heart would be partially behind him. He said he would be out of the house by Friday morning.

Fergus replied, "That's fine. My son and his wife will look at your house and DeLoach's Saturday. We're in no hurry for them to move. I doubt if they will move before Christmas. I hope they don't, so I can be with my grandchildren for the celebrations."

Fergus and Jenkins started back with a wagon load of supplies and the four mules. Jenkins was quiet, as if thinking about the future. For the first time in a long time, he felt his family had a future, which was a comforting thought.

They had to camp because of darkness. It was a sparse camp. Fergus bought ham and biscuits for their supper and breakfast. It showered during the night, but they slept comfortably under the wagon. The rain cleaned the air, but it looked like it might change to snow during the day. Fergus hurried as much as he could. The snow started as just a few flakes, but the black cloud promised a blizzard. The dark front fulfilled its promise before they arrived at Jenkin's place. Everyone hurried to unload the supplies. Mrs. Jenkins was overwhelmed.

The blizzard was too intense for Fergus to try to make it home. He hoped the snow would stop before the following day. The Jenkins had a tiny shack, but they made room for Fergus to sleep on the floor. Jenkins asked him about the yearling he said they could kill. Fergus was sure the family had eaten little meat for a long time.

Fergus explained, "Find one with my brand and butcher it. It should keep you in meat for the winter. We'll find you another in the spring for the rest of the year. Two should give a family of four enough meat for a year."

Mrs. Jenkins was almost beside herself to have something to cook besides the gruel she had fed the family three times a day for as long as she could remember.

The snow stopped during the night and melted enough by lunch for Fergus to make it home. Fergus was cold when he got home. One of the cowboys took care of his rig, and he went to the house. Everyone was glad to see him. He was gone longer than they expected, and they were about to send Wolf and others to look for him.

———————————

Christmas was near and Morgan was upset because the wedding dress had not arrived. Mary was upset at first but said, "I really don't care about getting the dress. I can wear one of my nice dresses and be just as married."

Morgan said, "No family member has ever had a nice wedding dress. You'll have one if I have to ride all the way to Cheyenne and get it. Besides, we've already paid for it. My only daughter is going to have a proper white wedding dress!"

Kamiah and the group had looked at the houses, and she was not impressed with either house. The furniture in the DeLoach house was obviously made by DeLoach. She had better furniture in her current home.

Fergus said, "Tell you what, stay where you are this winter. We'll build you a new house in the spring. You need to think about what you want. You can go furniture shopping after we finish the house, so think about that. I can't have my only daughter-in-law unhappy with her house. Thanks for being straightforward about your thoughts."

"I've thought a little about what I want. I want a large, nice log house."

"Okay. Why don't you and your mother work with Morgan to see if you can sketch the house and its floorplan? A rough sketch will likely be enough for a builder. I'll find someone to construct it just like you want."

The snowstorms swooped into western Montana regularly now. Jeb wanted to check on his herd. He and Colorado could stay in one of the houses.

Fergus said, "Take ten or so other cowboys so y'all can get it done quickly. I wish I could go, but I think I need to stay here with Christmas just around the corner. You need to start evaluating the cowboys there so we'll know whether to keep them."

Jeb thought Kamiah made a good decision about the houses. They were drafty and cold. The heaters and fireplaces did not warm the houses enough in cold weather, and the roofs leaked. It would be better to build new rather than try to repair the houses.

The cattle, on the other hand, were in good shape. Both ranches had very little hay, but many areas were blown clear of snow. The cows were proficient at getting through the snow to the dried grass below. Both ranches contained scattered thickets to shelter the cattle in the most severe snow. A ridge ran through both ranches, allowing the herds to escape the wind.

The counts Colorado and Jeb made in the fall were reasonably accurate. The cowboys were competent, but none appeared to be foreman material. Neither Colorado nor Jeb saw a good foreman in the group, including the current foremen. Neither got dirty with the cowboys, which did not sit well with Jeb. He was sure both men would have to be replaced, and Colorado agreed.

It was time to return home. Jeb decided to leave Dub to oversee the two foremen. Dub moved into the bunkhouse because the building was better constructed than the houses. Dub would be able to pinpoint the best cowboys and if either of the foremen were salvageable.

Jeb's children, Rowdy, Liz, and Joe, were happy to see him, as was Kamiah. Everyone was ready for a big celebration. Fergus and Morgan had made a trip to Butte to buy presents for all the children on the ranch. They trended to items like chaps for the older boys or fancy bridles for all the riders. Clothes were always a part of the Christmas presents. Boots were also a big item. Every year, fireworks were a significant part of the celebration, and Chinn had been working on some big blasters. Fergus ordered supplies for him to build something that did more than just boom.

Christmas Eve arrived with a big meal, and everyone was in the big house. Even Milam and Angus came over to spend the night. Many fireworks were expended, but many were saved for Christmas night. All the parents knew was that it would be challenging to get the children to bed. Fortunately, the gifts were in the big house. Many children were getting a horse to call their own this Christmas. They were all beautiful and well-trained. The girls tended to get louder colored horses, and the bigger boys received real cow ponies. The younger children received ponies and appropriate tack.

Juanita and Lotte made fantastic sweet rolls for breakfast. Everyone loved their shirts and chaps, but when the door was opened and they saw the horses saddled and ready to go, they immediately went to the horse they thought or hoped was theirs. The parents had to help some children identify the proper horse, and it all worked out. The older boys and girls rode out on the trail to get used to their horses. Rowdy and Colt were excited about their horses being capable of working cattle. Brody's kids were also enthusiastic about theirs. The younger kids were glad to have a mount that fit them. They could get on and off without help. The naming ceremony for the horses took hours of haggling, and a few little fights broke out.

Everything was smoothed over before lunch. The men laughed, and the women ripped their hair out about the arguments over names, especially the scrapes that broke out. The noon meal set a new standard for meals. A cured ham and a turkey were served, along with trimmings galore. Chocolate cakes and coconut pies were brought out when everyone finished. Most children dove into the fried pies filled with fruit, which were fantastic.

Chapter Ten

The fireworks on Christmas Eve were impressive. Chinn had done a magnificent job with the ones he made. Everyone was oohing and aahing with every blast. Milam and Mary were under a bearskin on the porch. They were so close that two or three additional people could have fit underneath the cover. Morgan noticed them but said nothing. She was relaxed and content except for the missing wedding dress. She would give the store until the New Year and then pay them a visit.

Milam and Angus planned to head home the next day, and Mary would accompany them. But a nasty blizzard rolled in, and they had to wait two more days before departing. Much of those two days were spent helping Kamiah design the log house she wanted. Angus helped with the design. He was surprisingly adept at making carpenter-friendly drawings of the interior and exterior. The house would be almost as large as the Bonner mansion. Chinn and Little Bird would move into their own wing of the house, which was nearly as large as their present house.

Kamiah was satisfied with the progress made in planning and delighted with the drawings. The plans included everything she wanted. In addition to an entire wing for Little Bird and Chinn, each child would have a separate bedroom. The master suite was as large as the Little Bird suite. Two extra bedrooms were included in case they needed them.

Angus said, "Jeb, it's a good thing you have lots of timber on your place. You're gonna need it."

Rowdy, Liz, and Joe liked their bedrooms, particularly the porch or balcony surrounding the second floor. A large common room was planned for their activities in the middle of the second floor. A room off the kitchen was included for a cook/maid. Kamiah was still determining exactly where she wanted the house located, but ten sections should have more than one excellent house site.

Angus, Milam, and Mary arrived at their house none the worse for wear. The trip was beautiful but frigid. The temperature would remain cold until a Chinook wind arrived to warm everything and melt the snow at lower elevations.

Mary spent time figuring out how she wanted the house arranged. It was well done for a man's taste. The first question was where she and Milam would sleep. They were talking about it one day, and Angus overheard the discussion.

Angus said, "You'll take the room I've been using. It's the master bedroom and Milam will be, or rather already is, the property owner. I'll use the nice bedroom downstairs so I won't have to climb those blasted stairs. They set my heart off." The issue was settled just as Mary had hoped.

After studying the interior, she decided not to make many other changes. A couch and a few chairs were moved, and a few things would be adjusted in the dining room. She wanted to make the big parlor a little more feminine but not too much. The more she looked around, the more it was apparent Angus did not change much after his wife died. Plus, she thought a ranch house ought to look a bit masculine.

She and Milam rode around and found a couple of cougar kills. Milam told Tall One to take the hounds out and chase the cougars. They needed to be run off into the mountains or, preferably, killed. Mary would soon return to Bonner's den and send Wolf to help.

Tall One and Wolf set out on their mission when Wolf arrived at the McCullough Ranch. They took a pack of six dogs and hit a fresh cougar trail close to the ranch house. The cougar scurried up a lone tree in the middle of a pasture. Tall One shot it, took it to the house, and returned to Wolf and the pack.

They soon chased another cat to a tree-lined creek bed. The cougar climbed a tree but jumped down before the hunters arrived. After a short chase, he treed again, but the hounds were right on his tail when he climbed the tree. Wolf shot it, and they decided to return home and start again the next day with a fresh pack of dogs.

They skinned the cougars and prepared the hides for tanning. The group dined on delicious cougar meat for supper. Ben Lilly had told them cougar meat was the best-tasting meat, and he was not wrong.

Wolf and Tall One started early the following day. A cowboy accompanied them to take anything they killed back to headquarters. The hounds struck scent only a few miles from the ranch house. It was a long chase before the cougar holed up in rocks that formed a little cave. The hounds tried to get to the cat, but the cat was fighting them off.

It was much easier to shoot a cougar out of a tree. One dog received a nasty cut on its face, but he did not quit. Wolf and Tall One, with the help of the cowboy, finally got the dogs away from the hole. Wolf used his pistol to try to shoot the cat. It took two shots to hit him in a vital area. The cowboy took the wounded dog and the cougar carcass back to the house. Wolf and Tall One took the other five dogs on a circuitous route to try to find another track.

The five remaining dogs took little time to hit a fresh track. This one acted more like a cougar should and treed after a long chase. Tall One shot it. The dogs were tuckered out after two long chases. They headed home, but the dogs hit another track. Wolf called them back with a horn Ben Lilly left with him. It was a cow horn, much like old timers used to carry black powder, but with the tip drilled out and shaped. When blown, it sounded somewhat like a hound baying. The dogs were trained to return to the horn despite wanting to keep chasing the animal.

The other hands had skinned the first cougar and placed the hide on a drying rack. Tall One's wife and sons stitched the hound's wound. They thought it would take several weeks for the wound to heal properly. She used a salve similar to Little Bird's to keep the wound clean. Cougar and bear wounds often caused nasty infections.

The next morning, they took a fresh pack of hounds to where they had called the pack off the track the previous day. It took the hounds a while to work out the track since the cougar had used the night to find new country. They struck hot after almost four hours of cold trailing. The huge male cougar did not want to tree, which made the chase long and tiring. The shot was anticlimactic after the cougar finally treed. They let the cowboy with them take the shot.

Cougars are not hard to kill if they can be sighted because they do not have tough skin or heavy bones. They are nocturnal and several of the cowboys had never seen one even though they had lived in cougar country most of their adult lives. Cougars usually hide during the day, and a rider could pass close by them and not see them. Their tracks are easily seen in the snow, but few cowboys really wanted to find one. Many stories were told around the bunkhouse about cowboys being killed by a cougar.

Wolf and Tall One hunted ten more days and bagged a cougar each day. They decided to move to Bonner's Den Ranch after giving the hounds a couple days off. The hunters actually needed rest more than the hounds.

They took ten hounds since a cougar had ripped another one on the side. The hounds were tough and did not want to quit, even when hurt. The pack hit a track on the way over, but Wolf and Tall One called them back. A couple of the young hounds did not want to leave the track.

Wolf and Tall One discussed which two hounds they would breed to raise a litter of pups. It was a difficult choice because all the hounds were good. They picked a male that Ben Lilly said was mostly Catahoula Cur. He was not a pretty dog, but tough with a good cold nose. The female dog looked nice, and Ben told them she was a coonhound. She was mainly white with black spots and ticking. In fact, Ben called her a bluetick hound. They would breed them as soon as she came into season, which should be soon.

Wolf and Tall One hunted for ten days on Bonner's Den Ranch. They hunted a lot near the two sections of rough land. The cougars always headed for the tangled land. Riding their horses in the rough land was dangerous, so they had to tie the horses and continue the chase on foot. It was uncomfortable approaching a dangerous cornered animal with five or six snarling dogs after it. They killed five cougars on Bonner's Den Ranch.

After a couple of days off to rest, they rode to Jeb's ranches. The ranches contained more trees, so hunting was easier and the chases shorter. They also found several bear dens, so they would need to work the area harder the next time they hunted, which would likely be just before the spring roundup.

Eliminating cougars from the ranches was important, but it was also enjoyable for the men. They had many volunteers for the hunts. Rowdy and Bear were especially insistent. Wolf promised they could go with them at least one day the next time they ran the hounds.

Morgan was all worked up over the wedding and fandango. She asked Juanita and Lotte at least ten times what food they would prepare and if they needed anything. It was getting to the point that everyone hid when they saw her coming, including the youngsters.

Morgan insisted she and Mary go to Cheyenne and maybe on to Sacramento. Fergus encouraged the trip so she would be out of his hair for a week or two. Perhaps he could manage to be out helping Jeb or something when they returned. Then, she reminded him that he needed to hire a builder to build Jeb's log house. He thought he could find one in Butte.

The three of them departed in late January. Much snow was on the ground, but the trail to Butte was pretty decent. After the women boarded the train, Fergus went to see Josh.

Josh said, "I know a man with a good construction crew. He's built huge log homes for several mine owners. You may be early enough to get him first this year."

Josh took Fergus to a warehouse and introduced him to the owner, Mike. Mike had yet to sign contracts for the spring, so Fergus would get him first.

Mike examined Fergus's plans and said, "It's big but not too complicated. We should be able to finish it in six weeks if you have men who can help transport the trees to the building site. We will need three or four teams of mules, but I only have two."

"I can handle the men and the mules if you can start soon." Fergus knew the farming operations would not get underway for at least another month or two.

"My crew and I are tired of sitting around town not making any money. We can be there next week, ready to start. It's still early, so snow will slow us down occasionally. Hopefully, we'll not lose too many days."

"Bring supplies and a cook, and I'll furnish a house. It's not a great house, but it will break the wind and might keep you dry. It has decent furniture. I'll also keep you in beef at no charge. The new house is for my son and daughter-in-law, but they'll probably not bother you much during construction. On the other hand, my wife might be a different kettle of fish."

———————————

Fergus headed back to the ranch to get Kamiah to pick the exact site of the house. He walked to their home and said, "Kamiah, the builder will start construction next week. You need to select the site soon — like in the next couple of days."

"I have it selected. It's on a little rise south of the Deloach house and has an excellent view. It has many big trees to take down, not enough for the whole house, but enough for a good start. I can show him the site and how I want the house to face."

"Good. You're ahead of the game. The builder says he can finish it in six weeks with a little help."

"Oh my, that's quick, but not too quick for me!"

Fergus got the best pulling six mules ready to take to Jeb's ranch. With Colorado's help, he also picked eight cowboys with logging experience. Some were not overly thrilled, but most were content to be doing something else for a while. The weather was cold with spitting snow. Everyone was thankful for only a slight breeze because big trees could not be cut down in high wind.

Kamiah met Mike at the building site, and they began by marking off where she wanted the house. Fergus thought she picked a superb location for the house, which would be positioned to catch sunlight throughout the day. Fergus and the men started felling trees inside and near the cabin's footprint. They used two-man crosscut saws to fell the trees and axes to trim the logs. They did not try to cut the logs to length or skin the bark off. They wanted the construction crew to be on site before they started those activities. Fergus was in the middle of everything because he likely had the most timber experience.

The construction crew arrived when promised. The first man to go to work was a blaster to remove stumps inside the footprint and close to the site. He was not part of the normal crew but worked for Mike on slow days at the mines. By the end of the first day, he had blasted out over half the stumps. The Sheffield mules drug the stumps away. All the stumps were gone on day two, and the ground was fairly level.

Mike put measurements on the drawings Kamiah supplied. He wanted to use full length logs as much as possible, especially around the bottom. The crew scraped the bark off and then burned the logs slightly to make them less susceptible to rot. The burning pulled a little sap to the logs outside, giving the logs a longer life, a trick Fergus did not know about. The foundation logs were set and leveled at the end of the fourth day.

The log preparation proceeded smoothly. Two cowboys felled the trees, two trimmed the logs, two others hauled them to a work area, and four men barked and burned them. Fergus and Jeb pitched in with whichever group needed help keeping up. The bases for the interior walls took a little time, but they were as critical as the base logs for the outer walls.

When the outline of the bottom floor became clear, Jeb brought Kamiah to ensure it was acceptable before they proceeded. Morgan also insisted on coming. Both women were satisfied with what they saw.

Mike asked them if they wanted a metal or traditional shake roof. Jeb replied, "What do you recommend?"

Mike hemmed and hawed but finally said, "The metal roof is easier to build and will not leak, but some people think the shakes are prettier. Metal will shed snow better, and the snow load could be a problem for a house this large. All in all, I think you would be happier with metal. We must decide now because we have to order it from Omaha or further east. It'll take a month to get here."

Jeb said, "Do I need to order it now?"

"Yes. Talk to Josh Doyle about staying on top of the order and delivering it as soon as it arrives. It will be a large order. Let me go figure out how large."

Mike walked to the side and started calculating. He first calculated the square footage needed to cover the flat footprint and then added the amount required to make a steep roof for snow. It was a lot of metal.

Morgan and Kamiah spent one night and returned home. Kamiah's head was spinning, but she was happy. Mike told her to come back in a week to ten days, and she would be able to see at least the bottom floor.

The weather cooperated reasonably well. It snowed several times but did not completely shut the construction down. Since the metal roofing would not be available until later, they used canvas to cover what they could. The way they used the ranch crew to cut and deliver the logs to the site was working well. The construction crew was able to spend all their time notching the logs and putting them in place. They used an interesting A-frame lift to get them in place, using one mule to provide the power. Mike had a good, hard-working crew.

Morgan, Mary, and Milam went to Cheyenne to get items needed for the wedding. Mary and Milam would be working on the roundup soon, and the wedding would occur immediately afterward.

As the wedding drew nearer, Morgan felt more pressure. Everything was pretty much together, but she was stressing about every little thing. The arrival of the wedding dress had helped earlier, but it seemed something would arise every few days.

Milam made the arrangements for their honeymoon. They would travel to Denver and stay in the Cannon Hotel.

Milam worried about Angus. He seemed to be getting weaker, and Milam wondered if he could make it to Bonner's Den Ranch for the wedding. Perhaps he would rally when the roundup started.

Milam, Mary, and Morgan talked one night about what they would do if Angus could not attend the wedding. Morgan thought they should get him to Bonner's Den early so she could look after him during the roundup.

Morgan said, "Juanita will feed him well. I'm sure we can get him moving better during the month y'all are on roundup. Maybe it'll keep him from missing the roundup so much. I know it's killing him not to be going out."

———————————

It was time to run the hounds to get it done before roundup. Wolf and Tall One decided to take two cowboys with them on each hunt. Having others gain a little experience with the hounds would be good.

They only had eleven dogs to run. The blue tick was going to have a litter soon. Colt took care of her and the puppies while they were running the rest of the pack. A dogs gestation period was only sixty-three days, so the pups should be born in about two weeks, which would be in the middle of the hunting.

Wolf and Tall One started on the McCullough Ranch. They chased mainly cougars again but got on a few bears. The bears were a nice size, and the first three they chased treed. The fourth one, however, scrambled into some rocks and chose to fight on the ground. Wolf tried to get a shot without hurting the dogs, but they were too close. Finally,

Wolf drew the Lilly knife and joined the fight. He jumped on the bear's back as Ben Lilly had done and plunged the knife as deep as he could. He then started moving the supersharp knife around inside the bear's chest. The bear expired quickly without injuring Wolf. When it was over, Wolf just sat there blinking his eyes and breathing deeply. He had not planned to jump into the tussle — he just wanted to save the dogs. Tall One and the two cowboys with them were duly impressed.

When they returned, Wolf's story circulated around like a flood on a spring night. Tall One took Wolf's knife to the blacksmith and told him he wanted one just like it.

The blacksmith responded, "I can build one, but it'll take a few days to get the curves just right. I have to first find a piece of steel to work with, which will be a big piece of high-quality steel. I think I have a steel rim for a wagon wheel. If I work it repeatedly, I can get a good blank to shape. I suppose the curves are important, right?"

"The curves are critical. If I use it, I'll be on the back of an angry bear. The curved double-sided knife will cut so the bear won't last long."

"You're telling me you're gonna' fight a bear with this knife? I thought you were smarter than that! I'll check the blade to make sure it is as good as I can make it. The steel has to be strong but not brittle, and it needs a little spring. It'll take a little figuring and work. May take a little longer than I said."

They chased cougars and bears on all the properties. Colt and Rowdy went on a couple of hunts. They saw Wolf kill a bear with his knife. Colt was so proud of his dad and did a lot of bragging to the rest of the youngsters. Half Moon was not so proud. In fact, she gave Wolf a piece of her mind, and it was not a happy piece. She would have put his blankets on the couch or porch if he had not been gone so long and was about to be away even longer.

All the ranches were bustling with activity getting ready for roundup. The roundup would begin on Jeb's ranches. They wanted to get a more accurate count of the cows and start using the new brand. It was a proud moment for Jeb when the first calf was branded and even more so when he was able to see his cattle in the pens.

Chapter Eleven

The hands assigned to bring the logs to the construction site worked hard to get enough to finish the house. The men would be needed on the roundup, which started in a week or so. Fergus brought a few more hands to help, and the stack grew more quickly. Mike told Fergus that two more days of cutting and hauling logs should be enough. Most of the rough logs were long enough to cut into two functional interior logs. The cowboys soon returned to the ranch to begin working the roundup.

Fergus stayed a few days at the building site but had to prepare for the roundup. The shoeing and things like checking gear had to be completed soon.

All the smaller ranches were rounding up their cattle to take to the work pens. Most had done their work before the big ranches took their cowboys to the catch pens. They first worked the smaller herds to get them out of the way.

Milam's herd was the next one worked on. More hands than usual were available, and some were already gathering McCullough cattle. Milam was glad they had already changed many brands from an A to A2M, which made this roundup easier. It still took two weeks to collect all the cattle running on the McCullough Ranch and work them through the pens scattered around the ranch.

The spring roundup took less time than the fall one because a cattle drive was unnecessary. The cattle were simply turned back out on the range. A few cowboys were assigned to keep those cattle from mixing with those not yet worked.

Fergus was reasonably impressed by Jeb's hands and thought they should be retained. He, Jeb, and Colorado decided to keep them all, but they still needed to look for a good foreman.

They sent Jeb's cowboys to the building site to help Mike and to bring Morgan and Brody's mules back to start the plowing. Fergus took a day to ensure Jenkins had the equipment they ordered and enough mules to break the land. He was glad to see Jenkins and his sons had already begun plowing where it was dry enough — they were at least a quarter complete. The plowing should be completed within a month. The Jenkins were ahead of the game because they had even planted part of the acreage and covered the seed with the harrow.

Brody and his farm hands had also begun plowing. The potatoes could be planted early, so they started with the hundred acres allocated for potatoes. They had enough seed potatoes left over, and hands were cutting the whole potatoes into pieces with an eye on them. Planting would start in a couple of days. Morgan and Brody thought planting would take about two weeks or a little longer. Morgan wished she could help Brody, but he had it under control. Oby was helping him stay ahead of the game even though he was too old to help with manual labor.

The cougar hunts had helped reduce the predation, as they had hoped. They found only a few kill sites. Wolf and Tall One took the hounds hunting to eliminate the few remaining cougars.

The roundup finally wound down. Milam and Fergus decided it was time to return home. Morgan was glad they were around to help with the wedding. Angus was already staying at Bonner's Den Ranch.

The band for the fandango would be composed of several cowboys who were quite good singers and musicians. The meal's centerpiece was a yearling that had been fattening for two months.

The roundup ended, and the cowboys returned to their home ranches. The wedding would be one week later. Mary could hardly believe the day was finally so near. Her waiting had seemed to last a lifetime, or at least most of hers. Even Morgan had settled down and was not bothering everyone with her worrying.

Morgan wanted to see Jeb's house, which should be nearly finished. The house and moving them in were her next projects, although Kamiah and Little Bird had it under control. The log mansion was beautiful. It was located in a beautiful setting and looked perfect. The metal roofing had arrived and was being installed. It was green and matched the logs and setting perfectly. Kamiah, along with Mike and his crew, had done a great job.

Liz gave Morgan a tour of the mansion. She was so proud of her room and all the rest of the house. Rowdy was on the range with Jeb and a crew of cowboys. He was already at home everywhere on the ranch. He had ridden over every square inch of it and knew it well. He was even beginning to recognize some of the cows and all the bulls.

The herds on Jeb's two ranches were a little different. The DeLoach ranch had more Hereford-looking cows, and the Belcher side had more crossbred Black Baldy's. They looked similar with white faces, but the Herefords had red bodies, and the Baldy's were black. Both were good breeds for the prairie.

Jeb wanted better bulls to add bulk to his cattle. He hoped to find some near Cheyenne during the summer. He planned to go as soon as the wedding was over, or maybe he could get Milam to look while he was in the Denver area.

Jeb talked with Milam and Fergus about bulls before the wedding. Milam replied, "I also want new bulls and will look for both of us. I can ship them back if I find any available."

Fergus said, "Denver is close to the rancher who sold me the Sheffield mules. If he has any mules for sale, try to buy some for Morgan and Jenkins."

Both men apologized for asking him to do things for them on his honeymoon. Milam replied, "It's okay. I was thinking about finding the Cannon ranch and looking it over."

Wedding day finally arrived. Surprisingly, Morgan was cool as a cucumber, at least on the surface. Fergus was a little nervous. Milam was the most anxious of all. He appeared as though he would burst. He was nervous when he woke up and his condition worsened by the hour. Juanita had prepared an excellent breakfast, which he did not touch.

118

Mary ate a big breakfast while she and Morgan calmly discussed the wedding and festivities to follow. The wedding was at two o'clock, with the fandango beginning immediately afterward. The hands had cleaned out the largest barn as well as possible and laid a large tarp for the eating and dancing. Since the women from the Butte saloons had enhanced the last fandango so well, Morgan hired them for the fandango. Strict rules about hanky-panky were still in place. The women were happy for the most part — they were getting paid for just dancing and talking.

Mary dressed in the barn's tack room. Only Morgan and Little Bird had seen her in the dress. No one else would see her until Fergus walked her down the aisle. Morgan knew she would be the most beautiful vision most attendees had ever seen. Having just finished a roundup, she was well-tanned, and the white dress fit perfectly in all the right places. She carried herself as the confident young lady she was.

The other women at the wedding party also wore new dresses. Fergus thought his little barn in Montana might have the prettiest women in Montana that day, from Maude, who was over seventy, to the babies. Liz looked particularly nice at nearly ten years old. She would break young men's hearts in a few years.

Fergus, Angus, and Milam dressed at the house and walked to the barn together. Angus stood with Milam, and Fergus escorted Mary. Rowdy and Wolf showed people to their seats. Liz was the flower girl, and Joe was the ring bearer. Most weddings on the prairie had no attendants, but Morgan had seen pictures of eastern weddings with attendants. The preacher was a bit overwhelmed with the ceremony. Frontier weddings were generally plain and simple, often conducted at an official's office with no attendants. After the wedding, most newlyweds returned home. But this wedding ceremony was definitely different.

Of course, the wedding should be different when the groom and the bride's dad were major landowners. Mary and Fergus started down the aisle when the band launched into the wedding march. Milam thought Mary was the most beautiful young lady in the state, if not all of the West, as she walked to meet him with a huge smile. Milam was smiling also, but his knees were shaking so much he was sure others could hear them knocking together. Angus moved a little closer to help stabilize him.

The vows were spoken, but Mary and Milam could barely remember them. They were married, which they had wanted for several years. Milam's knees settled down, and he could walk more or less normally. He was so proud of his beautiful wife. She was glowing and obviously in love with him.

Milam's aunts, uncles, brothers, sisters, mother, and dad attended the wedding. One brother, the banker, traveled all the way from St. Louis. Milam asked Fergus to spend time with him in case they decided to buy the bank.

The band started playing and Milam and Mary took the first dance. Then the floor, or rather canvas, was soon filled with dancers. The fatted calf was ready, and the cooks were carving delicious slabs of the meat. Potatoes were prepared almost every conceivable way, and many fresh vegetables from the extensive garden were available.

The dancing and eating continued all afternoon and was still going when the lanterns were lit. Mary and Milam managed to slip off mid-afternoon to put on more comfortable clothes. They were not used to dressing up.

They spent the first night at Bonner's Den Ranch and rode to Butte the next morning. Several other people accompanied them to catch the train or return to their homes in Butte.

Milam and Mary rode the train to Cheyenne and spent the night. Then, they caught another train to Denver, where they planned to spend several weeks. With the roundup over, Milam could take that much time to explore the Denver area.

The trip to Denver was uneventful. A few guys tried to hit on Mary but soon found out she could get her pistol out so quick that they did not know it was out until it was in their gut or face.

The Cannon Hotel in Denver was the fanciest one they had ever seen. The artwork was almost magical.

On their second day, the owner, Martha, sat with them at breakfast. It was the first time they realized her sons owned the Cannon Ranches and other property.

The couple enjoyed, walking around Denver, shopping, and eating at excellent restaurants. But the best restaurant was in the Cannon Hotel.

One morning at breakfast, the owner approached with a couple they had not seen in the hotel. She introduced them as Grant and Angelina Cannon, her son and daughter-in-law. They felt like they had seen them before and realized they were depicted in many art pieces. Milam also soon realized they were the owners of the Cannon Ranch.

Milam said, "I was hoping to meet you. Mary's dad bought two mules from you in Cheyenne — two of the biggest and strongest mules we've ever seen, and he wants to buy more. Do you have any to sell?"

Grant replied, "The Fourth of July Celebration is the big day for horses and mules in Denver. We always have a big auction. I think we have two Sheffield mules left to auction. We will also have a lot of horses to auction, races of all lengths, and pulling contests. Mary's dad was the one with the beautiful Appaloosas. If he brought a bunch of them, he could sell them all for a premium price. Probably hurt my sales, but maybe not."

"Do you think we can come out to look over your operation? Fergus keeps telling me about how you do it. You really impressed him in Cheyenne. I'm looking for Sheffield mules and bulls for our ranches. Maybe even a few cowhorses."

"That can be arranged. How big is your operation?"

"I own about ten thousand acres. Mary will inherit a ranch of a similar size, as will her brother. I'm a new ranch owner. My grandfather recently deeded his ranch to me. I have much to learn and hope to pick up some pointers from you.

Angelina checked out Mary, who was several years her junior. She immediately noticed that Mary was armed with a high-quality revolver and appeared comfortable with it. Mary wore her leather pants and looked like a frontier woman. Angelina thought they might have a lot in common.

Grant said, "We have plenty of room at our place. Why don't y'all ride back with us? We can leave after lunch. I have some business at the bank my brother runs. He and I are partners in several businesses."

"That would be wonderful! How long do you think we should prepare to stay?"

"At least four or five days. Let me go to the telegraph office. Another ranch south of here raises the big mules, and they will likely have more to sell. They have Sheffield Mules and another darker strain called Freedom Town Mules. They come from Shire horses rather than Percheron horses. They pull about the same and are just as good looking. Meet us here for lunch. Maybe Angelina and Mary can shop while I'm gone."

Shopping suited the women. They also wanted to talk about womanly things. Angelina asked, "I can't help but notice you're armed. Do you go armed often? I do. In fact, I'm armed now."

"Yes, I feel naked without my gun, and yes, I'm very good with a rifle and pistol. Had to show a couple of yahoos on the train how quickly I can get it into play."

Angelina thought, "*Sounds like something I would say. We're going to get along just fine!*"

"Is there anything you want to look at while you are here? We have decent shopping in Denver."

"I need a little furniture and accent pieces. His grandfather lived alone in the house for nearly twenty years. It's a little too masculine now, but I don't want to overdo the changes."

"I know exactly what you mean. A ranch should look like a ranch and not a gentleman's club, but a few niceties can help. Do you get many visitors at the ranch?"

"Hardly any. To get home, we'll take the train to Cheyenne, a different railroad to Butte, then ride a day to the ranch."

"Oh my, I thought we were isolated! Y'all really are."

"Yes, but before then, we mined gold in the Idaho mountains. The place was really isolated. I was born there, so I didn't know any difference."

"So gold is the basis of your wealth like it is ours? We do have a lot in common. I'm going up to freshen up a little, and we can head out in about thirty minutes."

Mary was ready when Angelina returned. She asked, "Who did all these paintings? You're in many of them."

"Two young women painted almost all of them. Neither Grant nor I are related to them by blood, but one of them, Lizzy, is like a sister to us. Lily Sheffield, a woman in Freedom Town, played a large role in her and Grant's lives. Lizzy was just a child when they met, and Miss Lily raised her from a young age. Grant was a young teenager when he met Miss Lily. He thought his mother and dad were dead at the time, so she provided a mother's love for him also. It's complicated. I'll tell you more about them at the ranch."

They walked into a furniture store, and it did not take long for Mary to find a couple of pieces she liked. They also stopped in a clothing store to look around. Mary had many nice clothes her mother had bought her. She found casual clothes that fit her lifestyle much better. They were made from the denim material they first saw in Sacramento. She bought both her and Milam a couple pairs of pants and shirts. She thought they could wear them anywhere. She found a denim jacket that was shorter than most — it would let her get to her gun quicker.

They stopped in a pastry shop in mid-morning to have coffee and a doughnut. They talked more and discovered they liked each other a lot. They were so much alike that it was hard not to like each other. They returned to the hotel to repack for going to the ranch. Martha said she could leave most of their luggage in a hotel storeroom so they could ride horses and explore more.

As they headed out of town, they stopped at a lovely mansion similar to the one they lived in. Clark, Grant's brother, and his family lived there.

Grant said, "Let me show you something a wealthy rancher might want."

He took them straight to the indoor toilet. It was still a novelty, although several houses in Denver had them.

Mary said, "My mother told my dad she wanted one after a trip to Sacramento. It would be convenient on a cold prairie morning or with children. Milam, you need to take notes on it."

They headed on to Grant and Angelina's ranch house. It was not much more than an hour at a steady pace. Suddenly, a snarling mountain lion was at the side of the road in tall grass. Instead of running away, it charged Mary's horse. She drew and fired, as did Grant.

Angelina said, "Girl, you're really fast, as fast as anyone I've seen, and both of you hit it square between the eyes. You'll do to ride the river with." Angelina and Grant were seriously impressed.

Milam added, "It reminds me how nice I have to be around her." Grant and Angelina chuckled.

Grant said, "Let me take the time to field dress it, and I'll send someone back to fetch the carcass. We might have cougar for supper."

Grant told them they were on the Cannon ranch a short time later. He explained how he and three other men had bought the original ten sections, but over the years, he had acquired all ten sections or at least the use of them. He mainly raised horses. They kept a small herd of cattle to use for training the horses. They also kept a herd of mules whose number was dictated by their number of Percheron mares. They also had a few Shire mares, which produced almost the same mules. "We'll show you around the place tomorrow."

"Did you send the telegram about mules to the other ranch?"

"Yes, but someone will have to take it to Freedom Town for an answer. We should get an answer tomorrow."

When they arrived at the house, Mary admired its clean lines and comfort. It was smaller than the McCullough Ranch house but used the space well. It had none of the trappings of a manor house, such as a large entertainment area, but it was comfortable. Angelina showed them to a bedroom that was less spacious than hers but plenty large enough with a good bed. They would eat at the bunkhouse.

Angelina said, "I'll now show you to a hidden gem on this place."

They went to the hot pool and washed the dust and tension away. It was wonderful.

The bunkhouse meal was fantastic. The steak and potatoes had a hint of Mexican spices. A selection of pies and cakes was also available. The cook said he would use the cougar in a hearty stew the next day.

Angelina said, "You have to watch this place, or you'll get too fat to ride." Mary nodded.

Grant and Milam sat on the porch with a glass of 'shine and a cigar. Milam commented on the quality of the 'shine. Grant told him it was made in Freedom Town by a former slave who made 'shine and rum primarily, but also several other varieties.

Milam said, "I just put a couple of things together. My grandfather and father-in-law keep his rum. Only a few people get access to the 'good stuff,' as they call it. They buy it from the railroad after doing a few favors for them. I should take them several cases of all his selections."

"The rum and 'shine are the best, but the others are also interesting. If we can get you mules from them, we can also pick up the booze. I also don't share the Freedom Town liquor with everyone. These Cuban cigars are sent to me by one of the original owners of this land, which we lease from him. He raises Paso Fino horses. He lives in Cuba and New Orleans and has a shipping company, so he keeps me in these smooth cigars. I ration them also."

They rode over the property the following day to look at the different herds. Most were cattle horses, a little shorter and more muscled than other horses.

Grant said, "They're tough as nails and strong. They can move sideways better than most horses can move forward. They're also swift in short races. We breed a little thoroughbred into them for speed. I bought a couple of Lexington stallions a few years back. The horse's base is the mustang, but we have put a lot of well thought out crosses in it. This is the basic horse I want to breed Fergus's Appaloosa stallion to. Appaloosas are popular around here. They may sell three or four times what a regular cow pony goes for."

They also looked at a herd of larger, taller horses. Grant said, "They have similar breeding as the cow horses but with a little more thoroughbred mixed. We use these for winning races. They are usually a little high-strung but are fast."

They went to see the Paso Finos next, "These are great horses. They can work cattle and are almost as smooth as a Tennessee Walker. Plus, they're flashy. For some reason, they've not gained much favor among cowboys. It's a mystery to me."

The last pasture they came to contained the Percheron mares and the two types of huge mules. About fifty young mules were in the pasture.

Grant said, "The mules are usually sold before they're born. I keep three or four Sheffield mules to put in the auction. Let's go back and talk about your father-in-law bringing a string of Appaloosa to the auction. They'll spice up the auction, and he'll make good money — maybe a lot of money.

Chapter Twelve

Grant and Milam returned to the house late in the afternoon and found a telegram waiting for Grant. Freedom Town planned to sell ten big mules. Grant replied that he had a buyer for at least six mules, and they would visit Freedom Town in a day or two.

Milam was glad he could buy the Sheffield mules. He knew Morgan would be pleased with him.

Grant said, "They may also have bulls to sell. Their bulls have a lot of Santa Gertrudis blood, which will quickly add size to your herd. They're really big and gain weight quickly."

"Excellent! We may have a full carload of bulls and mules to send back. It would make everyone back home happy. How long will it take us?"

"A couple of days. We can take the railroad to LaJunta and ride to the ranch. It's only a few miles to Freedom Town. You'll be amazed at what they've been able to do there.

Mary and Angelina decided to accompany the men to Freedom Town. The train ride was enlightening. The country looked like it could only support a few cows or horses per acre.

Grant explained, "The grass is very nutritious but insufficient to support many cows per acre. There's better grass close to the river, but not much."

They rented a large rig in La Junta so Milam could bring back a load of Doc's liquor. The road to the ranch was good because it was used often. Miss Lily and Gabe met the buggy and welcomed them to Freedom Town. Gabe managed the horse and mule herds. He had six Sheffield mules together to show Milam. Mary and Angelina chatted with Miss Lily in the fort/meeting hall. Supper would be served in about two hours. The aroma coming from the kitchen area was heavenly. Mary found her stomach growling but not too loudly.

Milam bought six mules and asked about buying five or six bulls to add size to their herds. Raul had more than six for sale because they had been used on the ranch too long. They would visit Doc's still operations and inspect the bulls the next morning.

Supper lived up to the enticing aromas. It was a superb Mexican stew. Mary and Milam had never tasted one just like it. It was spicy but delectable.

Cat and Willow Jones came in for supper, as did Angelina's mother and stepdad. It was a fascinating evening. The most remarkable thing was how the diverse ethnicities blended together. Mary and Milam could have stayed much longer, but they needed to get back on their honeymoon.

Milam picked out six bulls for him and six for Jeb. If Fergus decided he wanted bulls, they would each take four. Gabe said if they would arrange for a railcar, he would bring the stock to Denver in three days. Milam realized he would have to make arrangements with at least three railroads, one of which was narrow gauge. He decided to telegraph Josh to help with the arrangements and to get a message to Fergus about the shipment and the possibility of selling Appaloosa horses at Denver's auction.

He also bought five cases of rum, five of 'shine, and three of gin. He would share with Fergus but keep most of the liquor on his ranch.

When Milam returned, Mary asked, "Do you think we can finish our honeymoon, or do you have more errands for my family? We only have another week or so, you know."

"I have only one more errand to run. I have to telegraph Josh to get him to arrange stock cars to Butte and let Fergus know. At least the errands gave me a chance to rest up. You've been killing me!"

They caught the train to Denver early the following day. Milam slept almost all the way because Mary had decided it was time to reignite the honeymoon at the La Junta Hotel. She was quite a woman to be so young. The Cannon Hotel was ready for them. They hardly left their room for three days. Josh sent Milam a telegram letting him know the animals were cared for and that he would keep them until Fergus came to get them.

They spent the last few days exploring Denver. Mary arranged for the purchased furniture to be delivered to Butte and picked up the clothes from the general store. They had a wonderful time on their trip, but they were ready to return home when their last day arrived.

Mary and Milam slept most of the way to Cheyenne, where they spent the night. The ride to Butte was also uneventful until the engineer slammed on its brakes. A gang of robbers were stopping the train.

They saw only five robbers, and Milam and Mary prepared to tackle them. Two robbers jumped in the passenger car flourishing their revolvers. They demanded everyone's money and jewelry. Mary had no intention of giving up her ring. She shot one robber, and Milam tumbled the other one.

Two other robbers headed for the mail car while one held the horses. They shot the guard when they entered the mail car. Milam and Mary waited for them to jump off the train. They each put a robber down and waited for the man holding the horses to show up. He rode up expecting two people, but not the two waiting on him. They both shot him in the heart, with the bullet holes being about an inch apart. Milam helped the train crew load the five bodies in a cattle car and moved the log off the tracks.

When they arrived in Butte, the Sheriff inspected the bodies and said, "Each of these thieves has a reward posted, plus the railroad always pays a reward for stopping a train robbery. You should get two or three thousand dollars for ridding the country of these vermin. Come to my office, and I'll get you a draft for the rewards." The reward totaled over three thousand dollars.

Josh had a wagon ready to carry the freight. Milam gave him a bottle of each liquor type, which was plenty of pay for him.

Josh thanked him, saying, "Just pay the driver for his time, and we're even. Fergus picked up the mules and bulls a couple of days ago. He was happy, and Morgan was beside herself. You made your mother-in-law a very happy woman. You're starting off better than most of us married men do. It took me several years to just be accepted."

Everyone at Bonner's Den Ranch was happy to see them, especially Morgan. The twelve bulls were still in the ranch's bullpen.

The best news was that Jeb and Kamiah were ready to move to their new house. The only negative news was that Angus and Oby were still unwell.

Oby caught a cold that just kept getting worse. Little Bird prepared him several concoctions mainly based on alcohol and honey, but nothing seemed to help. Dr. Boyton had visited Oby and given him medicine that worked no better than Little Bird's. Oby had gone to bed almost a week ago and stayed there. He was frail, and Little Bird and Maude were worried.

Milam wanted to get to the McCullough ranch to see how Angus was doing. He would send a couple of cowboys back for his bulls. Milam also talked with Fergus for a long time about the Denver horse auction.

Milam explained, "If you could win a race or two, the value of the horses would rise even higher. Two ten-mile or longer races run up into the foothills and back. Actually, one is all the way to the top of a mountain."

Fergus knew just the horses to enter into those races. The two Appaloosa stallions were beautiful and fast over long distances. He would start preparing them for the races.

Fergus and Wolf picked out thirty horses to consider selling. Milam thought they would make a good contingent for his first auction. Morgan was happy with Milam for getting Fergus to try to sell some horses.

Mary and Milam departed for home the following day, driving the wagon with their horses trailing behind. They encountered Wolf and Tall One with the hounds about halfway home. One hound had gotten too close to a bear and was injured. They loaded the hound on the wagon along with the dead bear. Tall One had killed the bear with his knife. The danger was not too grave once a man knew how to grab the bear to ride his back. A knife like the Lily knife was necessary to kill the bear quickly. No one but Wolf and Tall One had tried the feat yet. Milam did not intend to, much to Mary's delight.

When they arrived at the McCullough ranch house, Tall One's wife took the dog to patch him up while two cowhands started skinning the bear. The cooks butchered the bear and planned to serve bear steaks for supper and make sausage with the rest. The fat was prized for many uses around the ranch, including softening and waterproofing leather.

Three ranch hands helped haul the large amount of loot inside. Angus looked no worse than when they last saw him. He and Milam sat chatted while Mary incorporated the things she bought into the decor. They were all having fun doing what they liked. Mary's additions subtly changed the house. The lamps and other items made it look like a woman lived in the house. Angus had moved out of the master bedroom suite.

Kamiah and Jeb were arranging furniture in their new house. Most of the furniture came from their old house and did not begin to fill up the new house. The kids, Rowdy, Liz, and Joe, had enough furniture, but the parlor and dining room looked bare. Kamiah had to buy many things for the bottom floor.

Kamiah and Mary talked about the furniture stores in Denver. Kamiah planned to go with Jeb and Fergus to the horse auction. She might spend all their income on her new house.

They moved everything they intended to move and then started with Chinn and Little Bird's things. Just as they were getting everything they wanted moved into the new house, Oby took a turn for the worse and died two days later. No one was surprised. Oby had lived a long and fruitful life. He had carved himself a beautiful wooden headstone and a matching one for Maude.

A rider was sent to fetch Mary and Milam. The funeral was held as soon as they arrived.

Fergus was concerned about Maude. She was pretty strung out and depressed. Oby had treated her better than Fergus and Brody's dad had ever thought about. Fergus talked to Mary about his concerns. She spoke to Milam, and they stayed a few days with Maude. As Fergus feared, Maude's health started going downhill. She died ten days after Oby passed. Fergus thought it was from a broken heart and loneliness, even though people surrounded her.

She was buried beside Oby with the carved wooden headstone on her grave. Life returned to normal soon after she was buried.

Fergus had to hurry to prepare the horses for the Denver races and auction. Morgan, Kamiah, and Jeb planned to go. Chinn and Little Bird thought about going, but Chinn feared the Tong might still be looking for him in a large city like Denver.

Fergus decided to take twenty-five Appaloosas for the auction: five stallions of breeding age, twelve mares of breeding age, and eight yearlings. They were all loudly colored, with fifteen being dark in the front with a blanket and ten being spotted all over. Josh was impressed with the horses when they trotted into his corral in Butte.

Josh commented, "They're beautiful and will command premium prices in Denver."

Morgan replied, "It's about time those horses generated some income. I'll tie him down so he can't bid on his own horses. This auction could be a game changer for the horse herd."

At the last minute, they decided to take Rowdy and Colt to demonstrate that the horses were safe for young riders. The two boys were ecstatic, but the other youngsters were a little disappointed. The adults would not have time to keep track of the younger ones.

The trip was uneventful. Robbers had been thinned out, so only a few were left to target the trains. The gang leaders often hired spies in Butte to identify cargo, but a crew from Bonner's Den Ranch was an effective deterrent. The primary issue was moving the horses from the narrow gauge railroad to the regular grade track in Cheyenne. Josh sent two men to help with the transfer.

The group arrived in Denver on the first day of July. Grant sent three cowboys to the Denver depot to help get the horses to his barn at the auction site.

Everyone checked into the Cannon Hotel. Morgan and Kamiah browsed the nearby furniture stores. Kamiah wanted Jeb and the boys to help, but they were busy with the horses. They would go with her to look at furniture after the auction. She would show them what she liked, and they would approve or disapprove. The men knew they would agree with her choices unless something was hideous. They expected all the items to be acceptable, and even if they thought something was ugly, they did not intend to say anything.

Each group member led three horses on a side street to the auction site. The trip through town created a stir because Appaloosas were seldom seen in Colorado. Grant rode in to ensure he knew which Appaloosas he wanted for his breeding program. Fergus gave him his first choice before the auction began. Two of the mature stallions would be running in the longer races. Grant recommended Fergus use experienced jockeys because many hand-to-hand battles occurred while the horses were out of sight of the judges. Grant offered two men who could ride and fight if needed.

The boys took the two racers to limber up each day before the races. They ran them ten miles only the first day, but not at full speed. They covered two miles the other days, with only a mile at full speed. Grant provided advice on strategy for the races.

He said, "You have a good chance in both races. They're as fast as any horse I've seen and are not lathered at the finish."

They attended several parties at the facility along with the cream of

Denver's high society. Clark and Margo, Grant's brother and his wife, were in their element at the parties. Fergus and Morgan were not at ease at the events, and Jeb and Kamiah even less so. The boys hid with the horses most of the time.

A few huge, impressive dogs guarded the stables. Grant told Fergus they were Comanche War Dogs. Fergus began to think he might like a couple of them on each ranch.

Race day arrived, and the boys and Fergus saddled the horses. The first race was the ten-mile race up the mountain and back. The road ran to the top of Mount Lady Washington, which rose to nine thousand feet. The route was actually eleven miles. A few Ute mountain horses were in the race, along with a few cow ponies.

The cow ponies took off fast and were in the lead after a couple of miles. The race then got rough, with several galloping fights among the jockeys. Fergus's Appaloosa took the lead at the turnaround point. He was sure-footed all the way down and won going away. No horse was within a quarter-mile at the finish. The results opened many eyes and made many men willing to pay top dollar for the Appaloosa.

The elevation change in the second ten-mile race was less severe. It was run on the foothills instead of the tallest mountain in the Denver area. The race started similarly, with cow ponies taking the early lead. The Appaloosa gained steadily until the seven-mile mark. He charged ahead as if the other horses were utterly worn out. One Ute mountain horse was near as they reached the nine-mile mark. The Appaloosa appeared to find a different gear and pulled ahead. The Ute horse tried valiantly but just did not have enough left. Fergus's horse pulled away steadily and won by two hundred yards.

Grant said, "Fergus, you're going to make a killing! I think your horses, even the young colts, will sell for a premium price."

The auction started the next day, and Bonner's Den Ranch horses showed first. Grant decided to buy a stallion that was the son of the racer in the steepest race for two hundred dollars more than the bid on a brother. He also took one of the younger stallions and four mares.

Fergus was in a great mood, and so was Morgan.

The other racehorse sold for over four hundred dollars, meaning the two racers brought in over a thousand dollars. The other horses, even the yearlings, sold for at least two hundred dollars. Fergus planned to return next year.

After the auction, several unsuccessful bidders approached Fergus to see if they could visit his ranch and buy horses. They should have talked to Morgan.

Fergus responded to all, "I'm not sure I have more to sell right now."

Kamiah, Jeb, and Rowdy went to look over the furniture. Neither Jeb nor Rowdy disagreed with any of her choices. The store would deliver the furniture to the train depot. It took almost an entire boxcar.

When they arrived in Butte, Josh's men unloaded the railcar onto two wagons. He sent two drivers and two other men to help unload the wagons. They drove to Jeb's place, unloaded, and placed the furniture where Kamiah indicated. Two cowboys helped rearrange it until she was satisfied. Kamiah was so happy she hugged Jeb and talked in the Nez Perce language.

Fergus and Morgan rode on to Bonner's Den Ranch. They found out Wolf and Tall One were out bear hunting. A bear got into the horse pasture and scratched one of the young foals, but it was doing okay after Half Moon doctored it. The chase started within sight of the ranch house about an hour earlier. Fergus decided he would try to catch them — he had never been on a hunt with the hounds.

He heard the hounds not far away and took off. The bear was an old boar that probably could no longer hunt successfully. The hounds had him at bay in a large pile of rocks. The bear had picked an excellent place to stand his ground and they could not shoot.

Wolf was getting ready to join the fracas when Fergus said, "Let me have your knife. I'm going for this one."

Wolf was unsure he should do it, "Fergus, that thing is almost as big as a grizzly. You're not as good as you used to be."

"Boy, give me the knife, or I'll use my own."

Wolf conceded and gave him the knife and basic instructions. Fergus jumped on the bear's back when it looked the other way. It was a good fight, but Fergus won. He had a few scratches but was not bleeding badly. Fergus had almost cut the bear's heart out in the fight.

He asked, "Where can I get one of those knives?"

Tall One said, "Our blacksmith made mine. I'm sure he'll make you one if you have some good steel. It must have the curve and be super sharp on both sides."

Wolf said, "I'm not sure Morgan will approve of you having one."

"Morgan won't know, will she?

Chapter Thirteen

When Fergus arrived home, he washed up as well as he could and walked inside. Morgan did not see him at first. When she did, she said, "What did you do to yourself? Did you get thrown from your horse?"

"No. I killed a bear with a knife."

"You did what? Are you crazy or just stupid?"

"Umm, I guess one or the other."

"You're too old to be fighting with a bear! Twenty years ago, maybe, but not now."

"Just wanted to let everybody know I could still do it."

"You old fool! The bear scratched you all over."

"Yes, but the bear is dead."

"Do you think I want to run this ranch by myself? I know dangers abound on the ranch, but old men don't have to pick fights with bears!"

"Can you lay off the 'old men' stuff a little?" Fergus knew he would not win the argument, so he poured a glass of rum and retreated to the porch.

The following day, most of the men knew Fergus had killed a bear with a knife. The men were generally pleased they had a boss capable of handling himself in a fight, particularly with a bear.

Fergus visited the blacksmith to ask him to make him a blade like Wolf's. When Wolf came by to get his horse, the blacksmith examined the knife again and wrote down a few numbers. He had a piece of good steel perfect for the project.

The blacksmith said, "It might take me a week or more because I have several other projects I need to finish."

"No problem. I may never use it, but it's useful if you need to do massive damage quickly inside your target. I became sold on it yesterday."

Morgan knew she had been on pins and needles recently because of the wedding and the deaths of Oby and Maude. Morgan was not as upset about Fergus getting old as she was about herself getting old. She understood the majority of her life was now behind her and it was depressing to face her own mortality. She had not realized how much having her two children move away would affect her. Fergus's stunt with the bear almost pushed her over the edge. She knew it should not have and that she should have known he would try it sooner or later. She loved that Fergus lived life to its fullest.

When Fergus returned to the house, she hugged him and said, "I'm sorry I got so upset. You just scare me sometimes. I can't lose you and live in this huge house by myself. I love you too much for you to take any unnecessary chances. I know I've been unpleasant lately, but I intend to lighten up. Why don't we find time to go up in the mountains or foothills and camp for a few nights? Maybe we can get our heads straightened out and rekindle our love."

"Hmm. Colorado does not need me to run the ranch. Why don't we leave tomorrow? Maybe Juanita can fix food to warm up. It'll still be cool at night."

"I'm depending on you to keep me warm at night, but we should probably take a couple of bearskins and a small teepee. I'd like to see the wild country y'all keep talking about. I've not had a good look at it."

"Let me pull our gear together. We'll carry the teepee on a travois. It'll keep us dry and warm without any trouble."

They left a little after daylight the next morning with an extra horse pulling the travois. They took the long way around to look over the range. Morgan had been so tied down with the wedding, or so she thought, that she had not ridden the range in several months. Morgan loved the fresh air and seeing the cattle grazing on the lush grass. She could feel her stress melting away by the mile. She thought, "*This trip is a good idea.*"

They set up the teepee on reasonably even ground at the edge of the woods. Fergus gathered wood for fires inside and outside the teepee. He stacked enough to burn all night inside and to have coals for coffee the next morning. After a supper of excellent soft tacos, they took a walk, holding hands to watch the sun go down.

Morgan said, "We seem to not have much time for each other anymore. With both kids married and moving out and Maude and Oby passing, we find ourselves almost alone. Surely, we can go on rides and walks together like we used to. Maybe we'll get to know each other again."

The fire outside was almost out when they returned to the campsite. The temperature fell when the sun dropped below the horizon, so Fergus lit a small fire inside the teepee. Morgan laid skins on the backside of the teepee so the fire was between them and the opening used for a door. It was not long before they were in the robes and getting to know each other again. It was the first time in a while Morgan was relaxed enough for the pleasures they were sharing. It was not the only time they got together during the night.

Fergus made coffee the next morning and stepped outside with a robe draped over his shoulders to watch the sunrise. Morgan quickly joined him. The bearskin robes were perfect to keep the morning chill at bay. They simply sat and watched the sun chase away the darkness. The sunrise was beautiful, something they had not shared in several years. Life had gotten in the way.

Neither were actually thinking of anything. It was as if their brains were simply coasting along, a wonderful feeling for them. After the sun rose fully, they went inside and dressed. They ate burritos for breakfast and rode along the property's western edge, just enjoying the day. They returned late afternoon by a route a little east of the path they took in the morning. They talked along the trail but not about anything important. They rode by pockets of their cattle, which gave them a wide berth.

Morgan said, "We've been fortunate but worked hard. I never thought we'd be able to ride for hours and still be on our own ranch, or we would have more cattle than one can easily count. Our children will have the same thing. Mary will own twice as much land and cattle as we do. Someone said she and Milam would be among the wealthiest people in Montana Territory. They're probably right."

The night went much like before, except a pack of wolves came uncomfortably close to the teepee. The howling a pack of wolves makes when hunting makes the hair on a person's neck stand up. Morgan moved as close as possible to Fergus, and Fergus brought his revolver a closer. Since they were awake, they let nature take its course once again. Both were as satisfied as husband and wife could be.

The next time Fergus awakened, he heard wolves snarling just outside the teepee. He grabbed his revolver, jumped through the opening, and shot at movement near the horses. He thought he may have hit at least two from the yelping.

Morgan began laughing as he built up the fire. Fergus demanded, "What are you laughing at?"

"You standing naked trying to scare off wolves and build up a fire. That vision may be what scared them off. It'll never leave my mind."

Fergus grinned and then started laughing. They let the fire build up and just kept laughing. The next morning, they found two deal wolves far too close to the teepee for comfort.

Morgan and Fergus walked along a small creek beside the campsite and saw trout feeding in several places. Fergus pulled hooks and lines from his saddlebags when they returned to the campsite. He cut two thin saplings and tied the line on with a hook on the thinner end. Grasshoppers abounded nearby, and they had fun catching them for bait. They caught four cutthroat trout, each between six to eight inches long. Fergus pulled out his small skillet and fried them for a tasty breakfast.

Morgan began wondering precisely what cowboys carried in their ubiquitous saddle bags. Fergus opened his to show her.

Fergus said, "As you saw, I carry fishing gear. Our ranch has many streams, and you can almost always catch a few. I keep the fishing gear in this small tin box. It's flat and takes up little room. I carry a clean shirt, pants, and rain gear. My heavy rain gear is tied behind the saddle to keep my sleeping gear dry. I always have a small coffee pot and coffee, a bag of flour for biscuits, cornmeal, and a small bag of beans. I have a little cured ham or some kind of pork to flavor my food. Jerky and pemmican round out the foodstuffs. I always have a couple of boxes of extra ammo, so I like to use the same caliber rifle and pistol. I want to be able to survive at least a week from the bags. Every cowboy packs his bag a little differently. A lot of thought goes into it."

"I've never thought much about it."

"That's because I usually pack your bag, often in concert with mine. You have a little bear fat in yours for your face and lips in case the sun starts to burn. I've lived out of saddlebags so often I don't think much about it."

Everything made sense to Morgan. She realized the saddlebag was necessary for survival and asked, "How did you teach the children to plan their bags?"

"I talk to them about it from the day they started traveling with me. I usually made sure they had fresh or dried fruit and nuts."

They packed up and started toward home at mid-morning. They arrived home about six o'clock, feeling relaxed and in love again. The camping trip was the perfect medicine for the couple. Fergus thought he would try to involve Morgan more in decision-making. Morgan intended not to let the small things bother her so much. They were sure they would slip up, but making the effort was important.

Not much was happening around the ranch. Brody was taking care of the potatoes and garden. He liked doing it because he could not do all the ranch work with one arm. Fergus rode to the Jenkins farm to check on the oats and corn. The crops looked good. The rains had come at precisely the right time and the harvest would be good.

Jenkins said, "You know, if we grew a little wheat and had a gristmill, we could make our own flour and cornmeal. We have plenty of room, and the creek flows year-round. A couple of small grindstones is all we need."

Fergus replied, "Hmm. I should have thought of that. Do you know much about gristmills?"

"I worked at a small one back home. It's easy to operate if the construction is done well. The critical element is the two grindstones. We would probably not need high output, but enough for the ranches y'all own. Of course, it takes a lot of biscuits and cornbread to feed the hands."

"Yep. I'll check in Butte in the next few weeks about getting us a gristmill built. I also want to discuss the bank with a few people before I go in."

"Gonna' buy a bank?"

"Maybe. The Butte bank is so badly run that I might pull the trigger. It's not making money, largely because they treat their customers so shabbily."

"I wouldn't know. Never had enough money to use one."

"Maybe you can make enough running a gristmill to need one."

Fergus rode home thinking about a gristmill and the bank. While contemplating the gristmill, he thought, "*Why not a timber mill? It's like a gristmill but with a blade rather than stones. If we could produce more flour, cornmeal, and lumber than we can use, we could sell to others. Hmm.*"

After caring for his horse, he walked inside to talk to Morgan. He shared his thoughts about the bank, gristmill, and lumber mill, "The main requirement for both a gristmill and sawmill is a source of power. We have many free-flowing streams to provide the power. We'll need to find someone to build them. I think the bank is being poorly run. Milam and Angus agree. I want to ride over to talk with Milam about these ideas."

"Surely you don't think you're leaving me behind. When do we leave?"

"How about tomorrow morning?"

She grinned and said, "I'll be ready at dawn. Do you have any ideas for my saddle bags? We might have to spend the night going, coming back, or both."

Fergus packed a canvas in case they decided to stop overnight. He put food in the saddlebags and literature he found in the few magazines around the house. One had the diagrams for a small sawmill, which he thought would be similar to a gristmill.

They made it to McCullough Ranch in mid-afternoon. Milam was on the range, checking his cattle and repairing the catch pens. Mary and Morgan sat and visited the rest of the afternoon. Fergus managed to catch a nap in one of the porch chairs. It was a pleasant afternoon for everyone.

They discussed Fergus's new ideas during supper. Milam liked them all but was most interested in the bank, as was Angus. Angus thought he might be able to get another grandson to live nearby.

Morgan and Mary knew almost to the dollar how much money they had to invest. They had enough to take advantage of all three opportunities. It would soon be time for the fall roundup when they would add a significant amount to their stash.

The bank should be profitable if management were changed. Fergus and Milam wanted to get the Cannon brothers to check on it. The gristmill should save them money. Each ranch used about a hundred pounds of flour a week and half that much cornmeal. The lumber mill would save them money for the construction projects they planned. A positive kicker was the smaller ranchers and Butte residents might buy flour, cornmeal, and lumber from them. With the railroad expansion, they could ship all over the West if the mills produced enough, which was a function of how large they built them.

The following morning, Morgan heard Mary outside, a little nauseated. She did not think much of it.

Fergus and Milam knew they needed to go to Cheyenne, and perhaps Denver, to follow up on the ideas. They needed to go soon so they could return before the roundup. Mary and Morgan decided to stay at the McCullough Ranch while the men checked out everything. They telegraphed Denver when they reached Butte. Grant and Clark said they would visit Butte to examine the bank's books. Clark could determine a bank's condition quickly and had done so on many occasions.

They visited Josh's office to see if he had any information on gristmills and sawmills. Josh said, "I've been thinking about building one or the other myself. Here's some catalogs with prices."

"Do you know anyone who can build a water-powered mill?"

"Yes. Mike can do it. You can order the lumber from Cheyenne and other necessary items from Denver. Finding the millstones could be an issue. You should be able to find good ones around Denver. I'm willing to invest or agree to do your hauling for you."

"Let's talk to Mike. I think we are going to do it."

Clark and Grant arrived in Butte the following day. Clark went to the bank, claimed he was a bank examiner, and asked to see the bank's financial records. The manager was too dumb to know Montana Territory did not have bank examiners. Clark was able to quickly evaluate the situation. The bank was losing money because of almost assuredly poor management. The mines used the bank to accumulate enough money to send to Cheyenne or Denver. Cannon Mining used the bank for the same purpose and often joked about how poorly it was operated. He told Fergus and Milam how much he thought the bank was worth, which was not much.

While Clark was reviewing the books, Grant looked over nearby land. He did not plan to buy any, but he always looked around. The land looked good, and he thought he might return later to buy a few sections. They did not purchase many ranches less than twenty sections, and he would likely buy more Wyoming land before focusing on Montana.

Milam sent his brother a telegram telling him about Clark's analysis and asking if he would be willing to run the bank. Bart would get a minor share of ownership and a good salary. The return telegram came back quickly and indicated Bart was interested. He would come to Butte as soon as possible to review the situation.

Fergus talked with Mike about building a gristmill. Mike said, "I can build it if we get detailed blueprints. The only things that must be done precisely are the waterwheel and the belts to transfer power to the blades or millstones. The carriage has to be steel. I'm sure we can buy one and have it delivered. Where do you plan to build them?"

"The gristmill should be close to the farm you saw, not far from Jeb's house. The sawmill will likely be closer to Butte and standing timber. We've not picked the exact sites yet."

"Doesn't make much difference to me. I was just wondering. It will cost more for materials the further you are from the railroad."

Fergus caught Grant at the boarding house before supper and asked if he knew where they could find good quality millstones. Grant replied, "I'm told a man in Denver does good work. I'm sure you can get good ones from him. He usually delivers his millstones and sets them up to ensure they work properly."

"Mike and I will go see him after roundup. Hopefully, Mike can start building the sawmill during the roundup."

Everything would be in place if Bart would take the bank job. He would arrive in Butte in a couple of days. Milam had a good feeling about Bart taking the job. He and Fergus planned to stay in Butte until Bart could evaluate the bank. Dutch and Colorado could handle the roundup for a week if necessary.

The cattle gathers on Jeb's ranch and the smaller ranches had already started. The gathers at Fergus and Milam's ranches would be in full swing in less than a week. Bart arrived two days after receiving Milam's telegram. He went alone to the bank and experienced poor service from the employees.

He asked in an intimidating voice, "Who owns this bank?"

He was directed to an office where a chubby little guy was napping in the middle of the morning. Bart asked, "Do you own this bank?"

"Yes, I do."

"How much do you want for it?" The little chubby banker stammered and stuttered for a while.

Bart continued, "Mister, with all the money you're losing, surely you've thought about selling. Now, how much do you want for the bank?"

"Well, I think it's worth twenty thousand dollars."

"No, it's not. My group will pay twelve thousand."

"That's too low."

"Then give me a realistic price so I can get my family moved here."

"How about fifteen?"

"I'll talk to my partners and get back in touch with you. Here's a thousand dollars and a contract that says we have thirty days to complete the deal. You cannot sell it to anyone else during the thirty days."

Bart went to talk to Milam and Fergus at the boarding house. He said, "I would have agreed to twenty thousand dollars like Clark said, but he took fifteen. That's okay with you, isn't it?"

"Yes, definitely. Are you going to join us and run the bank? We'll pay you one and a half times what you are making and give you five percent ownership. You will receive a nice bonus if you can get the bank to profitability."

"Yes, I'll take the job. We'll need to get a house built before my wife moves. I'll go home, pack all my personal gear, and return immediately. We must act quickly. If we delay, it'll go broke within the year and many people will lose their money. If that happens, no one will be able to revive it. I can be back in less than two weeks. I can stay in the boarding house until we get a house built. Is there a good builder in the area?"

"Yes. Mike has worked for me and is working for me now. He's a good builder and fast. We'll have a sawmill built in a month or six weeks. You might get the first lumber we cut. Bring back a set of plans Amber approves of, and he can build it. He built a log mansion for Jeb in about a month."

"Could I see it before I leave? She mentioned a log home, but a large one."

Chapter Fourteen

Josh took Bart to see Jeb and Kamiah's log mansion. Bart was impressed and thought his wife would also like it. Mike told him he could have a log mansion built in about three months, even with building the lumber mill and gristmill, if he had help collecting a stash of logs. Bart left word for Fergus that he would need help getting Mike a supply of logs. He wanted to build a log house, not a mansion like Jeb, but not a small cabin.

Milam and Fergus had returned to their respective ranches to work the roundup. All the ranchers who participated with them on roundups had record herds to sell. The plan was basically the same as in previous years. The narrow gauge railroad had many more cattle cars this year but not enough to ship all the cattle. Fergus decided to ship all he could and leave the remaining cattle on his pasture near Butte. They would sell over the winter to Butte residents and businesses. The mining companies would take most of them.

As soon as the herd was delivered to Butte, Jeb and Fergus started looking in earnest for cattle to fill out Jeb's ranches. They needed someone who wanted to get out of cattle ranching, which was a tall order. They spent three days in Cheyenne, finding only a few cows for sale. What they had to watch for was whether the cows were barren or still delivering calves. They checked each lead they heard about, but kept hearing about herds for sale in Kansas. It was primarily people who had been ranching but were converting to farming.

They rode the train to Kansas and found several herds for sale. Most were at relatively large ranches, but not large enough to make money raising cattle. They could make more money growing wheat on moderate-sized spreads. They bought five herds totaling two thousand head of already bred mother cows and a few bulls. The ranches sold their yearlings to the meat markets back east.

The cowboys from Bonner's Den Ranch and Jeb's ranches met the train in Butte to drive the cows to their new home, which took three days. The Kansas herds had never been in grass as good as they found in Montana. They did not want to move forward when they had so much to eat along the way.

Once the cattle arrived at the ranch, they had to change their brands to Jeb's. They were then scattered throughout the ranch. The cattle seemed to think they had died and gone to heaven. The only problem was that they had to be watched to ensure they did not bloat by overeating. The cowboys kept moving them around to make sure they did not lie down and die.

Milam returned to McCullough Ranch, so Morgan rode home. She expected to return to McCullough Ranch in the early spring. When Fergus arrived home, she had big news for him.

Morgan said, "Mary's pregnant! She assures me it happened after they married, likely on the honeymoon. Many people would be counting the months if we lived in a town. I'm not sure I'm ready for my baby to be having babies."

"Sounds like you need to get used to it. I suppose you'll be moving over there when Mary gets closer."

"Yep. Unless she comes here. We have more people to support her here. They don't have anyone but Rosalita to help. We can get Little Bird to help her, along with Juanita and Lotte. All have helped with births. Plus, we're closer to Dr. Boyton. I don't know if she'll accept coming here, but maybe she will."

"I'm sure you'll start working on her soon."

"You bet I will!"

Fergus smiled and shook his head, "We need to remember our promises to each other when we were camping. We have to think about each other."

"Remind me if I start ignoring us. I'm still worrying about my baby."

Fergus hugged her and said, "I know."

Fergus had work he wanted to get done before snow slowed everything down. He wanted to check on the grain and the gristmill and sawmill construction projects. He first rode to the farm to see how the oats and corn harvests were coming.

They were well into harvesting and ready to bring the first loads to the Bonner's Den and McCullough ranches. He returned to get more cowboys to help finish the harvest and deliveries. Harvesting would be much harder if it snowed on the grain.

The millstones were in place, and the water wheel was built, so the gristmill was almost finished. Fortunately, the creek they selected to build on maintained a reasonably constant depth in summer and winter. It was close to the farm so Jenkins could operate the gristmill. It would be a year before they had enough wheat and corn to make flour and cornmeal.

The equipment needed for the sawmill had been delivered. Harvesting all the timber near the sawmill would take years. Fergus bought a section of timberland. It was surprisingly cheap, only a thousand dollars. Josh bought a nearby section as an investment. Fergus now needed to find someone to run the lumber mill.

Bart had the bank running more professionally. Everyone who had worked there previously had been terminated on the first day. Two new people had been hired, a teller and a secretary. They were good, and everyone who walked in was greeted with respect. Deposits were up because many ranchers began using the bank when they heard the new owners were also ranchers. Bart was already looking for another teller.

All the new investments and Mary's pregnancy had Fergus's head spinning. Before he left Butte, he rode the sawmill site. Mike and his crew had moved to the site. He left a small crew to put the final touches on the gristmill. Mike thought the sawmill would be operating by spring.

Fergus sent a crew to begin cutting timber for Bart's house. Mike would first construct a bunkhouse at the site. It would be a long log cabin to house the workers in winter. Mike said he could have the bunkhouse completed in a couple of weeks because it was basically a rectangle with inside construction only for the kitchen and dining area at one end of the rectangle.

Fergus also had to find a cook for the bunkhouse. Everything they did caused Fergus to need more people to do ancillary things.

Many things needed to happen before the worst of winter arrived. Fergus hired a cook from one of the mines and a few miners who had done some logging. They would help build the bunkhouse and collect logs. Mike would not scrape the logs, which saved a lot of time. Having the bark on the logs could reduce the building's lifespan, but not too much.

It was becoming clear to Fergus that his days of being a cowboy were coming to an end. He recalled Grant talking about having too much to manage to do much work on the ranch. He now understood how it happened. He returned to Bonner's Den Ranch and found a little snow.

Fergus and Colorado spent much of the afternoon talking about various ranch issues. The bulls Jeb and Milam bought from the Freedom Town group had been divided into four bulls for each ranch.

The grain storage bins were full, even though the harvest was not quite complete. Fergus decided to put more oats on canvas on the ground and cover it with more canvas. The pile would be used first because it would be ruined if left on the ground for too long. The corn was stored near the gristmill and ground into cornmeal as soon as possible. Jenkins produced almost seven hundred pounds of excellent cornmeal to share between the ranches and the farm.

Fergus started looking for a place to plant more corn and wheat. He found and bought a hundred acres within a couple miles of the Jenkin's farm and gristmill. It should be enough for the three ranches and other operations like the sawmill. He also looked for someone to run the sawmill. Josh found someone with experience running a mill like the one they bought. Josh had met him when the mill equipment was delivered. He worked for the manufacturer but did not like traveling all the time. His name was Lance, and he worked in Utah at a similar mill.

Lance and Josh rode out to talk to Fergus. Lance was hired on the spot. Fergus later thought about the openings he needed to fill. The management roles had been filled, but he would need laborers in the spring. Josh posted signs around Butte about the jobs, and several miners decided to change jobs. He was sure they could find the others they needed in Cheyenne in the spring.

The winter was always filled with slack time, but that was changing. Some cowboys worked to get enough trees on the ground to open the lumber mill. The stack of logs was getting high. Only Lance knew how many trees they needed. He kept saying, "We need more." They continued felling trees when the weather allowed. It was easier to drag the logs on the snow, especially with the Sheffield mules. They would need more mules when the farming cranked up in the spring.

Angus, Milam, and Mary came to Bonner's Den Ranch for Christmas, as did Jeb's bunch. The house was just like Morgan liked it — full and loud. Fergus could take a little less noise and Angus a lot less.

Fergus and Angus found time to ride around the ranch in a buckboard. Angus liked getting out when he could. Fergus liked having fewer things to think about.

Mary was getting heavy with child. She thought it would be born in April or early May. The combined family talked for long hours about whether she should have the child at Bonner's Den Ranch or the McCullough Ranch. Milam wanted the baby born on McCullough Ranch, and Morgan lobbied for Bonner's Den. When Morgan laid out her case about having more women who had assisted with births, plus being closer to Dr. Boyton, Milam started to give in. He knew it was logical, but he wanted his child born in his house. Morgan pointed out that Bonner's Den Ranch would also be his one day, which slowed him down considerably.

After much discussion, they agreed the birth would be at Bonner's Den Ranch. Fortunately, no one left the discussion mad, which was good.

Christmas morning was approaching fast, and no big presents were under the tree. Everyone had received horses last year and rifles the previous year. Fergus and Morgan were at a loss for gifts for this year. The parents gave the children gifts, but the grandparents were a bust. They finally decided to take the older children to a big city soon. The younger children received a twenty-dollar gold piece.

Christmas morning was much like all the others. They had shot off fireworks on Christmas Eve and many more the next day, including some of Chinn's super boomers. The meals were superb, as usual, and joy permeated the household. Mary was happy and smiling at the thought of her new baby being there next Christmas.

The temperature was below freezing, and light snow fell. Fergus and Angus looked at the skies and predicted heavy snow by morning. They were seldom wrong.

The snow picked up steadily during the day and evolved into a blizzard by dark. It was an excellent day to sit in the house and do nothing. The cowboys fed the stock and broke ice on water troughs in the early afternoon. The cattle had enough water in the live creeks and grass under the snow.

Jeb was concerned about the Kansas cattle. They had undoubtedly lived in cold weather, but he was not sure they knew how to dig in the snow to find all the grass they needed. His ranch had more timber than the others, so his cattle had more cover. He checked on them before dark, and they were doing fine.

The next morning ushered in one of those frigid days, but as clear as a day can possibly be. It looked like a person could break through the blue sky and touch the sun. Fergus heard a cowboy call it a 'bluebell sky' and thought he was right.

A horse is not a warm place to be, but it was bearable with a bearskin robe. Heavy gloves and mittens were necessary, as were long fur coats that fell well past the boot tops. Headgear was needed that included a wool scarf for the neck and face. A fur cap covered the head and neck, leaving just a small slit to see through. The Bonner family did better than most because living in the mountains had taught them about wool, layering, and staying dry.

The weather was also brutal on horses. They needed a horse blanket to hold in the heat when being ridden. When in the open, they needed a wind break and maybe a blanket to keep warm and help them stay dry. Like most animals, they turned their tails into the wind and stayed close together to preserve warmth.

The calves were the most vulnerable. The mother cows tried to get them into tree lines for windbreaks. If rain and wind persisted, the winter kill could be bad, which did not usually happen on the Montana front range. Winter storms typically brought snow rather than rain, and the weather would get warm and sunny when it stopped snowing. The mountains would often bring a warm wind from the southwest. The country would then warm up, and all was good.

The day after Christmas was bone-chilling cold, but they needed to check on the cows and calves. Everyone who could go out rode in pairs. Thankfully, everything looked good on all the ranches.

As soon as the weather warmed and most of the snow melted, the McCullough's returned to their ranch, as did Jeb and his family. Winter moved by slowly, especially for Mary. They planned to return to Bonner's Den Ranch about the middle of February, which would be about six weeks before her expected due date.

When they returned in February, Mary rode with Angus in his buckboard. The buckboard was more comfortable than riding a horse, and they needed the space to bring various baby things.

Mary and Milam visited Dr. Boyton in Butte. He said everything looked good and agreed the baby would likely arrive at the end of April or maybe early May. He would come to the ranch when they notified him.

Mary also visited the general store, which carried more merchandise now that Butte was growing. She bought various items for the baby, such as soft blankets and a crib, thinking she was ready.

Mary's belly grew more prominent, and she began having trouble getting around. Fergus and Morgan gave up their bed because the stairs to Mary's old room were just too much. Milam returned to the McCullough ranch the first week of March.

Dutch said, "All is well. You don't have to worry. The things that might go wrong in winter can't be fixed without help from God. I'll send a rider if we need you."

After Milam returned, Mary awakened everyone with a yell one frosty morning, "Mother! Come down here! Dad, send someone for Little Bird and the doctor! I think they should hurry."

Coming from a sound sleep to wide awake is always a jolting experience. Even more so when a pregnant woman's yelling wakes a person up. Fergus went to the bunkhouse and sent one of the best riders to Butte for the doctor and another to Jeb's to get Little Bird, who had delivered almost as many babies as the doctor.

Morgan was calmer on the outside than on the inside. Fergus started a fire, and Juanita brought breakfast, which everyone said they did not want. But the enticing aroma changed their minds after a few minutes. Things were not moving very fast for Mary, but they were moving.

The pains were getting closer, and her water broke near noon. Little Bird said, "I think it will be close to sundown. She's mighty big. If I were y'all, I might start thinking about two babies. I think I feel more than one."

Milam, Angus, Fergus, and Morgan's minds went into a higher gear, but there was nothing to do except wait. The men paced back and forth, and Morgan checked and rechecked to ensure the blankets and hot water were ready. She had enough hot water to kill and dress a hog.

Dr. Boyton arrived in the late afternoon after a fast ride from Butte. He examined Mary and felt carefully.

He turned and said, "Little Bird, I think you're right. Both of us will need to work with Mary. Morgan, get someone to help you handle the babies. We will all sit and rest when we get them out."

The labor pains came harder and faster. Dr. Boyton and Little Bird checked on Mary almost continuously. The pacing men were making a track on the floor. Angus was on his knees praying — he had tired himself out pacing. He had taken four of his heart pills since daylight. Everyone was on edge. Even the horses were milling about. Jeb arrived as soon as he could after helping a couple of cows deliver their calves. New life did not begin easily sometimes.

Morgan kept thinking Mary was too young to have a baby. She blamed Milam for doing this to her. Finally, the men heard a newborn baby cry, followed quickly by another tiny voice. Dr. Boyton checked Mary while Morgan and Kamiah held the two babies. Everyone seemed to be doing okay. Mary was utterly worn out. Dr. Boyton gave her opium to help her sleep as soon as she had fed the babies.

Milam came in just as the feeding was over. Mary asked, "Have you seen our daughters? They're so beautiful."

Milam agreed, but like most babies, they were not yet beautiful but would break many hearts someday. After an introduction to Daddy and the grandfathers, the babies went to sleep. There was only one bed for the two babies, but they could fit in one tiny bed.

Morgan and Little Bird sat with Mary and the doctor. Milam and Fergus held the babies when they woke up. It was a busy night for everyone but Mary. The narcotic allowed her to sleep. Little Bird used some of her herbs to start the healing.

The doctor checked the babies the following day and thought they were doing fine. Mary was much better.

Dr. Boyton asked, "What will you name them?"

"Oh, mercy me! We've thought about only one girl's name. We'll have to decide on a name for two babies. Send Milam in here!"

Milam stepped inside with alarm on his face. Mary said, "We need another girl's name. We talked about Mora but didn't know we would need two girls' names."

Milam said, "Hmm, Mora is derived from your mother's name. My mother's name is Michell. What about Mica?"

"I like it! Mora and Mica sound good to me. They're strong names. A girl needs a strong name on the frontier." Many prayers were sent up for Mora and Mica, some from different religions and some from people without faith.

Dr. Boyton decided it was okay for him to return to Butte. He was the only doctor within a hundred miles, and someone always needed him. Mary would be in good shape with Little Bird and Morgan watching over her. He left a bottle of the opium in case she needed it. Little Bird used her herbs, which worked wonders for Mary.

Mary steadily got better. The twins gained weight rapidly and were healthy. They cried their share, but no more. They slept most of the time and Fergus and Milam helped care for them. Mary fed them, rocked them, and mainly loved them. They both had reddish hair. Not red like Fergus, but blond with a distinct reddish tint. They got prettier daily, at least according to their dad and granddads. Angus was the most smitten of all. He and his wife did not have any daughters or granddaughters. They had to keep telling Angus to let them stay in their bed and sleep.

Mary wanted Milam to go to Butte to buy another baby bed. Both babies in one bed were okay now, but they would soon outgrow it. He left early one morning in a buckboard large enough to haul the bed back.

Milam rode by the bank to see Bart before going to the general store. But someone had just robbed the bank, and Josh was organizing a posse!

A seven-man posse, including Milam, left town less than a half hour behind the robbers and had better horses. They closed the distance steadily. The posse caught the gang of five robbers at sundown. The robbers had posted a guard on their back trail. He shot Bart, but he was not hit badly. The posse stormed into the robber's camp and caught them off guard. The lookout was too far behind, and the others could not hear the shots.

After a short gunfight, all the robbers were down. Three were dead, including the lookout, and two were seriously wounded. The posse decided to make camp and care for Bart. The bullet went through the meaty part of his shoulder but did minor damage. Milam and Josh stopped the bleeding before he lost much blood. Bart felt good enough to eat a little pemmican and drink coffee. The coffee was laced with good rum — not the excellent stuff, but pretty good.

The wounded bank robbers died during the night. They did not get a lot of care but would probably have died anyway. They put the five men across their saddles and started back the next morning.

The Sheriff studied the bodies and returned to his office to look through his wanted posters. The gang members had papers totaling over five thousand dollars from a Wells Fargo robbery. Everyone agree Mora and Mica would split the money, and Milam would open their bank accounts.

Milam took Bart to Dr. Boyton. He cleaned the wound and doused it with alcohol and iodine. After wrapping the wound, he told Bart to go to the boarding house and get a good night's sleep.

Bart laughed and said, "I'll be up all night making sure we got all the bank's money back. So will the other employees. I'm sure we got it all, but we must make sure."

Milam sent a rider to Bonner's Den Ranch to tell them what had happened and that he was staying with Bart for a day or two.

Chapter Fifteen

Bart's teller and secretary helped him count and recount the recovered cash. It took all day, much of the night, and until almost noon the next day to ensure everything was balanced. It would have been a good time to rob the bank with all the money lying around in various stacks.

Fortunately, the robbers did not have time to spend any money. Bart thought, *"They gave their life for the money and didn't even get a shot of whiskey from it. I'm happy for the bank and our customers, but it's also very sad."*

After the money was returned to the safe, Bart decided to close the bank until the following day and sleep as much as possible. He wrote a lengthy notice and tacked it on the front door. He did not want anyone to think the bank was permanently closed because of the robbery, which could have caused a run on the bank.

Bart's shoulder was doing okay, but the all-nighter did not help. When he awoke the following day, he was stiff.

The doctor rechecked the wound, put more alcohol and iodine on it, and applied a clean bandage. He said, "You should take it easy for a few days. Your shoulder moves every time you move your arm and can't start knitting back together. At least wear a sling. Everyone will see how you risked life and limb to protect their money."

"Not a bad idea, Doc. I didn't think of that angle. I may wear a sling for a long time."

Mike had begun preparing the site for Bart's house. His main objective was to complete the sawmill, but he occasionally sent a few men over to work on Bart's place.

Mike told Bart, "I'll try to get your foundation and such done this winter so it'll have time to settle. We can start building in early spring, depending on the weather. I should have it finished and ready to move in about the first of June."

"I'll let my wife know she can plan to move in June. If she gets here a little early, I'm sure she can stay at McCullough Ranch for a while. What's the school situation around here?"

"Everyone teaches their kids at home. I've heard people talking about starting a school in Butte. We're getting enough residents to justify a small school now. It would likely have twenty or thirty children in various grades. But I'm not sure we have a proper teacher in Butte."

"Interesting. My wife teaches school in St. Louis. Maybe we could work something out. I'll send her a telegram to see if she is interested."

"Great! We can talk about it if she's interested. I can build a schoolhouse in time for it to open in the fall."

Bart sent his wife a telegram about the move-in date and the school situation. The bank was in full operation with Bart's arm in a sling. He began looking for another teller in earnest. He found a person who had worked as a teller in Omaha. She was a pleasant woman whose husband ran one of the mines.

Mary and Morgan decided Mary needed help with the twins. Juanita knew a woman who wanted a full-time job and invited her to visit Bonner's Den Ranch to talk with Mary. She was a young Mexican woman, Lena, who came from a big family related to Juanita, Lotte, and Rosalita. Mary thought she was perfect and hired her immediately.

The twins were nearly a month old, and Mary was ready to return to the McCullough Ranch to be with Milam. He had been visiting Mary and the twins for a few days each week but needed to prepare for the spring roundup. They loaded a wagon with Lena's and the baby's things, including a new crib. Mary had bought many additional items now that she had to care for two babies. Morgan and Fergus accompanied them to help everyone settle in.

Angus was happier than anyone to be returning to his home. The visit had been longer than he wanted. He wanted to sit on his porch and sleep in his bed, plus watch the roundup preparation.

Angus helped Milam and Fergus plan the roundup. They would work Jeb's cattle and other smaller ranchers' cattle first. Jeb had work pens of his own, so they would move certain small ranchers' cattle into his pens. Milam sent a rider to tell those ranchers where to take their herds.

Milam and Jeb were glad to have Angus and Fergus help plan the operation. Angus was even happier to realize he was still needed and appreciated. Colorado, Dutch, and Dub also helped with the planning. They initially worked on the porch so Mora and Mica could sleep without the planners interrupting them. After they kept coming in for coffee, Morgan told them to move the sessions to the bunkhouse. No one dared disagree with her. Besides, it was a good idea.

When the planning was completed, they decided to launch the roundup in five days. The chuckwagon was sent to Jeb's ranch with enough food for the first week, and it would be restocked each week.

Having over fifty cowboys working at Jeb's ranch made the work go fast. Dutch and Colorado sent their best ropers there because they were needed.

Fergus had to leave to ensure the farming was moving along properly. The Jenkins were making progress on breaking the land. A herd of cattle had been held on each plot for a month to fertilize the soil.

Fergus rode on to Butte to check on the sawmill. The mill was almost ready to begin sawing.

He also visited with Bart. The sling surprised him until Bart told him it was partially to show customers how hard he worked to protect their money. It worked because deposits had increased, and no one had pulled their money out.

Bart told Fergus about Amber moving in June and that she would begin teaching in the new school as soon as the schoolhouse was completed. The mine owners and the bank would pay for the schoolhouse and her salary. Fergus was surprised at the changes over only a few weeks since he had been in town.

Fergus ate lunch with Josh and Bart. He told them about Mora and Mica and how fast they were growing. He admitted he could not always tell them apart. Morgan, who saw them daily, could not understand why it was so difficult for Fergus. Fergus feared Milam would have trouble knowing which was which when roundup was over.

Getting all the news in town was good, but Fergus was anxious to return home. Angus was already drinking coffee the following day when Fergus entered the kitchen. Angus told Fergus he wanted to go to the roundup and spend at least one night.

Fergus and Angus sat on the porch, drinking coffee and discussed the issue. They looked up and saw a small herd of horses approaching from the north. When they got closer, Fergus saw the horses were Appaloosa, and eight riders were herding them. He eventually recognized two of the riders as Horace and Hank.

Horace and Hank visited every other year to bring Fergus his share of the gold they dug on Fergus's claims in the Idaho Territory. But Fergus did not expect to see eight riders and a herd of beautiful Appaloosa horses.

Fergus and Angus stood and waved to the approaching riders. When they neared the house, Horace and Hank dismounted, and the others held the herd a hundred yards away. The men walked to the porch, and Horace yelled, "Howdy!"

After shaking hands, Fergus asked, "What do we have here?"

Horace responded, "It's an interesting story. Can we put the horses in your corral before I tell it?"

"Certainly. Have y'all had breakfast?"

"No, we're hoping y'all have some leftovers."

"I'll get the cook to rustle up something."

The eight people returned to breakfast after the horses were put in the corral. Horace told their story during breakfast. He said, "The story has two parts. First, both of our wives' fathers passed on since we saw you two years ago. Their mothers moved in with us and brought their horses with them. The women heard Hank and me talking about living in warmer weather with much less snow. The women liked the idea and said they were ready to move to a place like that. So, we're headed to eastern Oklahoma or southeast Arkansas. We'll know when we get there. We want to buy property, raise horses, and rest our bones."

Horace continued, "The other story is about the gold. The gold dust soon began playing out when we returned to the claims. Our two oldest boys had been buggin' us about climbing up a little tributary to find its source, and we finally let them. It was a little dangerous because it was so steep. Took them all day to get to the top and back down. They brought back a small bag of white rocks with streaks of pure gold running through 'em. They told us the spring bubbled out of a cluster of big white boulders, and they could see gold streaks all through 'em."

"Hank and I climbed up to examine the rocks. We were dumbfounded! They were right about the white boulders gold veins. They had to be the source of the gold dust in the bigger creek. So, we went back up with heavy hammers and chisels to begin cracking the rocks. We found more gold than all of our years of prospecting combined! We've been workin' on them rocks for almost two years. Let's walk out to the corral so we can show you."

They walked to the corral, where they had unloaded multiple packs. Horace said, "Fergus, those two packs are your share of the gold."

Fergus picked up one of the packs and said, "My Heavens, Horace! That's nearly a hundred pounds of gold!"

"Yep, which means our share is three times that amount."

"Jesus above! Y'all are rich men now. I'm so happy for you."

"Thank you. Fergus, you've been good to us. You saved our lives, found us good wives, and gave us a chance to work hard and become wealthy. We can never thank you enough."

"No thanks needed. You deserve it."

"Still, we want to give you a token of our appreciation."

Hank waved to one of the boys, and he led a beautiful Appaloosa stallion to the corral fence. It was two years old and had a stunning white coat covered with gray dappling. Fergus thought it was the prettiest horse he had ever seen.

Fergus asked, "You're leaving him with me?"

"Yep. We're keeping his older brother. A man told us his color pattern is called 'leopard.' Thought you could make use of him."

"Absolutely! Thank you!"

When they returned to the porch, Horace said, "Fergus, we're not sure how to get to Oklahoma. Driving the horses would be dangerous and take a long time. Do the railroads go there?"

"Yes."

"We've never ridden on a train. Will they transport horses? Can you tell us what we need to do?"

"Yes, they transport horses. Do you remember Josh, the man who was with me when we helped you escape?" Horace nodded.

"Josh is in Butte and owns a freighting outfit. He's very knowledgeable about railroads and can help you buy the right tickets. Also, we own the bank in Butte. You should take only a little gold with you. You can put most of it in the bank and Bart, the president, can give you a bank draft to take with you. You can use the draft to open a bank account in Oklahoma."

"I like it."

"I'll ride with y'all to Butte and help make sure everything gets done right."

"Thank you."

Fergus left with the herd immediately. He helped Horace's group exchange most of their gold for a bank draft and a wad of paper money, and he and Josh helped them buy passage to Tulsa.

Fergus hustled back to the ranch to help Angus get to the roundup. He made Angus promise to sleep in his buckboard off the ground. If Angus caught pneumonia, he would likely not survive. It took them two hours to get to the pen where the work was happening.

The next day, Fergus talked Milam into taking Angus home and spending a night with Mary and the twins. She missed him, and the girls were changing rapidly. Milam feared he might not return to the roundup if he went home. He was almost right.

When Milam arrived, Morgan made him wash up in the bunkhouse shower. It was cold, but getting the trail dust off felt good and the clean clothes felt divine.

The babies were awake when he finally got clean enough to hold them. Mary was busy feeding the two, who sounded like they were enjoying themselves. As soon as she finished one, he held it. Milam decided to spend the night and get to know them better. He was thrilled being home but, at the same time, wanted to return to the roundup. As he expected, Mary begged him to spend more time at home.

Milam departed after eating breakfast and spending more time with the twins. He was working cattle before noon, and messing up his clean clothes.

The roundup proceeded well and quickly. The McCullough Ranch usually took about ten days to complete, but they would finish in seven or eight days this time.

Between working McCullough ranch and Bonner's Den Ranch, Milam and Fergus dropped by to see the babies and women. Fergus stayed for only a few hours while Milam spent the night. The men from Bonner's Den Ranch had almost all the cattle in or near the working pens. They had enough men to work two pens simultaneously, and the work went quickly. Fergus now had an informal count of the yearlings to sell in the fall. It would be the ranch's most significant sale ever.

After resting for a few days, Fergus rode to check on the sawmill. It was ready, and they had sawed a few logs for practice. It took four men to operate the big saw, with the sawyer controlling it. He determined the width of the board and, to a lesser extent, the speed of the saw. Lance intended to cut an ample supply of one- and two-inch boards with four and eight-inch widths. The saw blade could also be adjusted to cut lumber the size of railroad ties or mine timbers. They wanted to build up a supply of one-by and two-by lumber before sawing anything else. They would start drying the lumber while taking new orders for lumber. The timber they cut would make boards over thirty feet long, which would be cut to the desired length with a crosscut saw.

It took more men to work in the yard than to operate the saw. All the lumber was stacked with runners between the layers to dry in the sun. The stacks were beginning to grow before Fergus was ready to leave.

Several mine owners approached Lance about providing large support beams. Lance planned to start sawing them in about a month. Fergus and Lance the sawmill would be successful. Josh said he thought they could sell all the boards they could cut in Cheyenne. The city was really growing after the railroad arrived.

Fergus rode by the farm and gristmill on the way home. Jenkins would only have grain to grind in the fall, which meant the gristmill would sit idle until then. The Jenkins were working hard to get the fields plowed and planted. They had planted fifty acres of corn, followed by the same wheat acreage. A hundred acres of oats would be planted last. Little sprouts of corn were already breaking through the topsoil. Fergus was proud of the crops and how they would make the ranches self-sustaining.

He rode along thinking about the crops and not paying enough attention to his surroundings when a bullet took his hat off! He dove for cover, grabbing his rifle as he left the saddle. More rounds were fired at him from a cluster of boulders. He slipped out of sight from the boulders and began to work his way up the mountainside. An old mountain man never forgets how to climb a mountain. He began to run out of cover, but the attackers did not know where he was. He wanted to discover how many attackers he was facing and why they attacked him.

He finally spotted six young Indians, likely trying to prove they were grown warriors. Fergus preferred to avoid shooting them if possible. He did not want to cause an uprising by whatever tribe they were from. Fergus intended to slip behind them and capture the whole bunch.

He started moving toward their position and was thankful they were not seasoned adults.

Fergus dislodged a few rocks, but the boys ignored them. He was able to get close to their position without being spotted. He had the drop on them before they knew he was slightly above their position. He called out and told them to drop their rifles, which they reluctantly did. Fergus eased closer to them but still did not know their tribe. He tied them on their ponies and started toward Bonner's Den Ranch. Their horses were tied to a long rope so they could not run. He was only about an hour from home. Wolf and Half Moon would know the tribe and help decide what to do with them.

When he rode into the ranch's headquarters, the cowboys around came out of the bunkhouse with weapons drawn. Fergus said, "Get Wolf and Half Moon. When they identify the tribe, we'll put them in the oat barn. We'll take them to their tribe tomorrow. Shorty, you stand the first watch. Colorado will take the second watch, and I'll take the third."

Wolf and Half Moon approached and, after looking the boys over, told Fergus they were Blackfoot. Their reservation was not far away, but it was still a four-day ride.

One of the boys tried to break out during the night, and Colorado shot him in the leg. Everyone came running, including Morgan and Half Moon. They stopped the bleeding and patched the wound. Fergus, Colorado, Wolf, and two other cowboys saddled horses before sunup. They put the boys on their ponies and tied them securely.

Wolf said, "Fergus, the wounded boy is a chief's son. We can't let him get hurt anymore."

Before they left, Morgan walked over and said, "Saddle my horse. I'm going with you. He may need doctoring before we get there."

Fergus started to protest, but he received a stern look from Morgan. She said, "I'm going. Get my horse."

Fergus saddled her horse. They took a small wagon to carry the boys' weapons and trail food. It took four days of hard riding to get to

Blackfoot country. The chief's son's leg started bleeding, and he had to be bound again a couple of times. They put him in the wagon to make it easier on his leg. Fergus knew they were being watched as soon as they were in the Blackfoot territory. A group of Blackfoot braves soon approached and escorted them to their village, which was an uneasy ride.

All the braves knew the wounded boy was the son of Mountain Chief, one of the chiefs of the Piegan group. He was a fierce warrior in battle but usually did not initiate trouble. They rode into camp and found several Blackfeet spoke the Nez Perce language. One of them and Wolf served as interpreters. The usual courtesies were passed, and then the questions began.

The chief asked, "Why do you have my son tied like a dog in your wagon?"

He pointed to the hole in his hat and replied, "He and the other boys tried to ambush me. I got into the timber and slipped up behind them. We locked them in a building on my ranch. Your son tried to escape and was shot in the leg. We put him in the wagon to keep him from bleeding to death. Their weapons are in the wagon."

Mountain Chief turned his attention to his son. He was obviously not happy, "May I have my son back, or do you plan to take him to the white man's jail."

"We brought him to you for you to punish. He's just a boy and needs to learn much before he becomes a warrior. He is brave and would cut my heart out if he could."

"He will soon wish for white man's justice, and so will the others. I am in your debt for not killing them all, which is what I would have done. My warriors will not trouble your ranch or those of your friends. I am in your debt. Will you share food with us?"

Before Fergus responded, Wolf said, "We would love to eat with you, but then we must go. It is four sleeps back to our ranch."

The women soon began to serve bowls of thick stew to the visitors. They sat with the Mountain Chief and other minor chiefs. The stew was spiced with something hot, but everyone ate it. When everyone finished eating, Fergus and his crew arose to mount up and head home.

Once they were on the trail, Wolf said, "It would have been an extreme insult if we had not shared food with them. You made friends with a powerful ally if we ever need him. They will not attack your ranch or the others near us. They now know the red-haired one."

"What did he say to his son?"

"I don't know Blackfoot curse words, but I'm sure it was a severe reprimand with much foul language." They both laughed.

"It sounds like he will have a bad night."

"It will be more than one night." They had a hearty laugh.

Mountain Chief sent a group of warriors with them to ensure they encountered no problems while on the reservation.

When they arrived home, all the hands came to see what happened. Wolf told them the whole story, which caused much laughter. Some cowboys felt sorry for the young men, but Fergus did not. He needed a new hat.

Morgan was ready to visit Mary and the twins. Fergus went with her because the Blackfoot attack still concerned him. She was happy to have his company.

All was well at McCullough ranch, except everyone was concerned about Angus. He was having heart pains even while not doing anything. Milam was worried and sent a rider to fetch Bart.

Bart came to the ranch to see Angus, but his visit would be short because Amber and their children were arriving soon. Angus loved having more of his family around.

When Bart departed, Milam asked him to send a telegram to his and Bart's father, telling him Angus seemed to be going downhill. Bart sent a rider to Milam's house with their father's reply, "*Let me know what happens.*"

Morgan and Fergus decided to stay longer to make sure Angus

continued recovering. Bart received a telegram from Amber telling him she would wait until she could move into the new house, which would only delay her a few weeks. Bart returned a telegram telling her the house was livable and would be completed when she arrived.

Amber sent Josh a telegram asking about the schoolhouse. He replied that Mike would begin the schoolhouse as soon as her house was finished, and he was sure he would finish it by September.

Mora and Mica were growing and seemed very healthy. Angus took them to see the horses when they woke up most days. They slept all night, and Lena did a great job with them. Morgan, Mary, and Lena were finally getting more sleep and rest. As often happens with older people who have heart problems, he rallied with the family around. Although he was better, he was still popping his pills regularly.

After Angus's brief rally, he began to look worse. His color was not good, and he no longer took the girls to see horses. Fergus began bringing Angus's favorite horse to visit him and the girls, which was the high point of Angus's day. He seldom left the porch. He and Fergus had a couple fingers of the excellent rum most nights, often joined by Milam and Morgan.

Amber and Bart came out with their children as soon as they moved the furniture into the house. Amber liked the new home and would position the furniture where she wanted it later. Amber was not a good rider, and neither were their children, so they borrowed a large surrey from Josh for the trip. Josh also came with them to see Angus. Amber was excited about the teaching job. The land was still too sparsely settled for her preference, but she was sure she would get used to it.

Chapter Sixteen

Bart and Amber's children were Duke and Sheila, aged eight and six, respectively. Angus, Duke, and Sheila were tired and went to bed shortly after supper.

The next morning, they all ate pancakes and sausage for breakfast. Mary's twins woke early for their feeding, and Angus held each of them before they went back to sleep. Duke and Sheila sat with Angus on the porch and he talked to them about the 'good old days.'

Fergus slipped out to bring Angus's horse to the house. The kids petted the horse, and Angus found the strength to walk it around while they sat in the saddle. Duke wanted to ride by himself and did a surprisingly good job.

Angus said, "Duke, I don't need the horse anymore, and you need a horse. It's yours now."

"Thank you, Gramps! I'll take good care of it!"

Sheila's bottom lip protruded as she asked, "Gramps, don't it get a horse?"

Angus replied, "I have another horse for you. It's a golden palomino and the perfect horse for the prettiest girl in Montana." She hugged his neck.

Fergus walked to the barn, saddled the palomino, and brought her to the porch. Fergus agreed that it was the perfect horse for Sheila. She was a calm, smallish cow pony that was beautifully formed. Sheila rode it by herself, and she and the mare did well.

The kids rode the horses around the yard while Angus watched. It was hard to tell who was happiest, Angus or the children. After an hour, the kids were ready to stop riding, so Bart and Fergus took the horses to the barn, unsaddled and brushed them, and put them in their stalls.

They walked back to the porch and saw Angus slumped over. They started running to the porch and found Angus was not breathing. Fergus called for the adults to come to the porch. Morgan knew it was a problem based on his voice.

Morgan checked and could not find a pulse. His heart had just quit beating. Angus died surrounded by his family. Milam was grateful Angus had a chance to say goodbye to all his grandchildren and great-grandchildren. He was even able to pass along his favorite horses to his great-grandchildren.

Bart and Milam carried Angus to his bed to prepare the body for burial. The children cried aloud, and the adults also shed a few tears. Angus had led his life on his own terms until the heart problem slowed him to the point he could not do the things he loved.

Fergus asked Dutch to have the men dig a grave next to Angus's wife, which was where he wanted to be buried. Not much work was done on the McCullough Ranch for the rest of the day. They would bury him at noon the following day. Dutch sent a rider on a fast horse to tell the Bonner's Den Ranch riders of the death. Other riders were sent to other ranches to let them know. Most of the owners and a few cowboys came from each ranch.

McCullough Ranch was a sad place. Rosalita began preparing food for the group. The bunkhouse cook butchered a yearling and put half of it on a spit. Juanita and Lotte came to help Rosalita feed the family.

Bart and Milam put Angus's best clothes on him with help from Amber and Mary. The two grandsons would speak at the burial. Angus left a note about what he wanted at his service. In a little twist, he wanted his two favorite horses, which he had given to Duke and Sheila, saddled and in attendance. He had ridden those horses for his last five or six years. They decided to have the children hold the horses, with Dutch and Colorado backing them up.

The burial went as well as a burial can. Even the horses seemed to be standing at attention as a monarch of the West was put to rest. Milam and Bart delivered beautiful eulogies. Lena and Rosalita held the babies while Mary stood with Milam. They had grown to love the old man as a grandfather. Even the twins seemed to know this was not a time to create a disturbance. Fergus, Bart, and Milam helped Dutch and a few other long-time hands fill the grave.

The extended family members sat at tables set up for the occasion and talked quietly about Angus. As the day approached darkness, a large fire was kindled to provide light. The people from other ranches would camp that night and leave the next morning. Everyone told Angus stories well into the night. Milam and the other youngsters heard stories about Angus and his exploits fighting Indians, outlaws, weather, and stampedes they had never heard. Angus had been a rugged man in a hard land. Some of the stories about fights he participated in were quite harrowing.

The visitors from the other ranches departed early the next morning after a breakfast of biscuits and beef from the night before. Jeb and his group stayed to visit with the twins. Jeb told Kamiah they did not need any more children. Liz played with Mora and Mica all she was allowed to. She was good with the girls and loved it. She thought they did need another one because she needed a little sister.

Rowdy and Joe helped Duke and Sheila saddle their horses and ride near the ranch house. Riding came naturally to them, and their skill improved rapidly. Bart thought Angus was watching over them and may have been right.

Fergus and Colorado departed to let the immediate family spend more time together. Bart and Milam talked about their dad and why he had not come. He and Angus had never been close, and he left home due to bad disagreements. They did not know the details of the disagreements.

Bart and Amber decided to return to their new home the next day. The kids rode their new horses home and left them with Josh until Bart built a corral. Duke rode on Angus's saddle, and Sheila rode on a smaller saddle Bart had used as a youngster. Morgan decided to ride with them as far as Bonner's Den Ranch.

It was suddenly quiet at the McCullough ranch house. Milam rode around the ranch to grieve by himself. It did not take long for him to conclude that Angus was not having a good time when his activities became limited. He now grasped that Angus had always lived independent and free. Milam was sure he was now in a better place. He and Mary talked about Angus a lot when he returned home.

Milam went to work the next day. He mainly just rode and looked around the ranch, which was cathartic. He did it almost every day for a week. Dutch rode with him sometimes, and they discussed what needed to be done on the ranch before it was time for the fall roundup.

Milam rode to Butte to talk to the lawyer and ensure everything was done correctly for his inheritance. On his way, he passed Bonner's Den Ranch. Fergus rode with him to check on the sawmill, bank, and schoolhouse.

The sawmill was in full production, with large stacks of lumber drying. Lance was ready to begin sawing mining timbers any day.

The school building was erected. It just needed a few final touches before classes started. Josh had ordered desks and expected them any day. Amber had ordered books based on the number of children in each grade. She had also ordered a small library of classics and other books for lower-level reading. She knew of twenty-three students and expected two or three more.

While riding around checking on his various interests, Fergus realized he had worked himself into a job that did not slow down all year. He was used to the ebb and flow of ranch work, but everything had changed, and he still had to visit the gristmill. The mill was going to change things again when it cranked up.

Milam needed to spend a couple of days with attorney Eshee to get all the papers on the land and other property issues in order. Eshee was good at seeing that everything was in perfect legal order, which Milam needed. He still had a niggling feeling that his dad might kick up some dust. His dad was hard to like and harder to get along with.

Fergus rode to check on the farming operation. Jenkins had the grain farm under control. Everything was planted and growing well. They would plow and hoe the corn regularly until harvest time. Fergus talked to Jenkins about buying corn and wheat to grind and have it brought in by the railroad and Josh's freight wagons. Jenkins thought it was a good idea but pointed out he needed more storage buildings to handle grain and the resulting flour and cornmeal.

Fergus rode back to town to get Mike to build three storage sheds near the gristmill. He also asked Josh to find a carload of wheat and corn for the gristmill.

Fergus and Milam met in town and decided to spend the night and get an early start the next day. When they rode by the sawmill, Lance was converting to mine timber production. Three months of production had already been sold at a good price. Josh would haul the timber to the mines. Lance's orders would keep them busy until near the New Year.

They rode pretty hard going home. Milam planned to continue to McCullough Ranch and wanted to arrive before dark. Of course, dark came about ten o'clock this time of year.

———————————

When Milam arrived home, Wolf and Tall One were going out to see if a bear returned to feed on a carcass one of the line riders found. Bears usually fed at night and would sometimes feed several days on one kill.

Wolf and Tall One spent the night at the line shack and took the hounds to the carcass at daylight. The dogs hit as soon as they got to the kill site. The chase headed into the foothills. Based on the tracks, they were on a big boar. He was fast and ran in almost a straight line. They were far off the ranch at noon and moving higher, but the bear seemed to be slowing.

They moved into some timber and expected the bear to tree soon. He treed but jumped down before Wolf and Tall One arrived. He fought the dogs briefly before taking off again and clawed two dogs badly.

Tall One stayed with the two hounds to try to give aid. Wolf pushed his horse the next time to get there sooner. The two men knew it was partially their fault the hounds were hurt. They had to stay closer when chasing a big bear. The bear treed again after another hour. Wolf saw him climb the tree and shot it as soon as he had a clear opening.

Wolf returned to Tall One and the injured dogs. They always carried needles, thread, and bandages whenever they took the hounds out. The two dogs needed extensive repair work. One had some gut hanging out, and the other hound's mouth was ripped badly. They did the best they could to clean the one with his belly ripped, including using alcohol to wash the wound. Wolf stitched him up and put a medicated salve on it. They wrapped him tight to make sure he stayed closed.

Although the belly wound was the most serious, the face wound was more challenging to treat. They cleaned it as well as possible and began stitching inside the mouth. Fortunately, the hounds had loose lips. Wolf tried to use tiny stitches on the inside so it would heal quicker. The outside was sewn with larger stitches. They bandaged his head and neck as well as they could without pulling on the stitches. It was nearly dark when they finished the first aid. They camped where they were, sharing their food with the uninjured hounds. They withheld food from the injured ones.

The two dogs were carried home on a travois pulled by Tall One. The one with the face wound could have walked, but they decided it would be better to let him ride. Neither hound tried to get off.

When they reached the ranch house, several people examined the damage. A remote ranch had to have people who could treat animals. The closest veterinarian was in Butte, and he was primarily a people doctor, Dr. Boyton. Infection was the primary danger. The wounds were cleaned again, but the belly wound could not be effectively cleaned on the inside. The stitches were holding but were not very pretty. More of the salve was put over the wounds, and they were wrapped again. Both hounds were put in confined spaces.

Garry Smith and Danny Arnold

Mike finished building corn and wheat storage facilities near the gristmill. He was also building a storage barn to store sacks of cornmeal and flour. Josh found a railroad car of each grain and had them shipped to Butte.

The Jenkins men and the wagon drivers unloaded the wagons, which was a difficult job, but they were strong. With all the land planted, Jenkins started grinding flour the following day. The stones had to be set a little differently to grind flour finer than cornmeal. It took almost two weeks to grind the wheat. They produced nearly a hundred bags of wheat flour that weighed a hundred pounds each. It was a lot of flour, but each ranch might use as much as a hundred pounds weekly. So, they had enough for two ranches for a year.

The cornmeal was ground a little courser. I took only ten days and produced over a hundred bags at a hundred pounds each. It was enough to fulfill the needs of three ranches for a year. Those were good numbers to remember, especially for the corn, which would be for both animals and humans. Fergus thought the freshly ground cornmeal smelled much better than they bought in the general store.

They distributed the cornmeal and flour to the ranches at two bags of each per ranch. Fergus felt good about supplying their own needs. He was not sure he was saving money, but he was happy.

Jenkins caught Fergus and said, "While I was grinding the corn, I realized we're gonna' need at least two corn shellers. We could never shell enough by hand to supply the gristmill."

"I'll order a couple of the biggest shellers I can find. Should get them before we harvest our corn."

Fergus silently wondered what other necessary equipment he had overlooked. He rode immediately to Butte's general store and found they had a small corn sheller. An equipment catalog contained two larger models, and Fergus ordered two of the largest models. He was afraid they would be too large for one man to handle. The man at the

176

general store said they would be in before harvest.

Fergus headed for Bonner's Den Ranch to see if Morgan wanted to go camping again. He thought he could break away for a few days.

When Fergus arrived home, he asked Morgan if she was interested in taking a short camping trip. She thought for a brief moment and said yes. Brody did not need her help with the potato crop because he had four men helping him. Fergus went to pack the teepee, blankets, and cooking gear.

They went to the same place to set up camp. It was warmer than the last trip but still cool at night. They spent three nights and once again got to know each other. They both had been too busy to pay much attention to their relationship. Life had gotten pretty complicated for the couple. Morgan knew she would go see the twins soon. Fergus would soon be tied up with the fall roundup. Plus, the two mills were taking much of his time. They had not been exactly ignoring each other, but life was getting in the way. No matter how hard they tried, they could not devote enough time to themselves when so many depended on them.

They again caught a mess of brook trout to eat each night. They explored the foothills to the base of the mountains. The mountains looked beautiful.

Morgan said, "I want to camp in the mountains next time. We lived in the mountains for a long while, and I miss them sometimes."

"Me, too. I'd like to see how they look down here. They're taller and probably prettier than where we lived in the Bitterroots. I'll bet we can find lakes with big trout."

She said, "We're supposed to take everyone to a city this summer. We have to do it soon."

"I forgot about the trip! We can take them to Denver for July Fourth when we sell the horses.

"Good idea, but it's only a few weeks away."

"A couple of weeks! I had no idea it was coming so soon. I have got a lot to do to get ready."

"We should head back tomorrow. I think you need a little

rest anyway."

"I'm sure I do." Morgan grinned and hugged him.

They started back after a light lunch in the early afternoon. They would spend one more night because it was getting dark. They arrived at the ranch for lunch.

They had to let everyone know they were going to Denver for the Fourth. Fergus had to select the horses to take for the auction. It was easier this time since he knew more about what people wanted. He would take the same stallions for the races, and they needed to be exercised on long runs.

As soon as they returned, intense activity began. Everybody but Chinn said they could go to Denver, so the trip was on. Rowdy and Colt would help show the horses again. Fergus planned to take thirty horses to the auction. Many of the horses were yearlings or two years old, and all were flashy.

Fergus planned to enter the same two stallions in the long-distance races. He had two of his best riders run the horses daily. They started at a couple miles and worked up to ten miles before tapering down.

Fergus thought he should go to Butte to check on the sawmill, but he knew he did not have to. He would try to leave in time to visit it on the way to Denver. Everything came together, and the group departed on the last day of June. Morgan and Fergus would finally have a little time to rest on the train.

Most of the group would stay at the Cannon Hotel. A few, such as Rowdy and Colt, would always be at the stables. Several other hands would help with the horses. Fergus obtained compartments on the trip from Cheyenne to Denver, but none were available from Butte to Cheyenne.

They boarded the early train from Butte and arrived in Denver two days later. Fergus took enough hands to get the horses to the stables. The yearlings would be held in a pasture near Clark Cannon's house. Commanche dogs and several well-armed cowboys were in the stable area for security.

Grant arrived the first night. He brought the horses he planned to enter in the short races and compete in the cutting events, along with a few mules to auction.

The race events went much like the previous year in that the two Bonner's Den stallions won the mountain and flat ten-mile races. Many people were interested in Fergus's horses. The Appaloosas brought top prices even though they were young. Several people again tried to buy the racing stallions. One man made an offer that Fergus almost gave in to. He turned the offer down because they were his main breeding stallions. Fergus was not sure he had another stallion to plug into the breeding rotation. He would not tell Morgan how much he turned down for the stallions.

Grant again bought two young stallions, a yearling and a two-year-old. He offered to buy either of the two racing horses when Fergus needed to rotate them out of the breeding program. He understood breeding plans better than most people. Several of his best-looking young stallions sold for much more money than Fergus expected. The yearlings were selling for more than most top-end four-year-olds.

Fergus wanted to go home immediately after the auction, but Morgan wanted the children to see a play two nights later. She also wanted the men to see it. Morgan thought a little culture would not hurt the men. She had also bought tickets for a ballet. Everyone attended both events. The men would have preferred watching a rodeo, but they went along without complaint. The men enjoyed both the play and the ballet, but no one would admit it, nor would they actively complain.

———————————

Finally, they were back in Butte. Morgan and Fergus visited the schoolhouse. Amber was working to get everything cleaned up and ready. With the ever-present wind and dust, it would not stay pristine very long. The library books had arrived, and Morgan was impressed with their quality.

Fergus rode to the sawmill. The mine timbers were piling up, but the stacks of cut boards had shrunk drastically. It would be challenging for Lance to calculate the amount of each type of wood needed.

Morgan went to Bonner's Den Ranch while Fergus rode to check on the grain farm. The fields looked terrific. The corn was almost head high and beginning to tassel. The wheat and oats looked healthy. The rains had come at the perfect times so far. Bonner's Den Ranch still had oats and a little corn from last year. The amount he started the year with was a good target.

Jeb's cattle were in good shape. Fergus and Jeb thought they would need to cull a few of the cows to match the ranch's carrying capacity, which had been expected when they bought the herds. When Fergus reached home, Morgan rode to the McCullough ranch. Fergus checked with Colorado to see how things were going around the ranch.

Colorado said, "The bears are taking a few head, so Wolf and Tall One will start hunting them tomorrow. Hopefully, they can get it under control."

Chapter Seventeen

Fergus thought he must be losing his mind. He had planned to do two important things in Denver and completely forgot them. He wanted to return to Denver as soon as possible.

Fergus also wanted to figure out how to stop making all the decisions for the ranch and related activities. Good people were running the sawmill and gristmill, and he knew he did not have to visit them regularly. He was killing himself with details.

Riding a horse was a good time to think about such things. Fergus thought one day, "*Colorado can run the ranch without my help. Jenkins can grow the grain and run the gristmill without my advice. Lance can operate the sawmill, and Bart can run the bank. They're all excellent managers who can let me know if they need help. I have to stay out of their way. Each man knows more than I do about their operations, which is a humbling thought.*"

As Fergus thought about what he had forgotten to do in Denver, he decided it was an excellent time to head for Denver and get out of the managers' way. He decided to tell each one about his realization and what he wanted from them, and he wanted to talk to them individually. He thought they would be happy, and even though it would be hard for him, he knew he had to do it.

Fergus started with Colorado and Wolf. He explained that he was turning decision-making about the cattle operation over to Colorado. Wolf would be in charge of the horse breeding, which meant he would likely have to let someone else work with the hounds. They spent time discussing the new arrangements. Colorado would move into the house Jeb vacated, which would help ensure everyone understood he now held a higher-level position.

Fergus had similar discussions with Jenkins and Lance. Bart was already in charge at the bank.

Fergus thought he was ready to head for Denver and visit with Grant. He also wanted to visit Freedom Town to buy Sheffield or Freedom Town mules.

Morgan blessed the trip because she knew he needed a break from making virtually all the decisions for the ranch and other businesses, and she hoped it would stay that way when he returned. She decided to stay with Mary and the twins. She also thought she would later encourage him to take her on a trip back East.

Fergus sent Grant a telegram from Butte and boarded the next train. He would arrive in Denver in two days. Fergus asked Grant about staying at his ranch since Fergus planned to stay in Denver for about a month and wanted to discuss horse breeding with him. He also wanted to check on buying more big mules from him or Freedom Town. Grant telegraphed Freedom Town to let them know Fergus was coming to purchase mules and would likely buy as many as six if they had them.

The trip to Denver was uneventful. Most people quickly sized Fergus up as a man to avoid crossing. Grant was waiting for Fergus at the train station with an extra horse. They rode to the ranch after enjoying a scrumptious meal at the Cannon Hotel. Fergus was quite impressed with the chef's expertise.

Grant had no mules to sell, but Freedom Town had young mules they might part with. On the ride to Grant's ranch, they stopped at a barn just outside Denver so Grant could show Fergus three stallions he kept for outside breeders.

Fergus was impressed with the stallions and the concept and thought he could do the same thing in Butte. He had a stallion he was using sparingly at the ranch to avoid inbreeding. He thought the stud fees could be significant.

Angelina was ready for their arrival. She had set up a vacant cabin near their large cabin for Fergus's use. They ate steak for supper at the bunkhouse. Fergus had actually hoped for the Mexican stew, but the steak was his second choice, mainly because of how the cook spiced it.

After supper, the men sat on the porch and discussed Fergus's dilemma about being involved with every decision associated with the ranch. Grant said, "I had the same problem for a while. We have many mines scattered over a wide area, and I was always checking on them. The problem is I don't know much about mining. I was getting in the mine superintendents' way, and they are the ones who know what they're doing. Clark and I now get involved only when a problem arises. Clark gets all mining reports at the bank and can tell when something is amiss. One or both of us will visit a mine if he finds any discrepancies. You have to hire good people and let them work. Even with the horses, I let the foreman put together a breeding plan, and I only check to ensure I agree."

Grant continued, "Clark and I also divide our responsibilities. I usually select the land we buy. I have a good eye for grassland and where gold or silver may be hiding. He may look at the land before we buy it and then handle the legal aspects. But I pick the land. He has no real interest in the horses except to ensure we profit from them. It works well for us."

Fergus replied, "I have to think about dividing responsibilities and giving the people the authority to make decisions. I plan to stay here for a while to give them free rein. If I'm there, they always wait for me to decide. It's the way we have always operated. I must admit I'm the main problem because I keep checking their every move. It's going to take a while for me to change my stripes. I realized I had a problem when I returned home after the Fourth. I was so distracted by everything happening here that I didn't do several important things I planned. I'll get them done on this trip. I want to buy Morgan a ring. She's never had one to befit her station in life. I also want to return with several Sheffield mules and Comanche dogs. We used to have a great dog that I'm sure was part wolf. He was extremely protective of Morgan and Mary."

"How many dogs do you want? We'll have to check with Kate to see how many she has ready."

"Okay, let me think. I want one for Mary, Morgan, Kamiah, Amber, the bank, the sawmill, and the gristmill. I might as well get myself one, too. I think that makes eight."

"I'll send her a telegram to find out how many she has ready to go. You may have to wait to get eight, but I don't know. She's in charge of the dogs and their training."

"Before I return home, I also want to find out how you and your foreman keep up with your herd's bloodlines."

"It's quite a challenge. We keep everything written down. We keep records similar to what thoroughbred breeders use, and they go back multiple generations. We keep our crosses far enough away to avoid inbreeding problems. You must be careful when you have a great stallion because you want to use him as much as possible. We had to exchange mares one time with one of our other ranches. I'll show you how we do it. The main thing is to keep a written record of each breeding."

Grant and Angelina were not overly busy, so they decided to accompany Fergus to Freedom Town to look at mules and dogs. They took their young son when they rode to Denver and dropped him off with his grandmother, Gloria.

The threesome took the train to La Junta, where Gabe met them with a surrey. The surrey ride was enjoyable, until six bandits tried to stop the surrey and rob them when they were about halfway to Freedom Town. They had to be from somewhere else to brace Grant, Angelina, and Gabe. They would not have known Fergus, who was just as deadly. The confrontation lasted barely long enough to be called a fight. The robbers had their pistols drawn and got off only two shots, and both bullets struck the ground. The robbers all lay dead with holes in their chests or foreheads — several were hit more than once.

Gabe said, "Durn it! We might as well take them back to the Sheriff. Sorry for wasting your time, but the wolves and coyotes will get to them if we leave them overnight. I'm sure they're wanted for something somewhere. I would have left them for the animals in years gone by, but I'm trying to be a nicer guy." They chuckled at the comment but knew it was true.

As Gabe said, all six men had wanted posters on them. The total reward was two thousand dollars, which they divided equally.

The Sheriff said, "They must be from Texas or Kansas. Nobody around here would try to rob Grant, Angelina, and Gabe. I don't know Mr. Bonner, but he also looks pretty salty."

Grant replied, "Two or three of those shots were his. He may be the fastest of all of us. But we saw his teenage daughter shoot a few months ago. She may be faster than him."

The Sheriff smiled and nodded, "We need to put up warning signs at the border so new visitors would not brace you guys. They're not going to win."

"That'll make some people want to challenge us. Please don't put a sign up."

"You're right. Bad idea."

They arrived in Freedom Town just as everyone finished supper, but plenty of food remained. They ate chicken and dumplings to die for. The cornbread and peas were also quite good, and Fergus thought the cobblers might be the best he had ever tasted. He overate and enjoyed every bite. He had trouble going to sleep because he was so full.

After supper, Fergus sat and chatted with Miss Lily and Cat Jones for a long time. They remembered meeting Milam and Mary during their honeymoon trip. Fergus spent ample time bragging about his twin granddaughters.

Cat asked, "What color is their hair?"

"Red, of course. It's not red like mine, but reddish blonde. It doesn't glow red like mine. Don't know how curly it might be."

Fergus learned about the rigors faced on the Freedom Towner's journey from Louisiana and how Freedom Town had grown and prospered. Fergus told about his journey from Tennessee. Like many pioneers, they had many things in common, not all pleasant.

Gabe and Fergus rode out to look at the mules the next morning.

Gabe said, "We usually don't have this many we're willing to sell. The Freedom Town mules are not quite as popular as the Sheffield mules. Our people who drive mules don't understand why. They think the only difference is their coloring. They're darker and can be significantly darker than the Sheffield mules. They pull just as well, but most people prefer the lighter color."

Fergus replied, "Our first big mules, which Milam bought, are the darker Freedom Town mules. We don't care which color we get as long as they pull like the ones we have. A pair of these can do as much work as four regular mules."

Fergus picked out six of the strongest-looking Freedom Town mules. He could easily match them relative to size and coloring. Gabe would ship them to Butte, and Josh would take care of them until Fergus returned.

Fergus rode to Doc's liquor complex when the mule buying was consummated. Doc had been experimenting with different recipes for the various spirits. They were all good, but none touched his original rum in taste. The original 'shine was Fergus's second favorite. He ordered four cases of each to be shipped to Josh in Butte. Fergus instructed Josh to not let anyone else pick up his private stock.

Fergus visited with Kate the next day. She said, "I have four trained dogs now and will have six more in about a month. I need to train whoever will handle each dog. It's not safe for an untrained person to handle a Comanche dog. It could hurt someone if given the wrong command."

"Can you come to Butte to train the people? Of course, I'll buy your train ticket and pay you for your time."

"Works for me."

"Wonderful!"

Fergus and Cat rode around the Freedom Town range and talked the next day. Cat said, "I also had to learn how to push people into making their own decisions. For many years, everyone looked at me or Miss Lily to make all the decisions. It can wear you down so much you don't always make the best decisions. It seems to be a common problem as operations grow larger."

It was a good trip for Fergus. He learned more about managing people and diverse interests than ever before, which gave him many things to contemplate. Fergus found it interesting that every successful person he talked to shared the same advice.

Fergus, Grant, and Angelina returned to Denver. Angelina wanted to spend a few days with her mother before returning to their ranch. Fergus was simply amazed that cows could thrive on the near desert they rode through. He said something to Grant, who repeated the old story about the highly nutritious grass.

Grant leaned over and said, "But you notice I didn't buy a ranch here, right? We've never bought land like this." They chuckled.

Fergus told Grant he wanted to go up in the mountains to look around and decompress. Grant asked, "Would you mind if my dad rode with you? He's good in the mountains. He can get you out if you get lost. He spent three years alone up there, wandering around with amnesia. He simply didn't want to come out of the mountains."

"Certainly! I would love to have an experienced guide."

"He can be a little strange sometimes, but he'll return to normal. It's usually because he has seen something that triggers an old memory — it could be happy, sad, or frightening. Don't push him until he's ready to share with you."

Fergus and Dale rode into the mountains the following morning. They planned to spend ten days or two weeks. They rode surefooted mountain horses and led a mule with mountain experience. They climbed high into the mountains and made camp along a cold, clear stream. Fergus thought the mountains were beautiful and peaceful. He felt his mind becoming clearer each day. Fergus was also surprised when he realized he did not worry about Bonner's Den Ranch. Everything was so relaxing that he thought he should take Morgan camping in the mountains near Bonner's Den Ranch as soon as possible.

Fergus was pleased with his companion. Dale Cannon also

recognized a kindred spirit in the former mountain man and opened up after the first day. They swapped campfire tales about their experiences and became fast friends.

After a week, Fergus and Dale moved their camp to a higher location just to see different views. It grew colder as they rode higher, and patches of snow were scattered around evergreen trees and on the north side of the rises. It even snowed on them occasionally. After ten more days, they decided to start back down.

Fergus and Dale rode up to a small cabin, which Dale said was built for him. They spent the night in the cabin and enjoyed a restful sleep. They returned to the Cannon ranch house the next day, stopping at many beautiful overlooks on the way back. Lizzy was painting at one of the gorgeous vistas. Running across her reminded Fergus where he had seen some of the overlooks — they were depicted in many of the hotel's paintings. They talked with her and the young man with her, Fernando. She was a fascinating person, and Fernando provided protection for her. After they rode away, Dale told Fergus that Fernando was as good with his revolver as Grant and Gabe.

When they reached the ranch, Fergus visited the warm spring for a soothing soak. He realized he was the most relaxed he had been in years. He decided it was time to go home—he missed his family.

Fergus obtained a room at the Cannon Hotel and shopped in downtown Denver the next day. He was looking for a ring for Morgan. She had never worn a ring as far as he knew, and if anyone deserved one, it was her. He bought a wedding ring set. The diamond was a carat and a half. The gold band was not expensive, but the diamond was. As he paid, Fergus thought, *"I could buy a small ranch with that money."* But he was happy with his purchase. It was a perfect ending to a fruitful trip.

Fergus started back on the train two days later. It took two days to get to Butte. The mules and Freedom Town liquor were waiting on him. Josh had taken his payment out of the liquor and offered to help Fergus herd the mules to Bonner's Den Ranch.

Fergus rested in Butte for a few days. He and Josh departed and rode by the farms. The crops were beautiful, and Fergus thought they would have a bumper crop unless some disaster occurred. The two corn shellers had arrived and looked good. He left two big mules with Jenkins, who was delighted.

When they arrived at the Bonner's Den Ranch, Fergus talked with Colorado, who said the roundup would start in about a month. Fergus replied, "Remember that I plan to let you young guys handle the roundup. I may drop by to see how things are going, but you and Wolf will be responsible for the ranch's interests. I'll take a much smaller role in the ranching now. You don't need me except for occasional advice if you want it. You'll make the decisions. You won't have to check with me for every little thing."

Colorado was surprised but happy. He knew he and Wolf could do the job.

Since Morgan was still at the McCullough Ranch, Fergus rode to see her and arrived a little after lunch the following day. Morgan was worried because Mica was sick. She was not bad sick, but she had been congested for a week.

Fergus asked, "Do you want me to fetch the doctor?"

"I don't think so. Little Bird has been here for a few days. She made a concoction with a little rum and honey, which helped. I think she's better. Let's wait until tomorrow before we decide on the doctor. We're also keeping a small fire in the heater to warm water and herbs. It smells good and helps everyone's breathing."

Fergus talked with Little Bird, and she did not seem worried, which made him feel much better. He trusted her as much as he did the doctor. He washed himself at the cold shower near the bunkhouse before he returned to hold Mica. She was obviously not feeling well, but she seemed to be breathing okay. The room was warm, and the simmering water emitted a pleasant aroma. Fergus thought it was sage and a few other herbs he could not identify.

Mary was sleeping. Morgan said, "Getting her to leave the nursery has been a challenge. I'm sure you can help us with that. I'm worried about her. She's been asleep almost twelve hours and does not stir around much. I don't want to wake her yet."

Fergus replied, "She must be drained. The rest will help later if Mica takes a turn for the worse, but I don't think it will happen. You also look pretty tired. Why don't you try to catch a nap?"

Morgan nodded, lay down on a pallet, and instantly fell asleep. Little Bird slipped into the room and put her ear close to Mica's chest. All she said was, "Good." She and Fergus eased out of the room.

Little Bird said, "Her breathing is a lot easier. I think the steam is helping. The rum and honey have almost stopped her coughing. I think she'll feel better by daylight. Not recovered, but on the way."

"Great! I was really concerned when I arrived. I didn't even get anything to eat. I'll try to find a biscuit or something.

"Rosalita has something warming all the time. You might even find a peach cobbler in the kitchen."

Fergus returned later and found Morgan holding Mora. She said, "You're going to have to wake Mary up. They're getting hungry. It's been over eight hours since they fed. We're out of anything to feed them without Mary."

Fergus went to Mary's room to wake her up. He said, "The girls are calling you. They seem hungry, and all the surplus milk is gone."

"Hi, Dad. Welcome home. I'll be there in a minute. How long have I been asleep?"

"Your mom said twelve hours."

"Oh my! I can't believe it!"

"You obviously needed it. A person can stay awake only for so long. You have plenty of help to take care of Mica and Mora. Milam is cleaning up so he can help. I'm rested from my trip, but we cannot feed her. You feed them and go back to sleep. You have to keep your strength up in case both get sick."

Mary walked into the nursery and sat down with Mora, who seemed most insistent on feeding. She got her fill quickly and wanted to play with someone. Fergus quickly volunteered to hold her. Mica fed much more sedately and leisurely. She took twice as long as Mora.

When Mica finally finished, Morgan said, "Honey, you need to capture any milk you have left over so we can feed her at least once during the day. Dutch is milking a cow to supplement your milk, but I think it needs some of yours mixed with it. Little Bird agrees."

"I don't have much left over after those two gluttons get through, but I'll try."

As Little Bird predicted, Mica's lungs were less congested the next morning, and she breathed much better. In fact, she was crying as loud as Mora, which was beautiful music to everyone's ears.

Fergus had yet to give Morgan the rings. He asked her to come out on the porch to talk. She walked out and sat in one of the rockers.

Fergus walked to the front of her chair and kneeled to show her the rings he had bought, "It's a little late to ask you to marry me, but will you wear these rings to show we're still in love?"

She jumped up and said, "You rascal! I had no idea you were planning this! I love the rings and will wear them for the rest of my life!"

After a big hug, she said, "I have to show Mary and the others."

Fergus loved hearing the gasps and cries of surprise. He heard Morgan say, "I always told myself I didn't care about rings. But, deep down, I guess I really did. I'm so happy! Fergus, Jeb, and I were scrambling and running for our lives early on. We had neither the time nor money for fancy rings. Actually, we did, but rings were far down on our needs list. Plus, I'd hate to see the rings Hellgate Trading Post had in stock."

Chapter Eighteen

Mica improved so much that a stranger would never guess she had been sick. The twins were playing more and more. Fergus obliged them by getting on the floor with them. They laughed almost all the time he was on their level, as did he. One of their favorite things was for Fergus to lay on his back while they climbed all over him.

Morgan did not say much about her rings, but she made sure anyone she talked with could notice them. She had been at the McCullough ranch for six weeks and was ready to return home.

Fergus and Morgan prepared to head home in two days. Mary approached them and said, "Mom, they'll start the roundup in about a week. I think I'll come to stay with y'all. Dad says all the women need to go to Butte for a couple of days for some mysterious reason. Maybe we can go after the roundup starts."

"Sounds good to me. We've not had a fun women's confab in a long time. Of course, the smaller children will be around. I think the older boys will go to the roundup. Some of them are nearly your age."

"I'll bring Lena with me to help with the twins. The rest are at least five or six years old. Do you know why he wants us to go?"

"He's been very closed mouth about it. All I know is he's very pleased with himself."

Fergus was close enough to hear the conversation and just grinned. Their trip home was quick. Both were ready to sleep in their own bed. Juanita and Lotte were happy to see them. The house was as clean as it had ever been. If they had enough warning, they had been planning a big meal on the first night.

The meal was one of Fergus's favorites, carne asada. After two nights at home, Fergus said, "I have to go to Butte to set up things for you women. It'll take a week for the main characters to be ready."

He sent Kate a telegram with the date she should arrive in Butte. She replied that she would be there.

Josh said, "Let me know when they come. I may want to buy any leftovers for the freight yard. I don't think I have a problem, but it's better to close the barn door before the mules get out."

Fergus only spent one night and rode by the sawmill without stopping, which was difficult for him. Lance seemed to have everything under control. He also rode by the farm to check on the harvesting, which was going well. He was mainly interested in whether the shellers were working. They were, but it took a strong man to turn them. Fergus thought next year he would try to get them geared to make them easier to turn. He still had yet to find a water wheel drive version.

Kate arrived in Butte the day after the women arrived. Some children went to the schoolhouse where a substitute teacher worked while Amber was away. Lena and another lady kept the smaller ones at the boarding house.

Everyone who would receive a dog collected together in Josh's barn. Kate brought ten dogs into the barn. She talked to the group for two hours before she worked the first dog. The dogs were well trained, enabling her to work one dog at a time while the other dogs and people sat and watched.

The dogs going through their paces were fascinating to watch. She had them go into protective mode and make their intimidating low rumbling growl, which would stop most attackers. hey would do it on command or when they thought a person was in danger.

Everyone moved their dog through the various commands, including having the dog take down a person, usually by the arm. The last command Kate showed them was the 'go for the throat' command.

It took both a verbal and visual command. Kate emphasized that the dogs would use force, but not deadly force, if a stranger touched a child without a 'friend' command.

Everyone who received a dog was excited. The ranches were highly isolated, and the land was still untamed. They drew straws to see who got the first choice. Mary drew the short straw. No one could tell much difference between the dogs — all were large and looked menacing unless their tail was wagging furiously.

The last thing Kate showed them needed the twins help. Kate, Mary, and a few others walked to the boarding house. Kate thought all the dogs that would often see the twins should meet them now, including those owned by Mary, Morgan, Fergus, and Milam. Mary brought the twins outside, and Kate introduced the dogs to the girls and then let the girls play with them. They crawled all over the dogs without a single rumble. But a miner walked down the street, and Mary's dog suddenly became alert and eased between the man and the girls while rumbling a little. Mary and the others were impressed.

A celebration erupted at the boarding house after supper. Kate shared the story about how the dogs were originally given to Freedom Town by Comanche chief Quanah Parker, and she was assigned to train them. They were enthralled to hear of Quanah Parker, who was thought to be one of the most fierce war chiefs.

Kate said, "We were kind to him, and he returned the favor. One time the army asked our men to guide them in tracking Quanah down, and we refused. Instead, our men slipped away and warned Quanah about the soldiers."

Kate departed for home the following day on the early train. The new dog owners headed home after a hearty breakfast. Mary could not believe the dogs would play with the girls and then take a bad guy's throat out in a quick flash. Then she recalled Kota acting the same way with her. She decided to call her dog *Kota*. Morgan decided to call hers *Kelly* for Kelly Forks Creek.

When they arrived home, the roundup had started. Fergus went to help since he was still a good roper. They did not need his help, but he still did some roping. He got his noose around a large and wild cow. As she fought the rope, his saddle girth broke, and he and the horse went to the ground. It was a bad wreck, and Fergus emerged with a broken arm and leg.

A group loaded Fergus into a buckboard, and Jeb took him to Butte to see the doctor. The breaks were not good. The thigh bone and the upper arm were damaged. The doctor gave him a hefty dose of laudanum and set the bones. Despite the laudanum, setting the leg hurt like the devil.

The doctor splinted both breaks and said, "You should stay at my office for a couple of days and then at the boarding house for the rest of the week so I can check on you. Jeb, you'll need to take him home in a buckboard. He will not be able to fork a horse for months."

Josh replied, "Jeb, I'll take him home so you can return to the roundup. They'll need you with Fergus down. Is Morgan at the house?"

"Yes, and thank you. I need to get back to the roundup. Can you watch him before you take him home? He will not be a good patient."

"Sure, I'll watch him. If Dr. Boyton gives him enough laudanum, he won't be too tough to handle." Dr. Boyton kept him doped up for most of the week and gave him a large bottle to take home.

Jeb sent Rowdy to tell Morgan about Fergus's accident. She was distraught but decided to stay at home until Josh brought him. It took a lot of effort to get him inside and into bed.

Fergus thought, "*Well, this will ensure I'm not involved in anything for a while. Dr. Boyton said I should stay inside until the new year, which will be miserable.*"

Morgan gave him a large dose of laudanum, and he was out for several hours. His leg hurt intensely, even when lying still. Morgan knew he needed his leg raised to lessen the swelling. She got the blacksmith to put a hook in the ceiling and one on the nearest wall. She could then tie a rope to a sling on Fergus's leg, run it through the ceiling hook, and tie it to the wall hook.

After raising his leg the first time, she grinned at him and said, "I finally got you where I want you, hogtied to the bed. You better be a good patient if you ever want to get out of bed." Fergus saw no humor in his predicament.

The girls wanted to play with him, but they were too rambunctious. They were close to a year old and large for their age. Dr. Boyton sent a wheelchair home with him, but he could not move from the bed to the chair. Getting into the chair unassisted became his first primary goal.

The roundup was going well. It would be a terrific sales year. Colorado rode in occasionally to fill Fergus in. Fergus offered no advice to Colorado or anyone else. Between the laudanum and the pain, he knew he was not thinking too clearly.

No other significant accidents occurred at the roundup. The cattle were shipped before Fergus was able to stay off the laudanum. Milam completed the sale, and Colorado put the money in the bank. The sales price combined with what Horace and Hank brought Fergus meant he and Morgan were wealthy.

As Fergus lay convalescing, he thought about Wolf, who had been part of the family for years. He decided to set him up with a good horse ranch and cattle operation. He talked to Morgan, and she readily agreed.

Fergus later told Milam, "I want a ranch with five or six sections for Wolf. I want it close to this ranch so we can raise horses together. Could you look around and see if anything is available? Bart might be able to help you find something."

Morgan had the blacksmith attach another hook and rope to the ceiling above Fergus so he could maneuver to his wheelchair. He then could go to the porch without help, which helped his feelings tremendously. The fresh air and a little ranch dust helped more than anything. He could watch things around the headquarters without getting involved. He began to realize the ranch did not need him and, further, he did not need the ranch work. It was a huge revelation. He and Morgan talked about it a lot.

Morgan took Fergus to Butte to see Dr. Boyton. She did not mind taking Fergus alone. Having Kelly lope alongside the buckboard was a great comfort. Dr. Boyton removed the splints, and the bones seemed to be healing. Boyton was still concerned about the leg, so he put a lighter splint on it and told Fergus it would stay on for a couple of months, which was not exactly the news He wanted to hear.

When they left the office, Boyton said, "We got another redhead in town. He says his name is Bonner. He works for one of the mines and stays at the boarding house."

"I'll talk to him tonight. We might be kinfolks."

Fergus approached the man after supper, the only other man with red hair. They talked for a while and figured out they were not likely related, at least for many generations. He was from Ireland and came to the U.S. to attend the Colorado School of Mines. He was very proud of being from Ireland and talked at length about it. His description pumped Fergus up about seeing his ancestral homeland.

Fergus and Morgan talked later about taking a trip to Ireland when he could walk again. They had the time and plenty of money.

They returned to Bonner's Den Ranch the next day. Fergus took a dose of laudanum before they started so the pain would not be too much for him. Morgan and two cowboys got Fergus up the steps and back into his bed. He was worn out from the trip and slept most of the afternoon.

Fergus woke up excited about the possibility of visiting Ireland the following summer. Morgan was excited but wondered if she could be away from the twins that long. They were changing rapidly, and she did not want to miss anything. Morgan was afraid she could not avoid it with Fergus so fired up about the trip. It was a long time away, and maybe one of them would change their mind, probably her.

Milam dropped by one day after a trip to Butte. He reported that he found a six-section ranch between Bonner's Den Ranch and Butte.

Milam said, "Bart told me they were way behind on the loan payments, and he will have to begin the foreclosure process soon. He's sure they will sell for a rock-bottom price. They just don't know how to do farming or ranching. A few cows come with it, but they're not caring for them. I'm not sure when they branded last."

Fergus replied, "I'll send Colorado to check on their cattle. If it checks out okay, I'll likely buy it for Wolf. He's been with us a long time and helped collect much of the gold."

"Okay. Let me know if I can help."

Morgan thought they had talked business long enough. She wanted to hear about the girls. They talked for over an hour until she heard all the news. Milam told her the girls were pulling up and walking a few steps. She wanted to go with him so she could see them.

Milam said, "Mary wants to see Fergus. How about I bring her and the girls over for a week?"

Morgan jumped up and hugged him, "Oh, thank you so much! I just can't leave here now. Fergus needs a lot of help."

"We'll be back in two or three days. Maybe both of you women can get your visiting done in a week. Of course, we plan to spend a few weeks here at Christmas, which is coming soon."

Colorado rode up to the house and hailed Fergus. He said, "Fergus, the ranch looks good. It has good water and grass. I saw a few cows, but the owner is a lousy rancher who doesn't know much about cattle. At the right price, it's worth buying."

"Okay. Go to Butte and talk with Bart. Find out how much they owe the bank and ask Bart how much he thinks we should offer. Then, y'all make the owner an offer. I trust you and Bart to make a good deal. I'll write a note to Bart authorizing you to make the purchase."

"Okay, I'll leave in the morning."

———————————

Later that day, Jenkins brought a freight wagon full of oats to put in the storage facility at Bonner's Den Ranch. They would have at least three more full freight wagons, so they needed another oat bin. Colorado sent two cowboys to get the lumber to build one. He also sent a crew to cut timber for the bin's uprights. It would not take long to build it, especially if Mike and a few of his workers were available.

Mike and four workers came back with the lumber. Mike started on the bin as soon as they arrived, and he thought they could finish within a week. Colorado went to the house to tell Fergus what was going on. They would have plenty of oats for the year. Jenkins would start harvesting the wheat next. He would start grinding flour and cornmeal in about a week.

"I'm thinking about sending Jenkins some help to harvest the wheat and corn so he can start grinding. Snow could fly at any time now."

"Good idea."

"I can spare four riders to help for a few days, which should be enough to get the wheat with the harvester. I'll send a bigger crew to help with the corn, which will take longer. Snow would make it more difficult to harvest."

"Great! He'll need help each year when harvesting starts."

Colorado talked with him about the cattle and the ranch in general. Their conversation helped Fergus feel better, and he was taking less laudanum.

Morgan stopped Colorado on the porch and said, "It helps Fergus when you come to talk to him. I would appreciate it if you dropped by regularly to chat with him about ranch stuff. Not to get his approval — just to keep him in the loop."

"I'll make sure I drop by several times weekly."

Two weeks later, Jenkins had enough flour to take to all the ranches in the area. He left two one-hundred-pound bags at each ranch. He continued to grind flour until all the wheat was ground. All the cooks thought his flour was better than what was available in the general store.

When he finished grinding and bagging, Jenkins put the flour in the storage room. They worked on making it rat and mouse-proof, which was impossible. Jenkins put cats in the storage areas to help control rodents. It was time to start grinding corn. He thought he would grind about half of it and use the rest for animal food. It did not take but a few days to grind and bag the cornmeal. The aroma of freshly ground corn was almost intoxicating. A month's supply was delivered to each ranch.

Fergus saw Juanita put a half sack into the barrel she cooked from. He told Morgan he was ready for cornbread and chili. She passed the information on to Juanita, who told her chili was now on the menu.

Fergus was getting stronger, which was not necessarily a good thing. He wanted to do more. Thanksgiving and Christmas were arriving soon, and Fergus rolled his wheelchair up and down the porch. Morgan thought he was a pitiful sight pacing in a rolling chair.

Fergus wanted to be on his horse and riding the range, but the doctor said maybe by Easter. He wondered, "*How will I stay off my feet that long? Doctors can do it since they don't get out much anyway. I'll go mad.*"

His depression lifted when Mary and the girls showed up unexpectedly. He thought the girls would be as tall as Mary. They could walk and wanted Grandpa to walk with them. It killed him to know he could not. The girls pulled up beside his bed and talked gibberish with him. He could not understand it like a grandma, but he loved interacting with them. In fact, he loved everything about them. Woe be unto the boy who came courting when they grew up.

Rowdy, Liz, and Joe came to see him, and he loved their visits. He wondered if he could be away long enough to visit Ireland. He did not mention that to Morgan, or she would be all over it.

Colorado returned to the ranch one afternoon. He said, "Fergus, Bart made quite a deal. The owner was desperate to get rid of the ranch. He took Bart's first offer and has already left."

"Excellent! Thanks for your help. Wolf will be happy."

Fergus asked Morgan to fetch Wolf and Half Moon for a chat. Fergus said, "Wolf, you've been like a son to us, and your children are like grandchildren. I have bought a six-section ranch to put horses and cows on. You will be responsible for our Appaloosa herd and overseeing the new ranch. It will be yours when I retire or die." Wolf grinned and shook his hand. Half Moon gave him a big hug.

———————————

One Sunday after lunch, Jeb's, Wolf's, and Brody's children began arguing during lunch about whose horse was fastest. Fergus intervened and said, "The only way to settle this argument is to race. I'll put up a purse of a twenty dollar gold piece to the winner. Y'all will race about a mile. It'll start on the other side of the stallion barn and finish when you go by me. I'll determine the winner, and my decision is final. Everybody get your horse and get ready to ride. If anyone is fast enough, we may go to Butte and race. They have several races every weekend."

Shorty gave the signal to start. A few got a better start than others, but all the horses were fast. The kids charged down the road, kicking and screaming for more speed. Morgan yelled at Fergus for putting them up to the race. Elbert won the race and immediately started to brag and trash talk. It was not long before the scuffling began. Morgan did not know whether she wanted to help break up the fight or hit Fergus over the head with a piece of firewood. It was a good thing he was still hurt.

Fergus loved everything, including the tussle, which was part of the reason Morgan was so mad. She simmered down quickly after she had time to think. Horse racing, bragging, and fighting were part of the Western culture.

Fergus started wondering about having a rodeo for the kids. He kept his thoughts to himself until he was ready to battle with Morgan. Fergus decided to talk to the dads first. He caught them later in the afternoon to discuss the idea. Every daddy was in favor of a rodeo. They thought it would give the kids something fun to do.

Colorado was brought in on the deal and would find the cattle needed. The first Bonner's Den Ranch Rodeo would kick off the following Saturday afternoon. The events would include calf roping, team roping, bronc riding, calf riding, and a team event involving cutting. The animals and kids would be matched as well as possible, with the big kids getting the bigger animals.

Just before it started, two cowboys came to help Fergus into his wheelchair. Morgan knew something was up. She followed Fergus at a distance to see what was happening. She decided not to say anything about the early events of roping and such. Actually, Morgan was standing near Fergus and cheering the kids on. But when the riding events started, she was not nearly as happy.

"Fergus, what are you doing? You're going to break the necks of my grandkids and our friends' kids. I can't believe you're doing this!"

"Their parents are doing it. I've been in bed and couldn't help."

"Who gave them the idea?"

"How would I know? Maybe the meadowlarks told them what they wanted to see."

"Meadowlarks my rear! I know you're not innocent. If you were not hurt, I would take a club to you."

"Did you not enjoy fun? You were clapping and laughing as much as anyone. It gives the kids something enjoyable to do."

She conceded him a few points, "I'm just afraid they're going to get hurt on the bucking animals."

"Every cowboy has to ride a green horse sometimes. They better know how to ride a calm horse and one that's pretty raw."

"Oh, I give up! Try not to get anyone hurt. Let me know who's the best cowboy. I can't watch them falling in the dirt."

All the kids and dads enjoyed the afternoon. After the events were tweaked a little, the mothers would be invited to the next rodeo.

It was nearing Christmas, and all the grandchildren and 'almost grandchildren' would spend the holiday at Bonner's Den Ranch. Fergus was happy, and Morgan was even happier. Fergus decided to give the kids money. The girls also received some of the pretty stones Fergus found back in the mountains. They were pleased with their gifts.

At Christmas lunch, Fergus announced that he and Morgan would visit Ireland during the summer. He hoped to find some of their relatives, but it would be okay if they did not.

He said, "You folks and others have shown me you can handle everything about the ranch. The last several months have shown me I'm not essential to anything we do. I once thought I was, and I think some of you thought I was. No single individual is indispensable if they have good people working for them. We'll prepare to leave as soon as I can get around better. I want to go as soon as we can in the spring."

Chapter Nineteen

Morgan thought, "*Well, I guess we're going to Ireland. Hope we talk about it in depth before we leave. I have so many questions.*"

The rest of Christmas Day was a joyous time at Bonner's Den Ranch. Many songs were sung with enough voices to generate a great noise if not great music. Everyone sang with gusto, especially Fergus. Several cowboys came from the bunkhouse to join the singing. Fortunately, several people possessed good voices, and a few played the guitar well. While Fergus had a so-so voice, Morgan and Mary were excellent singers.

Fergus had an appointment with the doctor in early January. He hoped Boyton would tell him he could start getting around on crutches without cheating like he had been doing. Fergus really wanted to get in the saddle. He had ridden practically every day of his life before breaking his leg. The promise of being able to ride again made him follow Doc Boyton and Morgan's orders, more or less.

Morgan took Fergus in their surrey to see Dr. Boyton, with Kelly loping alongside. Morgan felt entirely secure when Kelly was close by. She was comforted knowing Kelly would inform them about any potential danger. She had not seen him in full protective mode but was optimistic about him.

It was cold, and Fergus and Morgan were huddled under blankets and a big bearskin. Before they arrived in Butte, four riders approached them from behind on the left side. Kelly loped back to the buckboard before the riders got to the wagon. He kept pace with the mules while looking back at the riders and rumbling.

The furs hid Fergus and Morgan's shotguns loaded with buckshot and the pistols lying on the seat. If the riders did not pass on by without incident, they would die at this place and time. They did not pass by. The bandits drew their pistols and motioned for them to stop. Kelly took one out before he knew his throat was missing. Fergus put two down with his shotgun, and Morgan blasted the other. They were even more impressed with Kelly – he had moved with lightning speed when he saw the bandits' pistols.

They loaded the four bodies in the surrey and took them to Butte. Morgan did most of the work and drove them to the Sheriff's office. After scrutinizing the bodies, the Sheriff thumbed through his wanted posters. Each bandit had a small reward posted. They were too dumb to have much on them. Riding up directly on a man and woman with fur over them was not a smart thing to do, nor was sitting on horses only a few feet apart.

Dr. Boyton said, "Well, you seem to have been following doctor's orders, except for shooting four road agents today."

"Doc, it doesn't take much effort to pull a trigger. You don't even have to aim with a sawed-off shotgun. Do you have a shotgun in your buggy? You would be a likely target for thieves. I'm sure many reprobates would love to have a bottle or two of your opium."

"It just doesn't seem right for a doctor to shoot a person."

"Doesn't seem right for someone to shoot a doctor. Or steal his medicine."

"I'll think about it."

"You might be more comfortable with a dog like Kelly to do the dirty work. They don't mind ripping out someone's throat if they plan to harm you. Kelly did that for us today. A pair of dogs like him would discourage any fool trying to hurt you."

"Hmm. I like the idea."

"I can get you one or two if you want them. Just let me know. The trainer will teach you to handle them."

Dr. Boyton told Fergus he could start doing everything but ride a horse. A horse and saddle put too much pressure on a healing thigh bone. He could ride in a buggy like Angus had done near the end of his life, which would have to do for now. Boyton also told him he could go to Ireland in the summer if he used crutches. It was not exactly what Fergus wanted to hear, but it was progress.

Morgan took the rest of winter and early spring to get ready for their Ireland trip. She was not rushing, partially because she dreaded leaving her grandchildren. But enthusiasm began to rise as the departure date drew closer.

They would travel by train to New York City and then by steamship to Dublin. Interestingly, the rail portion of their trip would take about as long as the ocean voyage. The vessels had recently gotten much faster. Even the ones with sails had engines for when they hit slack wind. Some ships could make the trip in about a week.

Fergus and Morgan planned to be away for around eight weeks. They would be in transit for a total of four weeks and spend about four weeks traveling around Ireland.

Fergus did not know which town his parents came from, so they decided to spend a few days in New York to examine immigration records for the Bonner name. Perhaps he could get a clue about their county of his origin. Surely, only a few Bonners came through during the years when he knew his dad had come to the U.S.

Fergus wondered which weapons he should take with him. He eventually decided to take his revolver and two derringers. Fergus joked about taking Kelly with them but did not want to clean up after a dog his size. He was sure they would be safe enough with the arms he planned to take.

The big day finally arrived, and they boarded the train for Cheyenne. Their luggage consisted of two large trunks and a couple of smaller pieces. Morgan's things filled about seventy-five percent of the luggage, maybe more. She was totally unapologetic.

Fergus took along photos of his parents when they were younger.

He hoped someone would recognize them.

The trip to New York City took most of five days and went smoothly. They encountered no problems on the train, and having a compartment helped. They walked to the dining car for a meal or two each day, and Fergus enjoyed a glass of excellent rum at night. They both slept well on the train.

New York City was enormous and amazing. The hotel clerk said over a million people lived in Manhattan, and Fergus believed he was correct. People were everywhere they looked, and the buildings were much taller than anything they had seen out West.

Their hotel was over ten stories. Morgan was not sure she could sleep on the higher floors, so they obtained a room on the fourth floor.

The following day, Fergus went to the building where they kept files of people who immigrated to the U.S. Morgan went shopping to see if she had forgotten anything.

A lady at the immigration department helped Fergus find records from when his mother and dad came to the U.S. He found their names on the second day. They had immigrated from County Maynooth, Ireland, and Fergus had a starting place. The woman told them he might want to visit churches in the area because they usually had good records of births and deaths, especially for Catholics.

Fergus and Morgan boarded the ship before noon the next day. They decided to board early to get settled in. They boarded at ten o'clock after a good breakfast. Both were concerned about seasickness because they had never been on the ocean.

The porter said, "Most people don't have problems unless we hit a storm. Try eating salty crackers for the first day. I think you'll be okay."

Morgan retorted, "I hope so. What do we do?"

"You may want to come on deck about noon to watch us push off and see the city slide by. It will take us two hours to hit the real ocean. Most people think it's the most exciting thing that happens until we approach land. We'll go around Ireland's southern end to Dublin."

"Thank you. It sounds interesting."

"You can find a schedule of activities at the main desk. It has the hours for all meals. You can eat in your room, but most people prefer to eat in the dining room. It's a chance to meet other travelers. You will be notified if we change the schedule due to rough water or bad weather."

They went on the deck a little before noon. The deck was a beehive of activity, especially near the gangplank. At noon, the sailors started working with the thick ropes, taking them off the stanchions and enormous cleats. Before long, the ship was loose, and a smaller boat was helping to turn it around. The engines were loud, and the smoke was thick, but the ship soon headed toward the ocean. It was interesting to watch the city slide by. The wind created by the movement made it feel cool.

Morgan said, "I'll bet it'll get pretty cold on the deck. We'll need a coat next time we come up."

Before long, the city was behind them, although they were still in a river rather than the ocean. It was apparent when they reached the ocean. The temperature dropped, and the waves began to gently rock the ship. The trip had officially begun.

Fergus and Morgan visited the dining room before returning to their cabin. They found plenty of sandwiches and other finger food. They sat at a table with other travelers and chatted for a while. Like Fergus, several people were going back to Ireland to find their roots.

After leaving port, not much happen — every mile looked like the last mile. Fergus and Morgan went to their cabin for a nap. Neither was used to a nap — too much work on a ranch. It was difficult for them to adjust to the confines of the ship. The waves reminded them of the tall grass back home.

It did not take long for Morgan to begin missing the grandkids. Rowdy, Colt, and Brody's kids were likely to drop by the house anytime, especially when cookies came out of the oven. They apparently had a sixth sense regarding warm cookies.

Fergus and Morgan settled into the ship's routine quickly. Neither had ever slept so many hours, which was delightful for them. Mealtime provide daily highlights, and they strolled to the dining room at least three times a day. Fergus enjoyed a drink and a cigar most nights. He even joined a card game a few nights and broke even on the trip.

On the fifth day, just before dark, a commotion on deck caught their attention. When they looked hard at the horizon, they could see land, Ireland. The weather had been excellent, but a few storms rolled in during the night. Fergus was not sure he could eat breakfast.

One thing they discovered was a bathroom connected to their cabin. Morgan was enthralled and asked many questions. One of those would be mighty welcome on a cold Montana morning. They kept a honeypot under the bed at home, but it was gross when the weather remained cold for days. Fergus thought, "*I might as well look into one of those when we return to New York City. I probably ought to look at more than one. Mary, Kamiah, Half Moon, Little Bird, and everyone else will want one if Morgan gets one.*"

The ship started the docking process late in the day, which was also interesting. Ireland was so green that it looked like an emerald. Fergus immediately thought of how many cows you could run on a section. He saw few beef cattle and a plethora of sheep. He wondered if they would have to eat one of those smelly things.

As soon as they began docking, Morgan returned to their room to pack. She was ready when the porter and two big stevedores came for the luggage. It would be well after dark when they got into their hotel room. Both were ready to be on dry ground. They decided to remain in Dublin for a few days to sightsee.

They enjoyed the time sightseeing in Dublin. The highlights were the Blarney Castle, St. Patrick's Cathedral, and the Jameson Distillery. Fergus thought the Irish Whiskey was good, but not as good as Doc's 'shine.

Fergus was anxious to get to Maynooth to check on his roots. They rented a horse and buggy for the month. The horse was well trained. It pranced and looked like a good horse. Fergus checked its shoes and the fit of the harness. Everything looked good.

The stable man said, "You seem to understand what's important for a happy horse. Many people don't, and they sometimes injure my horse."

"I own a large horse herd in the western United States. We're ranchers in Montana."

"How much land do you own?"

"Close to thirty sections, but some land was bought for my children."

"How many hectares is that?"

"Well, let me think. It's about twenty thousand acres. If I remember correctly, it should be about ten thousand hectares, give or take a few hundred."

"We have counties smaller than that. You must be a wealthy man."

"I've been lucky and successful."

"Did your father immigrate to the U.S.?"

"Yes. Our surname is Bonner."

"Maynooth is a good place to start looking for your relatives. It's full of Bonners and many of them have red hair like yours. Your wife doesn't appear to be Irish."

"We're unsure of her heritage, but it is likely English. Her parents died when she was young, and she doesn't remember any talk about their country of origin. Mine did not talk much, but I know they came from Ireland."

"Good luck with finding your relatives!"

It did not take long to travel from Dublin to Maynooth. They found a boarding house with comfortable rooms. Fergus talked to the owner, Sean, about his search for relatives. Sean recommended they go to a pub and keep their ears open.

"You should find many of them. Most have red hair, maybe not as red and curly as yours, but red if you look closely."

Fergus showed Sean a picture of his dad, but he did not recognize him. However, Sean thought he might remember the name Elbert Bonner.

Fergus and Morgan went to the largest of the two pubs in town. They ordered a pint and chatted with many people. A few people thought they might recognize Elbert, but no one was sure. It had been a long time ago.

They moved on to the other pub and ordered another pint. Again, Fergus asked around, beginning with the bartender. The bartender replied, "Yes, Elbert was a cousin of mine. Are you his son? You look like him with that shock of curly red hair. Many of us Bonners have red hair. The only thing more common among us is our hardheadedness. Most of us are strong-willed and will fight if you disagree."

"That pretty much sums him up. We did get along at times, but not always. I left home at a young age and moved West. He was killed in our Civil War. He supported the South, and I did not intend to fight for slavery or against my family. We butted heads over it many times before I left."

"Sounds like him. As I said, it's a family tradition. A group of our relatives is sitting over in the corner. I'll introduce you, but I warn you, a fight will break out in the group before the night's over. They're already arguing about something."

They walked over and started talking to what turned out to be a group of cousins. One said, "Our dads are brothers. I can take you out to meet him and some other aunts and uncles. They own a few hectares outside of town. Let's meet for breakfast tomorrow and ride out there. Do you have a horse and rig? Otherwise, I'll have to travel on my shanks mare."

"Yes, we have a rig that will hold three of us. What time for breakfast?"

"Let's say seven o'clock. How long do you have to visit?"

"We will be here for about a month."

"Good, that may give you time to meet most of your relatives." They all laughed.

Morgan was ready to return to their room, but Fergus wanted to visit longer. He escorted her to their Inn and returned to the pub. It was getting louder and livelier. After about an hour, the fight broke out between two Bonner brothers. Fergus tried to stay on the sideline, but that was an exercise in futility. The primary combatants were determined to see that everyone got punched. Fergus took a push and a fist to his face. He became embroiled in the melee and gave better than he received, but he was bleeding from his lip, eyebrow, and nose. The fight ended quickly, and everyone again seemed to be fast friends.

The bartender offered Fergus a towel to wipe off his face. He was proud he had held his own but feared Morgan would be angry. He waited until the blood stopped flowing and cleaned up as well as he could.

It took Morgan less than thirty seconds to realize he had been fighting. She was not happy and let him know it.

Clive met them for a quick breakfast and they hit the road. The relatives all lived near each other on small farms. It looked like they grew gardens and raised sheep. Western cattlemen generally did not like sheep. Most thought sheep ruined good grazing by eating the grass too short, which was not really true. The reality was sheep had a strong odor that was unpleasant to most cattlemen.

Clive left them at an uncle's house and went to tell the other relatives about Fergus. Everyone wanted to meet their brother's son. Elbert, the oldest, had left when they were young. The three sisters decided to prepare a feast if Clive brought them to their house last. They dispatched husbands and children to inform everyone and buy the items they needed. One item was a large lamb for the meal — they did not have time to kill and prepare one of their own, so they bought a whole dressed lamb.

It was a big day in the community where most close relatives lived. Everyone, relative or not, watched for a woman and a tall man with long, curly red hair. Not all Bonners were redheaded, but close to half were.

The meal was excellent. It was the first lamb Fergus and Morgan could remember eating, and he was surprised he liked it. The cabbage and potato dishes contained interesting spices and tasted very good. They enjoyed the day with family. A few people indicated they remembered Maude, but she was from another county. He got the location and wanted to find her side of the family.

They rode to Maude's hometown and found some of her cousins. Fergus could not detect any significant distinguishing features in her family members. They enjoyed spending the day and learning about her close relatives. Once again, they ate a meal, mainly vegetables and stew.

Fergus and Morgan headed back to their room after dark. As they rolled into the village, two men stepped from the shadows to stop their horse. They obviously did not know Fergus was armed with a revolver and derringer, and Morgan carried a derringer.

Fergus had his pistol out before the road agents knew he even had one. The two men got a gun barrel stuck in their faces when they walked up to the rig carrying clubs. Apparently, few people in Ireland carried guns. The two men quickly scurried back into the shadows. Fergus and Morgan laughed at the shock on the men's faces.

Over the next week, they explored Ireland without worrying about relatives. They simply rode and visited pubs along the way. The countryside was beautiful, with emerald-colored vegetation. After the run-in with the road agents, they ensured they were always armed. Fergus did not wear his holster since no one else did, but he kept it tucked in his pants. Both had a derringer in a pocket.

Clive invited Fergus and Morgan to a celebration on Sunday after church. Even more relatives and acquaintances would attend this meal. Clive said the main course would be corned beef, cabbage, and other side dishes. They attended church before the meal. Everyone wanted to meet them, and the minister recognized them during the service. They seldom received visitors from across the ocean. Many family members went to find work in the U.S., but few ever returned home.

The rest of the trip was uneventful, but satisfying. Morgan bought many items and wanted a few days in Dublin before packing. The wool sweaters made in Ireland were adorable. She bought one for almost everybody and two for each of the twins. She also purchased several high-quality wool blankets. While she was getting the woolen items, Fergus bought a large chest to put it all in. He was unsure he had enough room, even with the new chest. Fergus told Morgan they needed to pack the day before departure to ensure they had enough room. He expected to buy another chest before they boarded.

Sure enough, the day before departure, he went to find a middle-sized chest. Everything fit into the four chests and two duffle bags. Fergus closed the larger chests by sitting on the top, and Morgan closed the latches and locked them.

Fergus went to arrange for someone to take the luggage to the ship. He and Morgan would walk since they were only two blocks from the ship.

The trip to Ireland was mainly on smooth water. The trip back to New York City was quite different. They hit a couple of storms with vicious wave action. Neither ate much beyond salty crackers, and they did not usually keep it down. Both landlubbers were pretty miserable all the way home. Thank heaven for the indoor plumbing.

When they entered New York Harbor, they both praised the Lord. They took a room near the harbor to get their land legs under them. It took a while to get their guts to stop flipping every few minutes, but they were able to eat a light meal.

Fergus sent a telegram to Josh to tell him they were back in the country. Josh sent back: *PROBLEMS HERE. MCCULLOUGH RANCH HOUSE BURNED. EVERYONE IS OKAY AND IN YOUR HOUSE. MARY NEEDS HER MOTHER FOR COMFORT.*

Chapter Twenty

Morgan read the telegram, put her hand on her bosom, and said, "Oh, No! This is all we know? How did the fire start? Is anyone hurt?"

"All we know is in the telegram. I'm sure no one is hurt because Josh would have said so. We have no idea how it started. Since they're staying at our house, I assume theirs is not livable or burned to the ground. We can do nothing from here, so we need to hurry home. We can talk about what to do on the train and when we arrive."

"Agreed. Let's leave as soon as we can catch a train heading west. Maybe our stomachs will settle down on the train. I looked forward to shopping in this enormous city, but I think I'm taking enough for everyone."

"Based on those overflowing chests, you have plenty. We'll need to check the chests in the baggage car, at least the largest three. Do you need to repack so we have enough traveling clothes in our compartment?"

"I'm sure I do. I can't remember where everything is."

"Okay, the chests should be downstairs. I'll have everything brought up and then buy our railroad tickets. Hopefully, we can get a compartment in the morning."

When Fergus returned with the tickets, Morgan had unpacked the chests and rearranged everything. She was able to put all they needed in the bags, and the four chests could go to the baggage car. Fergus bought tickets for a six-person compartment. After everything was straightened out, they only had a few hours to sleep.

The porters arrived early the following morning to take the chests to the baggage car. Fergus and Morgan were ready to board the train, which was allowed two hours before departure. They had enough room

215

in the compartment, with plenty of space to lay down. They were sound asleep when the train pulled out. They slept until the sun was high overhead. Fergus thought it was the latest he had ever slept, even when he could not get out of bed. They were also famished.

The dining car offered a good menu. Both ordered a steak and eggs with all the fixings. Neither could eat everything on their plate because they had eaten so little during the last week, and their stomachs had shrunk. They carried the leftovers to the compartment for an early supper, even though neither expected to eat anything the rest of the day.

The countryside rolled by as they idly watched. Both were thinking of Mary, Milam, and the twins.

Morgan said, "What do you think about the housing situation back home?"

"I wonder what Mary and Milam want to do, rebuild or stay in our house? I'm getting used to not working so hard, and I like it. We've both worked hard constantly since we were young children. I want to enjoy the rest of our years. I think we have many more good years left, but my horse wreck made me reconsider many things. I've been thinking about living in the mountains again. Not to find or even look for gold, but to live comfortably in beautiful country. I'm just thinking about it right now."

"Hmm. I've had similar thoughts. I don't want to be far from our grandkids, but we must let our children grow into independent adults. You've done much in that direction, but I'm afraid I have not. This trip is the closest I've come to breaking myself of wanting to make their decisions. It's definitely something to think about."

They did not talk much other than sharing random comments about the countryside they were passing through. It was hectic getting across the river at Omaha with their baggage. After they crossed, the layover was long enough for them to rent a room, and they were both ready for a real bed. The railroad handled most of their luggage — they kept one bag of fresh clothes for the following day. The bathhouse was fabulous after supper.

They boarded the train to Cheyenne early, as they usually did. Nebraska was eerily pretty. It was mostly flat and almost featureless most of the time.

Fergus commented, "This is not the country I want to live in. It's mile after mile of grain crops. The land must be rich, but I like a little variation. Our ranch is mostly flat, but it seems to have character. I don't have a farmer's eye, as you know."

Morgan replied, "The more I think about living in the mountains close to the kids, the more I like the idea. I can visit Mary and the girls for a month at Christmas and a couple other times a year, and they can visit us. Rowdy, Liz, and Joe can spend time with us during the year. That'll be enough."

"I see you've also been thinking about it. We need to talk to Milam and Mary."

The countryside began changing as they neared Wyoming. Fergus commented, "This is more like it. I'm sure Wyoming has some beautiful places."

"Wait a minute! I don't plan to live this far from our family and friends."

"I didn't mean I wanted to live in Wyoming. I was just commenting. It was idle talk."

They spent the night in Cheyenne before finishing the trip to Butte. Fergus sent a telegram to Josh to ask about a wagon to haul their purchases and luggage. Josh said he would have it ready when their train arrived.

The wagon was waiting for them, and Josh volunteered to drive it. He also wanted to talk to Milam and Mary. They had to get moving on any construction they needed.

Fergus talked with Josh about moving to the mountains. Josh said, "I've been thinking about the same thing and like the idea. I know of a high spot with two mostly flat benches. It's about two sections and has magnificent views. A house would fit nicely on either bench. Plenty of timber is nearby to build a log cabin, or boards could be hauled up from the sawmill. It's not far from the timber sections we already own. I'm interested in it if you want a partner on the deal. I would love a small house up there just to get away and wind down."

They arrived home in the early afternoon. Mary and the twins seemed settled in at the Bonner's Dean Ranch house. After playing with the girls for an hour, they asked Mary about the fire.

Mary said, "The house and everything in it burned during the night. Koda saved our lives by waking me and the girls up. He helped me get the girls to the bunkhouse. The house was too far gone to save anything. A terrible lightning storm hit us at dusk. We think the lightning hit the house, and a shingle smoldered for a while. The wind came up later and apparently fanned the flames into a blaze. We don't know what to do about rebuilding."

"Good. We have a proposal you might be interested in. We'll talk about it a little later."

The girls had listened long enough to big people's talk and wanted to see what Morgan brought them. She was excited to show them, but it did not take too long for them to admire the woolen goods. Toys would have been more appreciated by them. But they put on the sweaters and did a fashion show.

Juanita was preparing a big Mexican stew, one of Fergus's favorites. Colorado saw them arrive and rode over to chat with Fergus about the ranch. The cattle and horses were in good shape, and the grain was growing well.

Mary later asked, "What about this proposal you mentioned? We're really torn about what to do."

Morgan explained, "Honey, we're ready to mostly retire from ranching and the related work. We don't need this mansion anymore. Fergus and I have decided we want to live in the mountains west of here. Josh told us about an available mountain property not far from here, which is about a half-day ride. We want to buy the land and build a nice log cabin. You and Milam can have this house and the furniture. It'll be yours in a few years anyway. We will still own the cattle, and when they're sold, we'll get twenty-five percent of the sales price. Y'all will get the rest and pay the expenses. What do you think?"

"I'll have to talk to Milam, but I like the idea. I'm sure he will need a small cabin on the McCullough Ranch to use when he's working there. Fortunately, the bunkhouse did not burn."

Fergus said, "Makes sense. I assume he'll be here tonight. We can tell him about our idea. We'll have to get the cabin built before the snow flies. Josh and I plan to visit the property and look around tomorrow. I doubt Morgan will want to go and leave the twins again."

When Milam arrived at dusk, Mary walked outside to talk with him. Fergus could tell they were having a serious discussion, which lasted for over an hour.

When they walked in, Milam asked, "Are you sure y'all want to do this? We're getting the best of the situation by far. If you're sure, we would love to take your offer. I don't have time to build a house like Mary would want."

"We discussed this a lot on the way back from New York. We're sure we want to move to the mountains and enjoy the solitude. We've always been mountain folks, and the mountains are beautiful. It's close enough for us to visit. In fact, it is not any further than Bonner's Den Ranch and McCullough's Ranch now — still about a half day's ride."

"Okay, we'll need legal papers drawn up."

"Josh and I are looking at the property tomorrow just to make sure. We'll be in Butte in three days, if you can come then. It shouldn't take long. I'll get Colorado to send someone to Butte to make sure Eshee and Mike will be there."

When she served supper, Juanita said, "Mr. Fergus, I need to talk with you."

"Okay, let's talk."

"I'm getting married. I know I'm too old, but I met a man who's getting too old for cowboy work. We want to find a quiet place with less hard work involved."

"Are you interested in living in the mountains? Morgan and I are building a smaller house in the high country. The two of you could take care of Morgan and me. We'll need a little help, but nothing like you do now. Think about it. I'd build y'all a cabin next to ours."

"We would love it! Count on us!"

Fergus and Josh rode out early the following day. Doc Boyton had given Fergus permission to ride a horse if he took it easy. Fergus was not sure the ride into the mountains could be called 'taking it easy,' but it would have to do. They traveled light with one pack horse carrying a little food and gear to prepare it. It was summer, and their only shelter was a tarp and bed rolls.

Fergus and Josh reached the lower flat shelf a few hours before dark. They decided to make camp there. The land was beautiful, and the scenery was as spectacular as he had seen.

Fergus also found a small cave. They decided to sleep in it because they heard the rumble of distant thunder.

They had time to ride around the area. About a hundred acres contained no trees, likely the result of a fire caused by lightning a few years earlier.

The hundred acres of grass were not like the land below, but it was still good grass. It would support a few cattle and horses. They also found three natural springs. One spring was warm, and the other two were cold enough to keep meat and other food from spoiling. Fergus thought the warm spring would be relaxing to sit in, like the one by Grant and Angelina's cabin.

A hard rain started just after dark, but they had dry wood and were snug in the cave. Fergus remembered using caves when he and Morgan left Pierce so long ago. Supper consisted of jerky, pemmican, and bread – they were satisfied.

The following day, the skies were as clear as a bell. It made one think he could reach up and touch it. The upper shelf was closer to two hundred acres and was even more beautiful. Some of the overlooks were breathtaking.

Fergus was sold but was unsure whether he wanted to build on the upper or lower shelf. The warm spring pulled him to the lower piece of land.

Fergus asked, "How many acres do you think are for sale?"

"As I remember the map, it's about two thousand acres. Most of it is mountains. Lots of game I'm told, mainly elk. If you want to buy, I will pay half as a partner so we can both use the land."

Fergus did not hesitate with his response, "Done!"

They spent the night in the cave again. Fergus shot a couple of grouse and grilled them on a spit. The supper was delicious. They left early the next morning and arrived in Butte mid-afternoon. They found Eshee and asked him to do the paperwork to transfer Bonner's Den Ranch to Mary. He and Josh formed a partnership to purchase the mountain property. Eshee said it would take him a couple of days to get everything together.

They went to find Mike to get him started on the houses. Fergus wanted a large log cabin for him and Morgan, about four thousand square feet. He also wanted a barn and stables of similar size. A log house of about fifteen hundred square feet would be built for Juanita and her new spouse.

Josh wanted a log house about half the size of Fergus's. Josh would haul two trailer loads of cut wood for the inside walls. Mike said he could have the cabins finished before severe snow fell. A cabin on McCullough Ranch would be built later because the snow came later at the lower levels.

Fergus was content with the plans and was sure Morgan would love the setting. The mountain man and woman were returning home.

The End

About The Authors

Garry Smith and his wife Charlotte have lived in Starkville, Mississippi for over forty years. They have been married for over fifty years. They have two sons, two grandsons, and two granddaughters. Garry was raised on a farm and worked many other jobs, including each summer for five years on offshore oil platforms. His adult life was mainly spent teaching management at the university level. He co-authored many textbooks and novels with Danny.

Danny Arnold and his wife of over fifty years, Peggy, live in Winston Salem, NC, near their son, daughter-in-law, and two granddaughters. Danny was raised on a plantation in Louisiana. His career was primarily spent in higher education as a faculty member and administrator. He is the author of numerous management, leadership, and marketing textbooks. His first western fiction, *Bad Cat Jones*, was published in 2021. He has also co-authored many novels with Garry.

9 781778 835384